The Cursed Unicorn

Published in the UK by Scholastic Children's Books, 2020
Euston House, 24 Eversholt Street, London, NW1 1DB
A division of Scholastic Limited

London – New York – Toronto – Sydney – Auckland
Mexico City – New Delhi – Hong Kong

ISBN 978 0702 30319 7

A CIP catalogue record for this book
is available from the British Library.

Printed by CPI Group (UK) Ltd, Croydon, CR0 4YY
Papers used by Scholastic Children's Books are made
from wood grown in sustainable forests.

3 5 7 9 10 8 6 4 2

www.scholastic.co.uk

The Cursed Unicorn

ALICE HEMMING

SCHOLASTIC

For Joss and Hattie

PROLOGUE

When the forest day is done,
And moonlight overthrows the sun,
A unicorn is said to roam.
Cursed: it lives its life alone.

If you see the unicorn,
Something will be lost or torn.
Meet twice and pain will come your way,
Be sure to run and stay away.

For if you meet three times: it's true –
The curse itself will fall on you.

MANY YEARS AGO . . .

IN ELITHIA

CHAPTER ONE

BARLEY MOON

In a calm sea, by a distant shore, a faint white Barley Moon lingered in the dawn sky. The peaceful island of Elithia was awakening for the day. She stood alone and proud in the sea, mist dancing around her like a sheer veil, revealing domed turrets which were smooth as pebbles washed up from the sea. A single straight causeway led from the mainland to the island. For two miles, it struck a sure line through the water, then joined a road at the island, where it ran past the peasants' houses, the bright silks of the circus and the dark shapes of the mulberry trees, directly to the palace.

At the palace, it met a tiled walkway lined with freestanding carved columns, bay trees clipped into perfect spheres and gentle flowing channels of water that were more decorative than defensive. Two knights, wearing tabards of green and purple, stood guard by the high arched gateway. Above, in Princess Celene's room on the first floor, pale light slanted through the lattice window, casting a starry pattern across her coverlet.

She was running away, feet pounding on the hard ground, heart thumping in her chest. She couldn't see her pursuer. She knew that she had to get away, far from all the people that she held dear. Otherwise this thing would hurt them too. She was alone, guilty and afraid. She swung around, ready to face whatever it was. She was brave; she could fight this threat. But she was not prepared for the sound of splintering glass. . .

Celene awoke and looked over the side of her bed to see her water carafe in jagged pieces on the floor. She must have knocked it off the nightstand as she turned in her sleep. She sat up, adjusting to reality, her heart still pounding. Why did she keep having that foolish dream? She wasn't a dreaming sort of person, yet this one persisted, coming back to haunt her every few weeks.

The door to the chamber opened a crack and Hester, the maid, poked her head around it.

"I heard a crash, Your Highness!" she said, looking into the room aghast, as if the ceiling had fallen down.

Celene sighed. "It was the water carafe, I'm afraid."

"No matter, ma'am, I'll soon get that cleared up." She walked in, carrying a silver breakfast tray.

Celene made to get out of bed but Hester tutted at the sight of her bare feet. "Careful, ma'am, you don't want to cut yourself on the glass. Let me sweep this up and I'll pour you some fresh water for your morning wash."

She set down the tray on the dresser and rushed forward with a pair of embroidered slippers, then scurried to the fireplace to fetch the hearth brush and shovel. She continued tutting loudly as she swept up the broken glass.

"Thank you, Hester. What time is it?" Celene slid her feet into the slippers, rubbing the sleep from her eyes.

Hester lowered her gaze and focused her attention on her task. "Just a little after sunrise, ma'am."

"*After* sunrise? Good heavens, Hester, why in the king's name didn't you wake me before?"

"When I popped my head in to check, you were tossing and turning and I felt sure you were having that dream again, ma'am – the one that you always have when the moon is full. I didn't like to wake you as it tires you so. This month is the Barley Moon, which is especially strong—"

"—What are you talking about, Hester? The dream comes randomly, not with a full Moon!"

"You'd be surprised, ma'am. I might not be learned with my schoolbooks but I notice patterns like that. And I know that dreams that come regularly, they mean something. Or they foretell something important—"

Celene waved her hand dismissively; she couldn't listen to Hester's ramblings directly upon waking. "I have no time for this! I have asked to be woken no later than sunrise. I like to be at the training ground as early as possible. Help me on with my things, will you?"

"What about your wash, Your Highness? Let me brush your hair, at least."

"No time for that." Celene's hair didn't need brushing. She kept it in a practical, sharp, chin-length style that fell into place by itself.

Her leather training armour was hanging ready in the dressing room. Celene wore it every day, unless she required chain mail for a tournament, or formalwear for some other royal occasion. Celene put on her soft leggings and linen undershirt and Hester helped her into the padded doublet and bulkier leather garments.

Hester continued fussing as she strapped the backplate to the breastplate. "You are losing weight. You should eat. I knew you wouldn't want a cooked breakfast but I brought you something light." She bustled back to the dresser. "Here, have some tea. It's ginger."

Hester poured a cup of the pale liquid and passed it to Celene, who took a grateful swig. Then the princess plucked a round, sweet roll from the selection on the breakfast tray, wrapped it in a linen napkin and put it in her pocket.

"Do take a little more than that," suggested Hester, holding out a bowl of sliced pear, but Princess Celene shook her head, smiling. "I like a portable breakfast." Hester sighed and returned to the broken glass, squinting to make sure that she'd picked up every tiny particle.

Celene left her bedchamber and ran down the stairs as quickly as she could.

AIMING FOR PERFECTION

At the training ground, Celene strung her bow, pulled back the string and let an arrow fly. It hit the circular target a little off-centre, with a *thock*. She couldn't quite shake off the feeling of last night's dream. It was as if something were out to get her and she should hide away. All nonsense, of course, but that was the problem with sleeping in: it upset her usual rhythm.

She rolled back her shoulders, cleared her mind and focused again on the straw target, sending the arrows flying towards it, *thock, thock, thock*. This time, two out of three arrows hit their mark. She shook out her arms as she went to retrieve the arrows. She would shoot again until she hit the centre every time.

Celene felt her neck and upper back relax and the tension from last night's dream ebb away. She felt bad for being short with Hester. Lovely, loyal Hester who only had her best interests at heart. But Hester didn't understand – no one understood – how seriously Celene took her role as commander of the Royal Knights.

She knew, at nineteen, that she was young to hold this position. She didn't want anyone to say, or even think, that she had been given this title because she was King Ellis's daughter. She wanted them to say that she earned this role because she was the best.

And that was why Celene was here, training, at sunrise every morning, no matter the weather, how she was feeling or what she had dreamed the night before. Celene refused to be mediocre, or even good. She was committed to being the most exceptional knight of them all.

She drew back her bow and fired three more arrows, each into the centre of her target. She smiled. Perfection. Now she was ready to move on to the next exercise.

THE ELITHIAN ROYAL KNIGHTS

After an hour's training, Celene returned to the palace through the back doors. She ran past the gallery, music room and library, along the corridor and through to the central open-air courtyard. It was a large, attractive space, with shining black and white floor tiles and planters of green ferns and hibiscus flowers. A little flavour of the Elithian countryside. In amongst the greenery was a tiered marble fountain, its water tumbling prettily over each level into a low reservoir. At the front end of the courtyard was a marble structure that looked like another fountain, but contained no water. It had a metal gnomon at its centre and was marked at regular intervals around its circumference with lines and numbers. The great moondial: an unusual but working feature prized by the king.

Behind this, towards the back of the courtyard, stretched the long, white table around which the Elithian Royal Knights met every month. Once upon a time, meetings would have taken place in the middle of the night by the light of the full moon. Night-time meetings were no longer considered practical but the knights still gathered here in the open air, next to the moondial, even when there was snow on the ground. Only pouring rain would keep them away, but in the two years that Celene had held the position of commander, it had not rained once on their meeting. A good sign, perhaps.

Today, the courtyard looked at its best. In anticipation of the meeting, royal attendants had hung regal green and purple banners from the internal balconies. The table was covered with crisp white cloths. Bowls of ripe fruit and jugs of water rested in the middle.

Celene sat at the head of the table as she always did. She was hungry now and glad of the roll in her pocket that she'd taken from the breakfast tray. She tore it apart and began to cram it, morsel by morsel, into her mouth. After she'd eaten three pieces, Rohan and Jade strode into the courtyard – they were early. She swallowed and slipped the uneaten remainder back in her pocket. They smiled, inclined their heads towards her and took their usual seats. There were no rules governing where the knights sat, yet they always chose their regular places. People were creatures of habit.

Rohan and Jade were twins, and although they were non-identical, the resemblance was plain to see. Celene had trained with them as a young girl and knew that they walked in time and talked with the same inflections in their voices. Right now, they even sat in a similar way, each with a hand to their cheek, one unconsciously mirroring the other.

Ardis, the royal sorcerer, was the next to enter the courtyard. He stood to one side, by the ferns, and didn't say a word. He never sat with them at the table, as he was not a knight himself, although no one would have minded. His supportive presence was always welcome at their meetings.

The other knights followed soon afterwards, right on time. They knew what Celene's expectations were and, despite her young age, respected her. Freda and Jorinda came in chatting. They were older than her – both quiet individuals who were happy to have found a place with the Royal Knights and as reliable as could be.

Then Nyaal and Kay, both fierce and brave. They fought each other all through training school, competing to be top, and were surprised, but gracious, when Celene outstripped them both in technical skill. Since then, they had been firm friends.

Behind them were the least likely pairing: Thorran and Alard. Thorran had been a knight for years, and commander before

Celene. While most couldn't keep to the pace of training as they grew older and were happy to retire, Thorran chose to keep going. His main duty was training and selecting the new recruits. Along with the king, he was responsible for each one of them making it through to the Elithian Royal Knights. He was supportive, offering advice only when needed, and Celene could not imagine the Royal Knights without him. Alard was the youngest of the knights. At only sixteen, he had a tendency to be rash, and could irritate Nyaal and Kay when the timing was wrong, but Thorran had taken him under his wing.

That was how they entered the room – in pairs – and that was how Celene thought of them: as five pairs that made one perfect whole. They sat facing each other across the stone table: Jade, Rohan, Thorran and Alard on one side; Freda, Jorinda, Nyaal and Kay on the other.

Celene, of course, had her own partner – Samara – who breezed into the courtyard, just on time. She could have sat on her own at the foot of the table but Nyaal and Kay shifted their chairs up a little to make room for her. She squeezed on the end, offering some comment that made them all laugh. She brought a certain warm light to every room she entered. Celene's best friend: kind, generous Samara.

Of all the familiar faces around the table, Samara was the one she would trust with her life. They had known each other from before they could walk. Samara's father had been her own father's most loyal knight but had been killed on a royal quest. Celene's father had vowed to look after Samara, and they had taken their lessons together: Celene, her brother Hero and Samara, all with the same governess. Celene nodded in her direction now. Some might think it strange that they could be formal like this and then revert to their childhood friendship, but for them it was normal.

Celene smiled. Now that they were all present, the meeting could commence. "Welcome, loyal knights—" she began, but a side door to the courtyard swung open, interrupting her greeting. Celene was surprised to see her older brother enter the room in his usual nonchalant fashion. Hero had two or three days' worth of stubble on his chin and was rubbing his eyes as though he'd just woken up. A few of the knights leaped up to greet him with pats on the back and embraces. Her brother was not a knight and was under no obligation to attend the meetings, but when he did, his presence was always welcome. Hero was tall, strong, gentle, kind, lazy and beloved by everyone, including Celene, although she sometimes wished she had his way with people.

"You're late, Prince Hero," she said.

"It is hard to keep to schedule when the one timepiece in the palace is correct only on nights when the moon is full and the sky is clear." He gestured to the great moondial behind Celene.

Celene smiled. "And yet, all other eleven people here managed to arrive on time."

Hero laughed. "You are right, of course, sister. This is one reason why I would never make a good knight."

Everyone laughed with him, including Celene.

Her father had tried hard to persuade Hero to be a knight before her, but Hero had neither the aptitude nor the inclination for fighting. He never had. As a child, he would play with spinning tops, hobby horses or toy castles, but never with swords or bows and arrows. As Celene grew older, it became clear that it was she, not Hero, who was the skilled fighter of the family. The king found a different role for Hero: as his personal advisor. This was in many ways seen as the top position and gave him a privilege unrivalled by most.

Hero waved an apologetic hand at Celene for the disruption and took a place at the table next to Samara. The whole row had to shuffle up again, despite the free space at the foot of the table. He leaned in to take a handful of grapes from the fruit bowl, despite the fact that no one else was eating. Celene raised an eyebrow and he threw a grape to her, which she caught in one hand, reflexes as sharp as ever. They exchanged amused glances, then he settled back so far in the chair that Celene half-expected him to rest his feet up on the table.

Celene put the grape down on the table and continued as naturally as possible, although she did feel a little self-conscious with Hero there. She was normally happy to be the serious, authoritative commander, but the presence of her older brother made her feel like an impostor. Hero's expression didn't help: there always seemed to be a smile playing around his mouth.

She tried not to meet his gaze. "As I was saying… Loyal knights, we gather here as we have always done, to remind ourselves of the important work we undertake for the kingdom every day. Our agenda is not long, but as always, there are some important matters to discuss. Firstly, the jousting tournament with the Western Isles. It is not until the spring, but we are hosting, and I would like us to be as prepared as possible. Jorinda, I believe you are going to tell us a little more about this?"

Jorinda stood and delivered the details of the future tournament, but Celene's mind wandered from what she was saying. Instead, she watched her brother and Samara. They were sitting so close that their arms were touching. She wondered why he had chosen that particular spot at the table when other places were available. As the other half of the Samara/Celene pairing, she wasn't sure that she liked the idea of a Samara/Hero pairing at all. She had a sudden urge to demand that Hero move to the spare place at the foot of the table, but then shook her head, dismissing the jealous thoughts.

Jorinda finished speaking and sat back down, and Celene moved on to the next item on her agenda.

"As we know, Thorran is planning to retire. Not yet, but within a year or two. This means that not only do we need to find a new trainer, but also another Royal Knight to join us around this table. Thorran, would you help us choose your own successor and a new young knight from the talented ranks of the training school?"

"I would be honoured, Princess."

"Thank you. We must never forget the next generation. The children out there playing with wooden swords and bows, as we all did, are the Elithian Royal Knights of the future."

Celene was in her stride now, feeling her usual confident self. Hero was still smiling but that was his natural expression. In fact, he didn't even seem to be looking in her direction at all. Unless she was mistaken, his smile was directed sideways at Samara, who was smiling back.

Perhaps no one was listening to a word she was saying.

She cleared her throat and moved on to the next, and possibly most important, item on the agenda.

"External threats are not a problem at the moment – we have friends on all sides – and although we should not rest on our laurels, our main enemy is to be found within the kingdom."

There was an uncomfortable silence within the courtyard. Nyaal cleared his throat and took a sip of water.

It was Ardis the sorcerer, standing by the ferns, who broke the silence. "You speak of my sister, Sidra?"

There were murmurs of agreement. Everyone knew whom Celene was referring to. Sidra – the dark sorcerer who had caused trouble in Elithia in the past. They just felt uncomfortable saying her name when Ardis was present.

Ardis sighed. "You do not have to be sensitive of my feelings on this matter. I am aware of the trouble that my sister causes in Elithia."

"Thank you, Ardis – we are grateful for your support," said Celene. "Yes. Sidra has been keeping a low profile since she was suspected of causing the fires in the city grain stores, but lately cockroaches have been plaguing the east of the city. They were first spotted in the house of a schoolteacher who had a dispute with Sidra. Once again, Sidra is rumoured to be behind it, but it is hard to prove."

Alard, their youngest knight, spoke, cheeks pink. "She has forever been a blight on Elithia – worse than the cockroaches themselves. I say banish her and be done with it!"

"The problem is that she keeps on just the right side of the law. We cannot banish her on the strength of hearsay – it is not the Elithian way." Samara was always more measured in her responses.

Nyaal agreed. "And you know what they say about keeping your enemies close. At least while she is here, we know where she is and can monitor her."

"Yes, and we have Ardis here to help and advise whenever we need him. Nyaal, Kay, do you think you could keep an eye on her and check nothing untoward is going on?" asked Celene.

They nodded seriously. Celene knew that she could trust them to do this without harassing Sidra, who had a right to live with the same freedoms afforded to the rest of the city.

She moved on to the last item, grateful to change the subject to an easier matter.

"Many of you have been focusing on skill and accuracy in your training but sometimes we forget simple stamina. Incorporate long runs and rides into your schedules. Play to your strengths. If you struggle with a sword, then work on your lance. Not all of us can be experts at everything."

Apart from me, thought Celene. *I plan to stay an expert in every discipline.*

"Remember, this may be a time of peace, but the Elithian Royal Knights should train as hard as we would if we were at war. Discipline, organisation and strength are key. You know that my expectations are high, but this will bring out the best in you."

All around the table, the knights nodded and mumbled their agreement. Celene felt lucky to lead such a trustworthy group; it was hard to imagine any problem that they would not be able to fight together. She took a sip of water.

"Does anyone have anything else they wish to share?"

Hero raised his hand, a flicker of amusement dancing around his eyes. Raised hands were not necessary at these meetings but Celene nodded in his direction and he announced his news in a loud voice.

"I will be going on important diplomatic business with the king. We leave next week and during the king's absence Princess Celene will be in charge of the kingdom."

Would she? This was the first Celene had heard of any such trip. She should not be hearing about it for the first time along with the others. She felt herself redden slightly but smiled and nodded towards Hero as though she knew and approved. She did not want her annoyance to be obvious to any of the others.

"It is noted. Well then, if that is everything? This meeting is dismissed. Thank you."

Ardis and the knights filed out of the courtyard, nodding to Celene, making their way to the training ground, the castle, the stables. Samara was the last to go. She and Hero smiled at each other and then he stood to speak to her. They were speaking quietly, whispering, almost.

"I will see you later," interrupted Celene, loudly. They both turned to look at her. "At the stables," added Celene, making it clear that her words were intended for Samara.

Samara smiled. "See you there," she replied, and turned to leave. Hero watched her walk from the room and raised a hand in a gesture of farewell.

Celene was puzzled. They had all been friends as children, when they schooled together, but for years Samara had been her special friend. She had assumed that Hero saw Samara as another younger sister. Now she wasn't so sure. She would ask him about it, but there were other more pressing issues to address – Hero's mysterious diplomatic journey, for one thing.

Hero poured two cups of water and passed one to Celene, smiling as he did so. "Well done. I'm always impressed to see my little sister lead a meeting with such confidence."

That was typical of her brother. He always said something charming, was free with his compliments. It often made it difficult to stay cross with him, but this time, she brushed it away. "I have been commander of the knights for over a year. I am used to these meetings now." She added, "I was surprised to hear that you are going away with our father. Neither of you mentioned it."

"I only heard about it myself this morning. You know what father is like. He probably thought he'd already told us both."

"And where exactly are you going?"

"I can't quite remember. Somewhere to the east? I think we are meeting another royal family. I must admit that I did not pay quite as much attention as I should have done when he spoke to me about it. He rambled on about a lot of things."

"So you are going on a mission with the king but you have no idea where or why?"

Hero shrugged sheepishly. "I suppose that's right."

"Do you even want to go?"

"I'm happy to. I enjoy travelling. Different sights and sounds. Lots of time to let the mind wander."

Celene rolled her eyes. Time to let her mind wander would not have been her first concern if she were going on such a trip. "I need details. I am going to see our father now."

They left the courtyard together, but at the bottom of the stairs, Hero turned to head outside.

"Where are you going?" asked Celene.

"To the stables," said Hero.

This was a little odd, because Hero was not a natural horseman, and tended to stay away from the stables unless necessary. Celene wondered if he was going to see Samara, but dismissed the thought. Her brother could see whomever he pleased, as could she. And right now, she was going to see her father, to get some explanations.

KING ELLIS

The king was in the first place she looked: the library.

The library was a dark and dusty room, lined with books from floor to ceiling. Ladders were placed to allow access to the upper shelves, and the king was perched precariously near the top of one, reaching out for a red-spined book.

Celene said nothing – she didn't want to cause him to wobble and fall – but he raised his hand in a gesture of greeting.

"Hello, my dear. One moment." He removed his book from the shelf and climbed down carefully.

Celene waited until he'd reached the bottom of the ladder before speaking.

"I have been lecturing your knights on how we shouldn't rest on our laurels because it is peace time. Yet here is our king, not at the training ground or the treasury, but pottering about in the library."

Her father smiled. "Hello, Celene, it is good to see you this morning. You are right, of course, but we should not forget that intellect and learning are as important to the kingdom as military excellence. Sharp minds are essential." The king kissed her lightly on the cheek and took a seat at his favourite desk, nodding to invite her to sit on the other side.

Celene picked up his book. "And what is it that you are reading to improve your intellect?" She read the title on the cover: "*Happy Houseplants: surrounding yourself with thriving greenery.*"

The king shifted his glasses higher up the bridge of his nose and looked a little embarrassed. "Yes, well. A relaxed and happy king is also of benefit to the kingdom."

Celene raised her eyebrows and sat down. "At least your leafy subjects are in good hands."

Her father pushed the book to one side. "Why do I think you haven't come here to discuss houseplants?"

"Hero came to our meeting earlier. He seems to think that he is accompanying you on a diplomatic trip, although he doesn't know where."

King Ellis removed his glasses and rubbed his temples. "We have hardly talked about it, that's why. It's not of great importance. We are simply visiting the sea people to discuss their new settlement."

Celene pursed her lips. The nomadic sea people had lived on houseboats out at sea near to Elithia for many years. Their relationship had been tumultuous in the past, because of arguments over borders and resources, but it was currently good. Celene would be fascinated to meet them and see their plans for a permanent site: it seemed that her father was playing down the importance of the trip. "Why did you not tell me of these plans?"

"I sent Hero just now to the Knights' meeting to inform you."

"But he didn't know the first thing about it! He never does."

Her father smiled amiably. "What do you need to know?"

"When exactly are you leaving? For how long?"

"We will be leaving on Wednesday and returning within a fortnight."

"Why so long? It is only a day's journey each way."

"The sea people have asked that we spend a significant stretch of time with them so that we can appreciate what they are trying to achieve. It is a good sign that they want us there."

Her father smiled again and raised his eyebrows, inviting any further questions.

Celene had many more bubbling up inside her. She might as well get them off her chest now. "I want to know why you have chosen Hero to accompany you, and not me, when I have always paid much closer attention to political issues."

The king sighed. "Perhaps you should be asking yourself why I have chosen you to stay. It is a great responsibility to be left in charge for a fortnight."

"We both know that it is in name only. The council will be here to deal with anything that comes up in your absence, whereas a trip like this doesn't happen every day."

"There will be other trips in the future, other ways for you to learn and gain new skills. This time, I am taking Hero. The decision is made."

He picked up his book again and opened it, indicating that the conversation was at an end. That may have worked with others but it didn't work with Celene. He was her father as well as the king, after all, and she wanted to have this conversation. "I love Hero, you know I do, Father, but he will never make a king. He does not even *want* the crown, whereas I will be a committed ruler one day."

The king placed his book page down on the table. "You forget that I am still a relatively young man and I am planning to live for a few more years yet. I have therefore not made any firm decisions regarding my successor. Anyway, your brother is older than you and traditionally the eldest child is first in line to the throne. Until he indicates to me directly that he wishes to give up this right, then I shall continue to treat him as heir."

"Well, he won't speak to you directly. He hardly considers what will happen in the future. He hardly considers anything at all."

"Which is exactly why, on this occasion, I feel that Hero would be more suited to accompany me."

The king clearly didn't want to be having this conversation, but Celene did.

"*Why*? What is it I am lacking?"

The king sighed. "You have many enviable qualities, Celene. You are organised, strategic and fair-minded, not to mention your great technical skill as a knight. Yet, there are traits you possess that might not be so beneficial, and more you must learn."

"Tell me. I am always ready to learn. I strive to improve, which is why I train every day."

The king laughed. "This is a good thing, Celene, and it will serve you well. But it is also part of the problem. You are too rigid in your ways, too controlling. There are some things that you cannot plan or train for and that only experience of life will teach you. There will be times when life will take you by surprise and you will realize that you cannot control everything."

Celene sighed. This conversation had not gone the way she had planned. "Perhaps so, but this is not one of these times. I must leave now before Samara thinks I have forgotten her."

"Of course. Now give your father a kiss."

Celene planted a reluctant kiss on his cheek and headed off to the stables.

AT THE STABLES

Celene stomped down the slope from the palace to the stables, thinking about what the king had said. She worked hard every day and did everything she could for her father and the kingdom, yet he never seemed to recognize her efforts. Her brother did virtually nothing, and good things seemed to fall into his lap. It was so unfair.

When she was about halfway there, she spotted Hero waving up at her, grinning. She raised her hand, without smiling. He was heading uphill, away from the stables and towards the palace, so their paths crossed. He stopped, but she kept on walking.

"Did you see Father?"

Celene nodded.

"And he explained everything?"

She nodded again; she didn't feel like discussing it. "I'm late to meet Samara," she said, over her shoulder.

"And I'm late to meet the king! I'd better find out where we're off to," he said, grinning and waving again.

Celene didn't respond or look back, but kept going along the pebbled path, bringing her feet down hard with every step. Was Hero so unaware of her displeasure? He hadn't given a single thought to how she might feel about any of this. At least Samara would understand.

Samara had nearly finished grooming Breeze, her horse, and as she brushed his tail, her long dark tresses were indistinguishable from his. She looked up as Celene approached. "I was wondering what had happened to you. I was beginning to think you might be unwell."

Celene and Samara had been meeting here for a daily ride since they were young girls. In ten years, Samara had arrived first on just a handful of occasions. Celene greeted her own horse, Morus, with a soft touch of her knuckles to the front of his muzzle. She embraced Samara, even though it had been less than an hour since they'd seen each other.

Samara finished with the brushes, passed them to Celene and began to attach Breeze's bridle. Celene brushed Morus firmly, starting at his neck. Morus loved to be brushed and scratched, particularly around his shoulders. When Celene reached that part, he lifted his head, half-closed his eyes and pointed his ears back. They had grooms who would do this for them, but both Samara and Celene liked to do it themselves: for them it was an important part of bonding with the horses.

"I had an audience with the king," said Celene, raising her eyebrows at her friend. She wouldn't talk to any of the other knights about private family matters – this was one of the downsides of being part of the royal family – but she knew she could trust Samara with anything.

"Problems?"

Celene sighed, continuing to brush in a circular motion towards Morus's hindquarters. "I cannot believe my father. He *knows* that I would make a better ruler than Hero. He *knows* that Hero has never wanted the throne, yet he continues to invite him on royal business – without me. Why would he do that?"

"I don't know."

"The only reason I can see is that he prefers Hero. He is his favourite."

"No! I don't think that is true. Your father loves you both. He is a fair man. Maybe he thinks that Hero would be good in this type of situation. People do warm to Hero. He's calm, and gracious. . ."

Samara broke off with a smile, and turned to place Breeze's saddle on his back. Her hair shielded her face, but not before Celene saw pink spots appearing on her cheekbones. Celene waited for her to turn around and then stared at her.

"What is going on between you and my brother?"

Samara reddened deeper. "Nothing."

It was obviously a lie and Celene felt a prickle of betrayal. She understood Samara's reluctance to tell her. The pair would not be allowed to have a relationship while Samara was serving as a knight. However deep their friendship, Celene still ranked higher than Samara and could strip her of her title of Royal Knight if she so chose. But Celene would never do that to her friend. She would let her remain a knight even if she were to marry. Samara was her best friend and she wanted her to know that she could tell her anything. "I don't mind, you know. Some people might mind but not me. I like the idea of having you for a sister."

Samara smiled.

"I wouldn't even tell my father. I can keep a secret."

Still, Samara said nothing.

Celene moved around to Morus's right side to finish grooming him. She felt strange. She had always trusted Samara with her own secrets and now she felt excluded by the two people she loved most. On top of the news about her father and Hero's trip, it felt like a double betrayal.

"There's honestly nothing to tell," said Samara, without looking Celene in the eye. She clearly didn't want to talk.

Celene clenched her teeth and turned away from her. "Fine: I can see you won't discuss it. We're nearly ready to get going anyway."

Celene finished equipping Morus for his ride in silence and then they mounted the horses and walked out of the stables together, hooves clopping in unison on the cobbles. As soon as they were clear of the buildings, Celene broke into a trot. Her daily ride was an essential part of her training, and also the part of the day that she loved best. All Elithians were good riders who grew up around horses, but the knights were better than most. Celene could draw a bow or use a sword as she rode. She could duck low to avoid a flying missile, or even, in an emergency, jump from her saddle.

Celene squeezed her legs, urging Morus to canter, then leaned forward to gallop almost straight away. It felt better to be travelling fast, leaving the palace and all her worries behind her. Out here, with the wind whistling past her ears, she could forget about her brother, her father, and any responsibility. Morus cared nothing of her status of princess or commander of knights; he just wanted to enjoy his morning ride. She felt jealous of how easily he ran, and how quickly, with so little effort.

But Samara and Breeze lagged behind, and Celene was not sure why. Samara was the only one of the knights who was a better rider than Celene – she was quicker, sharper. It had crossed Celene's mind that if it weren't for her status as princess, then Samara might have been the commander rather than her. But then Samara had always lacked a certain drive. She might have been a good leader, but it wasn't something that she wanted.

Right now, Samara was holding back. Celene wasn't sure if it was because she felt Celene's annoyance with her, or because she had some kind of injury that she hadn't shared. Celene was beginning to wonder quite how much Samara kept from her.

BY THE MULBERRY TREES

They galloped for a few miles, leaving the palace, the stables and the training ground far behind them. Celene led the way past the peasants' houses, through the fields and along the empty shingle beach. This was the part that Morus enjoyed best, and Celene gave him a good romp through the water, the white foam frothing at his hooves. Then they headed back uphill.

At the top of the hill, Celene slowed and waited for Samara to draw level to her. They allowed the horses to nibble at the grass at the outskirts of the mulberry woods, the distinctive dusty smell of the mulberry leaves scenting the autumn air.

It all felt normal again: the ride had cleared any tension between them. Samara took a swig of water from a flask – she was always well prepared – and passed it to Celene. Then she reached out into the branches of one of the trees.

"They're ripe, look." She plucked a few of the large purplish fruits and handed one to Celene.

Celene chewed, enjoying the sudden tangy burst of flavour, refreshing after the ride. "Mine's sweet," she said. Some had a sour taste but it was difficult to tell until you bit into one. She had another sip of water and then passed the flask back.

Samara ate her own fruit and inspected her fingertips, which were now stained with juice. It looked a little like blood. She stared up into the branches. "The best ones are always near the top of the tree. Do you remember when we used to climb up there?"

"Yes," said Celene. Of course she remembered. It felt like yesterday. She also remembered the time that one of the brittle branches broke, sending Samara plummeting to the ground. She remembered how she and Hero had both slid out of the tree, exchanging fearful looks for what they might find on the ground. But, apart from a cut on her temple, Samara was fine. They had taken her to Ardis, who had applied benzoin oil and patched her up. Celene didn't recount the tale now. She didn't want to relive the fear of thinking that she might lose her best friend.

So she stayed quiet, although Samara now seemed to be in the mood for chatting.

"It's incredible to think that those trees feed the silkworms that make Elithian silk. They raise the silkworms on mulberry leaves down in those barns. Thousands of the creatures, munching away. Apparently, when there are so many of them, it sounds like the patter of rain on the roof."

"I'd never really thought about it," said Celene. She was not sure where this conversation was heading. She jiggled Morus's reins and began walking again.

Samara followed. "Do you ever think about what you'd do if you were born into a different life? If you were a farmer or a circus performer, instead of a princess?"

"No," said Celene, not inviting further conversation. Samara worried Celene when she spoke like this. She was the best knight they had – good at everything she set her hand to – so why was she talking about leading a different life?

But Samara continued to look dreamily into the distance. "I do," she said. "When I look at the rows of mulberry trees, I imagine what it must be like, spinning silk from the cocoons as so many of our people do. Raising a family and thinking only of day to day routines. Or performing as a bareback rider in the circus tent, training all day and enjoying the applause at night."

"But you are so good at what you do. You are not made for a simple life."

"I am sure that many of the people in the cottages were not made for a simple life either. Some of them could be expert riders or hunters if given the chance. Wouldn't it be fun to all swap roles for a short time, and to see if we enjoyed the alternative?"

Celene did not agree. She had her eye on one role only, and she wasn't sure what she would do with her life if that option were unavailable to her. She remained silent as Samara gazed off in the other direction. "Perhaps not a silk spinner – that work can be tough. Perhaps a seamstress. I was always good at needlework—"

"I must go now," interrupted Celene, turning her horse back in the direction of the palace.

"But we have only covered half our usual route. Don't you want to continue around the woods?"

Celene shook her head. She was frustrated that Samara was so keen to twitter on about mulberries and silk making but seemed to evade questions of any real importance. They could talk another day. Maybe next time they met, Samara would be keener to share what was going on in her life.

Celene headed back towards the palace, feeling more alone than ever.

CHAPTER TWO

FAREWELL TO HERO

Before long, it was time for Hero and her father to depart on their trip. They were taking a small ship with a basic crew, as they would only be gone for a fortnight. Despite this, on the morning of their departure, everyone at the palace seemed to be involved with helping them pack. Maids and footmen scurried around carrying piles of clothes, food and provisions. Great trunks were brought from the palace to the harbour, where the ship was moored, hung with silks. Even Hester was helping Hero instead of Celene.

Celene watched it all happening without feeling any excitement.

She went to her father's quarters to say a brief farewell, and then set off for the training ground as usual. She didn't want to wave the boat off, or see Hero, but as she was leaving through the back door, she bumped into him. He was wearing his smartest princely clothes.

"Goodbye, my sister," he said, enveloping her in a hug. "Good luck being queen in our absence."

"Don't jest about such a thing." She prised herself free from his grasp. Sometimes Hero could irritate her like no one else. It seemed to her that he was delighting in the fact that he was leaving and she was staying.

He stood back with a surprised expression on his face. "I'm not jesting. I hope it goes smoothly while we're away and I look forward to seeing you when we return."

How could he be so blind to her feelings? She wanted him to understand that this mattered to her, even if he was indifferent about the trip. "I hope that your mission does *not* go smoothly. I hope it is full of calamity and that your lack of political knowledge shows you up. Then perhaps father will take *me* next time as he should have done this time."

She pushed past him, her eyes stinging with angry tears.

Hero called after her. "That is unkind, Celene! I didn't know you felt that way. This one trip hardly matters. There will be other trips – other chances for you."

"You're right, I shall enjoy this time without you. At least I will have my friend back." She felt like they were children again, arguing over a favourite toy.

"I don't know what you mean. Won't you send me on my way with good wishes? Come and wave off the ship!"

But Celene raised her chin in the air and strode onwards. She wasn't going to wave him off or wish him well; she was going to pretend that he didn't exist. And she would use their absence as a chance to train harder than ever before.

TRAINING AGAIN

Later, at the training ground, Celene was training with the lance. It was her least favourite weapon but that was only because she hadn't put enough hours in. She practised now against a shield and dummy suspended from a pole, working on her thrust and tilt.

Normally, training blotted out all other thoughts from her mind, but this morning, anger was still making her hands shake. She shouldn't have been so rude to Hero. It wasn't exactly his fault that her father has chosen him as his companion on this trip. But if only he would tell her father that he had no desire to be king, then it would make her own path to the throne much easier. She just didn't understand.

Part of her wondered if she should have gone to wave them off but it was too late now. She jabbed at the dummy unsuccessfully. Had it been a real assailant, it would have overpowered her in minutes.

"Good morning." She heard Samara's voice and glanced at her briefly as she approached. She was not looking quite as radiant as she had at their last meeting. Her hair was unbrushed and she had dark smudges of tiredness under her eyes. She had probably been at the docks, saying an emotional farewell to Hero. Celene sighed loudly at the thought. Why did everyone think her brother was so wonderful? She didn't say anything and continued poking half-heartedly at the dummy.

Samara stood back and watched for a little while, then when it became clear that Celene wasn't going to stop, she ventured, "How are you?"

"I could be better. I am commander of the Elithian Royal Knights and I simply cannot master the lance. What about you?"

Samara looked thoughtful. "I am well. Sort of. I miss you, though."

Celene stared at her. "I see." Now that Hero had gone away, Samara was lonely. Now Samara wanted to talk, whereas a week ago, all Samara had wanted to discuss was silkworms.

Samara twisted the end of a lock of hair around her forefinger. "There is something I would like to discuss with you and I was wondering if you might come for a longer ride with me this morning? It is such a beautiful day and it feels like a long time since we've properly spoken to each other – spoken about things that matter."

Celene went back to jabbing away at the dummy. She had a good idea of what – or whom – Samara might want to talk about, but she didn't particularly want to listen to it today. She already had so much on her mind and felt that any sort of deep conversation might make her cry. "That sounds wonderful but I can't. I am busy looking after the kingdom."

"Please come. You can miss the rest of your training this once. You said yourself that you are not up to your usual standard this morning."

"Which is exactly why I have to train."

"You train every day."

"I do. And I have been meaning to ask you: If I am acting queen in the king's absence, then we should also have an acting commander. Will you step up to that position?"

Samara paused and let the hair unwind from her finger. She looked surprised. "That is very sweet of you, Celene, but I am not the right person. I do not want that level of responsibility and I . . . I have other things on my mind right now. Why don't you ask Nyaal?"

Celene bristled. "I happen to think that you are the perfect person for the role. I don't understand why people don't take these opportunities when they present themselves."

Samara sat down on the ground with her knees drawn up to her chin. "Why does it all matter so much to you, Celene?"

"It matters to me because I want to be queen. I wouldn't mind if Hero wanted to be king but he doesn't. Not really."

"Maybe he doesn't know what he wants yet. We are all still so young."

Celene stopped unsuccessfully fighting the dummy and stood, breathing deeply. "That is my point exactly! I have known since we were children that Hero finds happiness easy. Hero doesn't need to have a plan because he can do whatever he wants in life. He can travel the kingdom, making friends wherever he goes, throw glittering parties to impress the world. Whereas I am ordinary."

"You are many things, Celene, but not ordinary!" Samara laughed, but Celene didn't smile along. She blinked back tears.

"Hard work is all I have. I don't have your natural skill, or Hero's charm. I will never be the most popular and I have to work hard at what I do. But as long as I stick to my plan and don't make any mistakes, I can be the best."

Samara looked up at her with her big brown eyes. "Life doesn't always go exactly to plan. Don't you think you are setting yourself up to be unhappy if things don't work out?"

Celene sighed, frustrated that Samara was questioning everything she said, rather than just offering a bit of support. "Things *will* work out. And the first thing I must do is prove to my father that I am a capable ruler."

"He would never have left you in charge if he doubted that."

"In reality, if there were any sort of emergency, the king would return immediately to make any necessary decisions – or delegate to the council. It is my brother that he chooses to have at his side."

"It doesn't mean that he doesn't trust you."

Celene threw her lance down. She couldn't concentrate, and this conversation wasn't helping.

"Since when are you an expert on my family and what they think and feel?" she snapped.

Samara reddened and looked at the ground.

Celene regretted her words instantly. "I didn't mean it. It's just, it doesn't have to concern you. It is a family problem and I will discuss it with my father and Hero on their return."

Samara nodded and stood up, picking up the lance as she did so. "Perhaps I could help with your training? We could practise against each other."

"No. We would be unevenly matched and I prefer to train with the dummy. We'll talk another day."

Samara passed her the lance and walked sadly away. Celene watched her go. She would talk to her when she was less frustrated with her father and Hero. For now, she would train and shoot and ride and run.

CHAPTER THREE

THE KING'S SHIP

Elithia was a calm and peaceful kingdom; Celene had grown up knowing that she had all the time in the world. Even if *now* was busy with training, there would always be *later*: time to do all those things one had been meaning to do, time to have that awkward conversation, time to apologize. But sometimes, life took an unexpected turn and all that time was no longer available.

The king and Hero had been absent for five days. Celene was in the drawing room, eating her luncheon in an armchair. She had a simple bowl of soup and bread balanced on her knee, as it had seemed excessive to request a formal meal for one person.

"How is your soup, Your Highness?" asked Hester, who was busying herself around the room, dusting ornaments and plumping cushions.

"Delicious, thank you, Hester." Celene suspected that Hester's main reason for being there was to keep her company. She had not spent much time with anyone since her father's absence, apart from brief meetings with the council, and she appreciated Hester's concern.

The drawing room, like most other rooms in the palace, had a sweeping sea view, which was one of the advantages of island life. Hester was rearranging the curtain tiebacks, when she stopped for a moment, squinting into the distance.

"I can see the king's ship, ma'am."

Celene finished the soup and put the bowl down on a side table. She joined Hester at the window, adopting a similar squinting expression.

"It can't be. They are not due back for another week, at least."

But as the ship sailed closer and its crisp outline came into view, she saw the green and purple Elithian flag fluttering from the mast, complete with royal crest. It *was* her father's ship. Back too early. She thought back to the conversation she'd had with her father in the library.

"The sea people have asked that we spend a significant stretch of time with them so that we can appreciate what they are trying to achieve. It is a good sign that they want us there."

So was it a bad sign if they were returning early? Celene's first thought was that maybe Hero hadn't been quite as charming as her father had hoped. Perhaps he had disgraced the sea people with his lack of political knowledge, and they had withdrawn their hospitality. She felt amused and then immediately ashamed of herself for even thinking such a thing. She thought of the last words she had spoken to Hero before his trip:

"I hope that your mission does not go smoothly. I hope it is full of calamity. . ."

What if something was really wrong? Her father was not old, but he was not a young man, either, and he had suffered problems with his chest in the past. He probably shouldn't be out at sea past the warmer summer months.

Hester's face reflected this concern. "I do hope everything is well with King Ellis," she said, clasping her hands together.

"Let's go down to the port and meet the ship," said Celene.

"It will be windy down there. Shall I get your winter cloak?"

47

"Please do," said Celene, looking out of the window again as Hester scurried off. The sea was still and the ship was sailing gracefully towards Elithia, a white line trailing behind her like a tail. From this distance, it was impossible to imagine there could be a problem.

She would go to the port and welcome her father and Hero with enthusiasm. She would enquire about the trip and make positive and helpful remarks, no matter whether the visit had been successful or not. That would make up for the lack of a proper farewell.

AT THE PORT

Hester was right: it was windy down by the docks. A salty breeze whipped across the water like a slap. Celene pulled the hood of her cloak right over her head and down to her eyes. This kept out the cold and also indicated to anyone who might bother her that she was not in the mood for small talk. Hester acted as a human shield, standing solidly beside Celene with her own winter wrap folded across her chest.

A small, giggling group of young women gathered nearby to welcome home the king – or more likely the handsome prince Hero.

They held posies of deep pink asters and handfuls of flower petals. A royal ship, however small and however unexpected, couldn't dock in Elithia without a welcome party. The girls didn't try to talk to Celene, and although she was glad she didn't have to make conversation, she still felt a pang of hurt. They would no doubt try to speak to Hero when he disembarked.

As the ship drew nearer, she dropped her sail, and the crew brought out the oars to row her in. The king and Hero were nowhere to be seen: below deck, probably. One girl with bare arms broke from the group, ran to the perimeter wall and threw a handful of petals into the water, as a gesture of welcome and good fortune.

Suddenly, deep cackling laughter broke the happy atmosphere.

"All is not well on board that vessel, and it is too late for flower petals in the ocean. I have seen dark times ahead for Elithia!"

The girls, Celene and Hester all looked for the source of the voice, and saw a figure dressed in black, lurking some distance away. It was Sidra, the sorcerer they had been discussing at the knights' meeting. Sidra, who was infamous in these parts and caused trouble wherever she went. She was short but stood as if she were six-foot tall, her long purple hair flowing over her shoulders. The girls turned their backs and ignored her but she moved closer.

Hester swatted the air in front of her, as if trying to rid herself of a pest. "Get away from here – this is a welcome party, not a funeral procession!" she cried.

Sidra cackled again. "A welcome party that might not be as happy as planned. I cannot see the royal family waving from the deck, can you?"

Celene looked away from Sidra, not wanting to engage in conversation and worried that her expression might give away her own anxiety about the ship. She saw Nyaal and Kay, in full armour, marching down towards the docks. She made eye contact with them and gestured subtly towards Sidra to let them know that she was being a nuisance.

They marched towards her. "Is everything all right here, Sidra?" asked Kay.

Sidra narrowed her eyes. "I have a right to stand on these docks with everyone else."

"Yes, as long as you don't stir up any trouble," said Nyaal, moving between her and Celene.

Sidra raised her hands up in a gesture of surrender. "I have finished here anyway. I only wanted to watch the ship come in." She turned to Celene. "Farewell for now, Princess. I shall leave you to greet your family. No doubt I will see you soon." She swept away, still laughing to herself, and Celene avoided looking in her direction.

She shivered. Were Sidra's words true, or was she stirring up trouble? She would love to dismiss such thoughts, but she had known as soon as she saw the ship that something wasn't quite right.

Then she caught sight of her father on deck. He had emerged from his cabin and stood facing the harbour. The wind whipped his longish hair around his face and his travelling clothes flapped about him. His face was red and weathered and he looked unusually tired, but well: fit and healthy.

Celene breathed out deeply. Perhaps things had gone dreadfully wrong with the sea people. Perhaps they were on the brink of war, but if he was well, then the rest didn't matter; they could solve any problem together.

Hester was clinging to her arm and she turned to smile at her maid, expecting to see relief on her face; but Hester was still looking towards the ship, her brow wrinkled.

She turned to Celene and whispered,

"Where is Prince Hero, Your Highness?"

HERO'S RETURN

Hester was right; Hero should be on board, with his easy smile, waving to his welcome party.

But as the ship drew nearer and finally set anchor, Hero still didn't appear on deck. Celene met her father's gaze and his stony expression confirmed her suspicions that something had happened to her brother. He disembarked and came straight over to greet her. He kissed her cheek; his face was even colder than hers.

"Father, where is Hero?" she whispered.

Her father shook his head in a small, barely-there gesture. "Let me see to this welcome party and I shall explain everything."

He turned to the group of young women with a broad grin.

"Thank you, thank you, for such a warm welcome back to the kingdom. Prince Hero is on a separate ship. You will see him in good time but for now, return to your work. Go on, be gone now."

He spoke in a gentle but firm voice and the group dispersed, wilting flowers still in hand.

Once they were gone and Celene and Hester were the only two left at the harbour, he turned to his boatswain and nodded. "You may bring Prince Hero up now."

The man gave orders to some unseen crew members and after

a couple of minutes, Hero's head and shoulders emerged from below deck. They appeared to be half-dragging him out from his quarters. Once he was up on deck, two men propped him up under his arms, and led him to the gangplank and off the ship. He could barely put one foot in front of the other; his head lolled to the side and his mouth was slack.

Hester gasped. Celene didn't make a sound but was just as shocked: it was difficult to process what she was seeing. Hero was not the type to look unwell. Even when they had battled childhood diseases, she had been the one to suffer the worst symptoms. He had been the one sitting up in bed playing puzzles and enjoying the break from his schoolwork. And now he could barely stand.

"A blanket!" demanded the king. "Keep him warm." Another man obediently tossed a blanket from the ship and it was tucked around Hero's shoulders.

They walked past where Celene was standing and she reached out to touch his arm. "Hero? What is the matter?"

The two aides continued marching him forwards. "Sorry, Your Highness, but we've been given strict orders to help him straight up to his chamber."

They continued past Celene towards the palace and she turned to her father, who was massaging the bridge of his nose with one hand.

"What happened to him?" she asked.

He paused before answering, and she could see that he had tears in his eyes.

"Oh, Celene, I wish I could answer that, but the truth is, we don't know."

They followed Hero and his aides up to the back door of the palace. Celene thought she caught the sound of more low laughter coming from the harbour but, because of the breeze, she couldn't be sure.

CHAPTER FOUR

THE BITE

Once they were inside the palace walls and Hester was occupied with other tasks, the king was able to speak more freely. The trip had been a success, he said. The outward journey was calm and the sea people had welcomed them warmly. Hero (it was no surprise) had been received particularly well, charming the royal family and the people alike. The accommodation was basic: they had slept in tents and low cots, but the people had put on dances and seafood feasts, and music and speeches. It was looking like the best diplomatic trip imaginable.

Then, on their third evening, Hero had started slurring his words. At first, his father had put it down to the free-flowing wine, which their generous hosts had poured all evening; but it soon became apparent that this was not the cause. Hero mentioned a pain in his arm and they discovered a bite. It looked like a mosquito bite, but the sea people had never seen anything like it before.

Hero had quickly deteriorated, sweating with fever and crying out in pain. The king had made a swift decision to sail him straight back to the comfort of his own home. On the journey back, the pain seemed to abate but he had become drowsy and unresponsive – the state in which he appeared now.

Within two hours of returning home, he fell into a deep sleep from which nobody could rouse him. His sick bed was prepared and a nurse, Dev, was employed to tend to him around the clock.

The next morning, Celene asked to see him. She went with her father and they sat together by his bedside. Hero lay on his back, the sheet pulled up to his chin, his face pale and motionless as he slept. He had no fever, no sweat on his brow, and was breathing steadily, as if he were in a normal slumber. It was so strange to see his face without its usual wide smile.

"How is the bite?" whispered Celene.

The king nodded to Dev, who folded back the sheet, loosened

the ties of Hero's shirt at the neckline and pulled it down to reveal his shoulder and upper arm. The bite was swollen and angry. Its crusty red centre was circled in white and then red, which brought to mind the target that Celene used for shooting practice.

She winced and drew back. "It looks bad. What can we do?"

"That's just it, Celene – we don't know. We've removed the dressing and he no longer appears to be distressed or in pain, but we can't rouse him from this sleep." The king had bags under his eyes and a pained expression. He looked as though he hadn't slept.

Celene thought for a moment. This was just a problem that needed solving, like any other. They needed to think it through and there would be a solution – there had to be. "Has he been seen by an experienced healer?"

"Yes. Three healers visited him last night. All of them examined the bite and none of them had ever seen anything like it before. They each had their theories as to what it might be, but none of them knew for certain."

"Somebody out there will know," she said. "You just need to find the right person."

"I know that! But where do I find them?" Her father moaned quietly: a low, pained sound. His eyes were shiny with tears.

The nurse left the room for fresh water, probably to give them some privacy, Celene thought.

The king closed his eyes and lowered his head. He stayed like that, as though thinking deeply.

Celene wasn't used to seeing her father in such a state. She rested her hand on his shoulder, patting it gently. "Everything will be all right," she said.

The king did not move and his voice was muffled. "Hero is very ill, Celene."

"I know, I can see that. But all he needs is time, is it not?"

"He may not recover from this."

Celene shook her head. She could not believe what she was hearing. Just over a month ago, she and Hero had gone out sailing together and had been laughing in the early autumn sunshine. Even at the last knights' meeting they had been joking together before his announcement about the trip – and now she was being told that he might die.

"Not recover? But he is young, fit and healthy. He doesn't even look that ill!"

"You are right, Celene, and we will do everything we can to help him, but some things are beyond help."

"What do you mean? You are a *king*. Use your power." She thought for a moment. "Has Ardis seen him?"

"Yes, he came as soon as we returned. But Ardis is a sorcerer, not a healer. There was nothing he could do."

"What is the difference? He can magic up springs and make apples grow on trees, can he not? Why could he not heal my brother?"

"It is different. That is not where his skills lie."

"I will go to him myself. Perhaps there is something he needs – some magic ingredient, some herb. If that is the case, then the knights will find whatever it is. I can't believe the situation is entirely hopeless."

"Hero was bitten by something from the east. We have sent ships back to search the forests, to identify the insect, to find a cure – but it could take years."

"I don't believe that," said Celene. "We have the money to pay for a fleet of ships, or hundreds of people if necessary. I will start with Ardis and see what he has to say. Goodbye for now, Hero."

She kissed her brother swiftly on the cheek, rose from her chair and strode to the door of the room. A thought struck her.

"Can he hear what we are saying?"

The king was sitting back in his chair, eyes closed. "I don't know. Can't you understand? This illness is a mystery to me."

HERO

Yes! Father and Celene. I can hear what you are saying.

I was bitten, I remember, although I don't know what bit me. I felt pain, but not any longer.

I wish you weren't worried about me. I wish you weren't sad. I want to open my eyes to tell you, but I am too tired and you are too far away. It feels as though I am under water, the waves washing over me. Maybe, like the sea over the Elithian causeway, the tide will turn, the water will ebb away, and I will return to you. Until then, I will enjoy this feeling. I am weightless, floating.

AT THE MARKETPLACE

Celene felt a new sense of purpose as she went to consult Ardis. Her father was tired after their voyage. He would no doubt soon see sense, but in the meantime, she had not given up hope and was sure that Ardis would be able to help. His quarters were on the other side of the marketplace and she went alone. Hester would accompany her if she asked, but Celene didn't think she could cope with her chatter today. In Elithia, it was quite common for the princess to be seen out and about near the castle, and Celene would be given space by her people. The weather was mild, drizzly, uninspiring. She walked briskly, with her head down, lost in her own thoughts.

Celene should have been kinder to Hero when he left, should have wished him well. It was not his fault that their father chose him for the journey. And had that journey even mattered after all? Now, it seemed not. If he died, then her final communication with him would have been angry silence.

But Hero wouldn't die; she had faith in Ardis. He was wise, experienced, kind, and had always been there to help her family in the past. She quickened her pace, eager to get to him, but caught the toe of her shoe on a cobblestone, and stumbled. She was falling, but then a hand was immediately at her elbow, catching her before she hit the hard ground. That was typical of Elithia: even when she thought her people were giving her space, they were really all keeping an eye out for their princess.

She turned to thank whoever it was and saw a tiny frail figure in a hooded cloak: an old woman or man, perhaps. This was surprising, as the hand which had supported her, and was still holding her elbow, felt strong and capable. She reached into her pocket to retrieve her purse and offer a coin or trinket. A gift from a princess was always well received.

But then the figure looked up and, without the cover of a low hood, Celene saw a sharp face and distinctive, dark purple hair. And she heard that laugh again.

"Sidra!" she gasped, shaking off her hand immediately, and stuffing her purse back into her pocket. "Be gone. You are not welcome in these parts."

Sidra laughed and straightened up, pushing back her hood a little more, to reveal a smooth, unlined forehead and pale blue eyes with spiky lashes, like spiders' legs. "I am most offended, Princess Celene! That is no way to talk to me, and after I thought you were going to reward me for my kindness."

"I do not have time for your antics, Sidra."

"Ah, and I know why. I have heard all about your brother's misfortune. That is why I came to find you."

"Who told you?"

"As sure as moths are drawn to the light, bad news seems to flutter to my door. So many people suffering from terrible life-threatening illnesses or losing loved ones." Sidra smiled. "Their bad news finds me and I am overcome by an urge to help."

"I have heard of the kind of help you offer," said Celene coldly. She thought of Madam Reddy, from the east of the island, who was said to have made a pact with Sidra long ago, when her eldest boy was ill with a terrible fever. Against all odds, the boy recovered, but she changed. Madam Reddy had always been such a warm and humorous person but the sparkle vanished from her eyes. People said that she had paid Sidra with her very soul.

Sidra narrowed her eyes. "If my help is so terrible, then why do so many people come knocking at my door? Because they know that my power is strong, that is why."

Celene tensed and tried not to listen to what Sidra was saying. "I tell you again, be gone, or I shall report you to my father."

Sidra lifted her hood once more. "Don't worry, I know how it works. Your royal knights will soon appear to escort me away from the precious princess." She seemed ready to leave, but then turned to Celene again and spoke. "You are so angry. I see that. But I understand: guilt can make a person angry."

"Guilt? Why should I be guilty?"

"Only you know the answer to that, Princess. But I saw your face at the harbour and I recognized what I saw. I understand only too well how the jealousy of your brother has grown within you. I too have a *perfect* older brother. You are going to see him now. He was always the centre of attention, while I was ignored."

"We have nothing in common, Sidra."

"So you say, but I can guess how you wished Prince Hero away. And now that wish might very well come true."

"I don't have to stand and listen to this," said Celene, striding away.

But Sidra sidled along beside her, still talking in her ear. "My brother Ardis will not be able to help you with his plants and herbs. Hero is beyond that now. I have my ways of knowing, and I have seen him walking towards death's door. He will be there before you know it."

"Ardis is the most powerful sorcerer in Elithia."

"Perhaps, Princess, but you forget that we first learned our magic together, at our mother's knee. He knows what to do but he will never be brave enough to do it. You need someone who is not afraid to communicate with dark spirits. I am the only one who can help you."

"I do not want your help."

"You say that now, but by the time the next full moon rises you will have changed your mind. Hope will desert you; it has already left your father. When that day comes, you know where to find me."

"I will not be visiting you now or ever. Goodbye."

Sidra stopped walking and laughed as Celene continued her

journey through the market square. Her voice followed, sharp and clear.

"See you soon, Princess."

NATURAL MAGIC

Celene worried about what Sidra said, about her guilty feelings around Hero. But she knew that was what Sidra did: she played with people's insecurities and manipulated them into getting what she wanted. Celene was too strong for that. Anyway, she had many options. As she had told her father, they were the royal family: they could access the best healers and sorcerers. Money was no object and they would make Hero well again.

She did not normally visit Ardis in his own quarters. Usually, he was summoned where he was needed. But this was an emergency and Celene did not care to send official messages. She knocked sharply on his door. He opened it slowly, looking unsurprised to see her, and invited her to step in.

His quarters were decorated in cool colours: blues and greens. A large window let in lots of light. By the window, an Elithian silk wall hanging fluttered in the breeze. Plants trailed from shelves, climbed the walls and brightened dark corners. It was a little like being in a garden, but inside.

Ardis was barefoot on the natural matting and Celene removed her shoes without being asked: it seemed the respectful thing to do.

He greeted her with a warm, perhaps pitying, smile. He took a small glass and poured in what looked like water from a jug. Celene took a sip. It was minty and refreshing.

"Welcome, Princess."

"You know why I have come?"

He nodded. "Your brother is unwell."

"Ardis, can you help us? Please?"

"I am sorry, princess, but I have already examined your brother. There is nothing I can do; a greater force is at work."

"That is what my father said, but I cannot believe it. You have so many skills."

"We sorcerers like to show the power of our magic. Some of us more than others. We like to hear the gasps from crowds when we make objects appear or disappear."

Celene tapped her foot, waiting for Ardis to get to the point. She needed answers, not speeches on the history of sorcery.

"I can make a plant flower. . ."

He picked up his staff, which looked like a young upturned

sapling, and tapped it on a pot some distance away. Pretty violet flowers sprang into life on the bare green leaves.

"Or I can make them fade. . ."

He tapped again and the flowers shrivelled, turned brown and fell from the ends of the leaves.

"I can turn the plant into a teapot and the teapot into a plant. . ."

Ardis performed the tricks as he explained,

". . . but I am only using the magic which resides within the plant. Do you understand?"

Celene understood, but she wasn't particularly interested, as it had nothing to do with her brother. "I just want to know if you can help him. There must be something, some plant, some rock, *something* that will cure him."

"But, Princess Celene, I have answered this question. I cannot help Prince Hero. There is a treatment for almost every poison, if you know where to look. Normally the antivenom can be found from the same source as the poison, but in this case we do not know what creature has bitten him or what the cure might be.

"I am touched by your dedication to your brother, but I must warn you: where death is intended, death *will* prevail. The best thing you can do for Hero right now is to be with him, continue to speak to him, and to hope that he hears you, wherever he is. It might be that the best thing you can do is say goodbye."

Celene stared at Ardis and shook her head. She had not expected Ardis to admit defeat in the same way as her father. Surely he knew a way? Sidra's voice popped into her head: *He knows what to do but he will never do it. You need someone who is not afraid to communicate with dark spirits.*

"I refuse to accept this. I have seen and heard of greater magic at play. I know that other sorcerers can do what you refuse to do – bring people back from the brink of death. When you say you cannot, what you mean is that you *will* not. You are afraid."

"This is not true," said Ardis with a sigh. "The sorcerers that claim to do such things are not people of magic; they are thieves – criminals. They are evil! Even my sister. Especially my sister. If you take something from Death, then Death requires so much more in return. These sorts of pacts benefit no one in the end."

"But it can be done?"

Ardis shook his head, not looking up at her. "We mortals should not meddle in the matters of the afterlife. It is too dangerous – the cost is too high."

"I don't care what the cost is!" shouted Celene. "I will pay any price."

"No riches in the world can stop death, child."

"I am not talking about riches. What about if I gave you something else? I have heard that others have paid with their very souls—"

"No! You cannot think such thoughts. You have not been listening to me, Princess—"

"—No, you are not listening to me!" said Celene, trembling with frustration. "If you think I will be content with your answer then you are wrong. You have known me since I was a child and you should know that whatever I do, I do it well. And right now, my intention is to cure my brother of his ailment. As commander of the knights and Princess of Elithia I insist upon it. So I ask you, one last time, will you do what I ask of you?"

Ardis sat and put his face in his hands. Then he looked up. "No. I cannot."

Celene lifted her chin. "Well, no matter. I know what to do. There is someone who will help me, even if you won't."

Ardis sighed deeply. "Please do not go to my sister. The magic she practises is not true magic. True magic harnesses the power of nature and works with it. She tries to go against the natural order of things. It never works."

Anger bubbled up inside Celene. She wasn't really considering consulting Sidra, but she was offended that Ardis wouldn't help her. "You advise me on what I should and should not do, yet you will not help me yourself?"

"Beware of my sister. Everything that Sidra does benefits her, and her alone. Do not go to her, my child. I know you are hurting, but on this occasion you should let nature run its course. Sometimes, we must trust that everything will work out exactly as it should. What will be, will be. That is the way it has to be."

Celene turned and put her shoes back on her stockinged feet without looking once in Ardis's direction. She let herself out.

"Do what you can to help your brother, but promise me that however bad he gets you will not go to Sidra," Ardis called after her.

But Celene left, without any such promise.

ROYAL VISITORS

The following morning, Celene's presence was requested in the throne room, where some visitors were expected. She rarely went into the room, which was used perhaps three or four times a year. Maids were rushing around uncovering and polishing the furniture. As Celene walked into the room, one of the maids whipped a white dustsheet from a cabinet, revealing the Elithian glass crown. Celene stared at it as she always did. It was a beautiful object, delicate and well-crafted from the finest crystal glass so that it projected little rainbows from any angle. Since she was a little girl she had been desperate to wear it, to see how it would feel upon her head, but it was never allowed. The glass crown was too precious, too fragile, to be worn by anyone but the Elithian monarch on coronation day.

Her father coughed, drawing her attention. She was surprised to see him sitting on the throne itself: a giant, wooden seat decorated with carvings of heart-shaped mulberry leaves. If he was sitting on the throne then the visitors must be important. Luckily, they had not yet arrived, which meant she could speak freely to her father. She was unimpressed by the situation.

"Why are we hosting visitors when Hero is ill?"

"I have taken your advice, daughter, and sent for some of the wisest healers I could think of. I recalled that Queen Audrey of Essendor was once struck by a similar affliction, yet she made a full recovery. By luck, some of her council are travelling in these parts and I have reached out to them as our neighbours and friends."

Celene nodded. That did sound like a sensible decision.

"Before they arrive, I must ask you something: I understand that you have been asking questions about Sidra and her magic?"

Celene felt a flush rise in her cheeks. "Has Ardis been speaking to you?"

"How I came to hear of it is not the point, Celene. The point is that no good ever came from Sidra – I hardly need to tell you that—"

The king was cut short as the herald walked in to announce their visitors.

"Queen Audrey and her people are here, your Majesty."

The king nodded and settled back in his chair. "Please bring them straight in."

Celene stared at her father open-mouthed. "The *queen* of Essendor herself is coming?"

"I took your advice and used my influence. What good is it being a king if I do not occasionally use my power for the good of my family?"

Celene nodded and drew herself up tall. She had heard much about Queen Audrey of Essendor, who, despite only being about Celene's age, was said to have restored peace to a troubled kingdom. She was known to be caring and fair but also strategic and calm under pressure. These were all qualities that Celene herself aspired to, and she prepared to show her best side to such an inspirational figure. Maybe one day they would rule neighbouring kingdoms.

But when the Essendor royal party entered the throne room, Celene was staggered at how strange they looked. A small elfin man with green and red speckled skin, and a lanky, startled-looking man flanked a young girl. Celene nodded a greeting and looked behind them for Queen Audrey.

It was not until her father rose and took the hand of the young girl in the centre of the group, that Celene realized this was in fact Queen Audrey herself. The queen was about a head shorter than Celene, who was not particularly tall herself, and slight, with cropped brown hair and large brown eyes. If Celene had passed her in the street she would have assumed that she was on her way to the schoolroom or to knights' training school.

She realized she was staring and dropped a small curtsey. Queen Audrey smiled kindly and offered her hand to shake. "A pleasure to meet you. I am so sorry to hear about your family's misfortune."

Celene didn't know how to reply. It sounded as though someone had died, or as if a great calamity had fallen upon Elithia, whereas in fact Hero was just ill. It was a temporary problem, not a great tragedy.

"We hope you and your aides will be able to help, Your Majesty," she replied confidently. "With the right treatment, my brother will soon be well."

Her father shot her a sideways look. "All in good time, daughter."

Her comment had probably gone against the royal etiquette. Perhaps they should be pouring tea from the silver teapot and making small talk before discussing the real reason for the visit. Hero would have known this instinctively, but it was not Celene's way. They all knew why Queen Audrey was here, and time was of the essence.

Queen Audrey didn't seem offended in any way. She smiled again. "I do hope we can help. I will attend to your brother as best I can."

Still, the Essendor party didn't go straight to Hero's chamber but had refreshments first. All Celene's muscles were tense and her mind drifted away from the conversation. She couldn't touch the tea or sweet treats put before her. She felt herself staring at the three visitors. Would they help her brother? They didn't look up to the task.

At last, the king and Celene led the queen and her two odd companions to Hero's chamber. They moved to follow them in, but Queen Audrey turned and raised her hand.

"Please," she said. "I think it is better if we see the prince on his own."

Celene wasn't sure about that. What could they possibly be doing that required Hero's sister and father to stay away? But the king nodded his agreement and so Celene was left standing with him outside the bedchamber. The nurse, who was also dismissed, walked to one end of the corridor and began studying a portrait there. He obviously didn't want to intrude on any conversation between the king and his daughter.

Celene was not used to the feeling of being shut out: the royal family were normally the only people allowed behind certain doors. It felt unnatural and unnecessary. Her father looked as though he felt the same. There was no chair or stool out in the corridor so instead he paced back and forth. This angered Celene and she tried not to look in his direction. She tried to listen, to hear anything that was going on in the chamber, but the door was heavy and she couldn't hear a thing.

After some minutes, the small greenish man cracked open the door, his expression unreadable. "Her Majesty bids you enter now."

Queen Audrey stood at Hero's bedside, paler than before and breathing unsteadily. Whatever she had done had taken some effort on her part. She shook her head gently and Celene's heart tightened.

"Here," she said, beckoning them. "I have healed the puncture wound."

She uncovered Hero's upper arm, where the swollen bite had been. Now the skin was smooth and unblemished as it had been before the trip. Not a trace of the ugly wound or the swelling. Perhaps the treatment had been more successful than Queen Audrey's expression suggested.

"So he is better?" said Celene. "He will awaken soon?"

But Queen Audrey shook her head again. "The wound has healed, the poison has gone, yet still he sleeps. I fear that the poison has spread deep within his body – possibly even reached his heart. There is nothing more I can do."

Celene couldn't believe what she was hearing. "How can this be? I thought you had experience of such matters. You fell into a deep sleep yourself and yet you were cured, were you not?"

"My sleep was brought on by dark magic. Magic is treated with magic. It seems that the cause of your brother's malaise is to be found in the natural world. There is no magic for us to fight."

"So a tiny bite from an unknown insect is more powerful than a spell from a dark sorcerer?"

"I'm afraid that is sometimes the case, yes." Queen Audrey used a gentle tone.

Celene didn't like the sympathy in her voice. She was looking at her the way people looked when someone had died. And Hero was not going to die. "I find it hard to believe there is nothing more you can do," she said, her face flushing with hot anger. "You were in this chamber for no longer than ten minutes, which is not enough time to do *anything*. It would be encouraging to know that you had at least tried to help us, otherwise what was the point of travelling all this way?"

The king stepped in front of Celene, with a glare. "That will do, daughter."

Queen Audrey did not seem offended by the outburst. She placed a hand on Celene's forearm.

"You remind me of my sister, Alette. You are a good sister to your brother. I am sorry I can't help your family this time but I hope you will remember the kingdom of Essendor if ever you need me in the future."

Anger still burned within Celene. She had heard of Queen Audrey's elusive twin sister Alette, who had given up her title and right to the throne. Celene would never do such a thing. Anyway, Queen Audrey had no right to compare her with anyone; she barely knew her.

"I must go. I must not waste any more time," Celene said, and stalked out of Hero's bedchamber without saying a proper farewell. The door slammed behind her. It seemed that the healers were in agreement that there was nothing to be done, but maybe it was not healers that Hero needed. Maybe it was a different kind of attention.

TRUE LOVE'S KISS

True love conquers all. Celene had heard many times how true love's kiss had the power to raise someone from a deep sleep, change frogs to princes, or work any number of miracles. And Celene had a good idea of where she could find Hero's true love.

Samara was at the training ground, putting on her armour while her page polished her shield. Celene hadn't seen her once since Hero fell ill. For the first time ever her training schedule had been abandoned. The knights all knew the situation but other than that it had been kept quiet. Until they knew more there was nothing to report.

Celene watched her for a short while before approaching. Samara looked a mess, with dishevelled hair and tear-stained cheeks.

But then she looked up and saw Celene. She rushed over to meet her and held her for a few moments. "Celene! How is he? It must have been so terrible for you."

Celene shook her head stiffly. "Still asleep. Apparently there is nothing anyone can do to help him."

"He's not going to—"

"—I don't know, Samara. But not if I can help it. I need you to do something."

Samara's lip wobbled. "What can I do?"

"You love my brother, do you not?" Celene asked bluntly. She had never asked Samara this before.

Samara did not respond, just looked at her with wide eyes.

"Don't try to deny it! To you he is worth more than your knighthood. And he loves you?"

She nodded then, a small but distinct movement.

"So go to him. True love is a powerful thing. It is supposed to awaken people from slumbers, curses and illnesses! Go now and help my brother."

The visitors and the king had left, so once Samara had removed her armour, Celene led her to Hero's chamber. She stood by the door as Samara took tiny steps towards him, clasped her hands to her mouth at the sight of him, then sat in the chair by his bedside and held his hand. Celene glanced at the nurse, who raised an eyebrow. "Leave us," she said quietly, and he obeyed.

Samara leaned towards Hero, as if to kiss him. Celene held her breath. But Samara didn't kiss him. She whispered something and moved his hand towards her belly.

Was there another secret, a bigger secret, which Celene was not party to?

Still, he did not wake.

Samara began to sob, tears streaming down her face. Celene stayed, frozen, by the door. Why was it that everyone else seemed to be crying? Her father, now Samara. When she looked at Hero, she felt like doing many things: shouting, hitting someone, breaking something, but not crying. There was a hard knot in her chest that was getting in the way of everything. She should possibly go to her friend but she could not.

In the end, Dev returned and led Samara gently away from the bed, towards Celene.

"It didn't do any good," she sobbed. "I don't know if he will ever wake up."

Celene knew she should offer some words of comfort to Samara but she couldn't. If she spoke, she would say the wrong thing. Like, "*You don't love him enough.*"

HERO

I feel your warm tears falling softly on my face and I hear the secret you whisper in my ear. I want to respond, but you are so far away. I will try to wake up and be with you again but right now I am tired and need to sleep. I must sleep for a long time.

MORE WORTHY

Afterwards, Samara fled and Celene felt shaky. They never argued and it felt wrong to be short with her. But she was so frustrated: no one else seemed to be taking any action to make Hero well.

She decided to go out to the training ground for an hour, to clear her head. But on the stairs she almost ran into her father, who was on his way to his chamber. He didn't hug her as he normally might, and his expression was tight and unsmiling. It was surprising for Celene to see him so agitated.

"I never want to hear you speak to a foreign visitor in that manner again. I was left to apologize for your rudeness after you left. And I hear from the nurse that you dragged Samara to Hero's bedside. She is your friend; you have known her your whole life – how could you upset her like that?"

Celene paused, unsure whether to betray the loyalty of her friend and her brother. But the king should know. Then he would understand.

"There was a reason for my actions. One hears how true love's kiss can awaken a person. I have not mentioned it before but there is something between them: Hero and Samara. They have been keeping it a secret."

She left this information hanging in the air, expecting shock and surprise, but the king sighed heavily. "Of course I knew about Hero and Samara. It has been plain for years that those two are made for each other."

Celene blinked. Plain to see? For years? How was it that her father knew, but she, Samara's best friend, did not? The king continued.

"Celene, I realize that you are very upset by Hero's situation. I know that you would do anything in your power to help reverse it, but I am telling you to stop being so impolite to everyone who is trying to help us."

"I am not a little girl to be ordered around," replied Celene indignantly. "I am the commander of the Royal Knights and I may speak as I wish!"

"I am the king and *your* commander and it would help you to remember that."

"But Queen Audrey and her party should never have come here. Their visit was a waste of time. While we were entertaining them, we could have been finding someone who could actually help Hero."

The king sighed. "I was trying to help your brother by inviting Queen Audrey. She is known far and wide as a sensitive monarch and a great healer. We are lucky that she understands your anger comes from distress at your brother's condition."

"Oh good – I wouldn't want to offend an adolescent queen and her pet elf," said Celene sarcastically.

"It is this attitude exactly that concerns me, Celene. You tell me that you are equipped to accompany me on sensitive royal business and then you behave like this!"

"Hero wouldn't let you down in such a way, I suppose."

"He would not."

"Then it's a shame he is not here. I suppose you would be much happier if he were standing here now and I were the one lying unresponsive upstairs. In fact, everyone would be happier if that were the case."

Celene turned and fled. Her father called after her but she did not respond – she didn't want to talk to anyone.

She could not dislodge the thought from her head: Hero was more worthy than she was. It was a shame that she hadn't accompanied her father on the trip. Then she would have been the one lying ill and everyone would have been much happier: her father, her best friend, and all the knights who loved Hero so well.

Maybe what was needed was a great sacrifice. If there was a way to give herself in his place then that is what she would do.

She knew straight away whom she should speak to.

But first, she went to visit her brother, to tell him what she meant to do. Once again, she sent Dev away, then sat by Hero's beside.

"I'm sorry for what I said before you went away. You are more worthy than I and you deserve to live and thrive and grow to be king."

She could not imagine saying these things to him under normal circumstances but now everything was different.

She placed her hand gently on top of his.

"I know that you are in there somewhere and you are waiting for someone to wake you up. There is one person here in Elithia who has that power. I am not afraid to approach her, but I know that I will need to make a great sacrifice." She thought of Madam Reddy and how she'd changed. "I just want to let you know that when you awaken, I might not be the same sister that you knew."

She planted a kiss on his forehead and sat back to look at him one last time. For a short moment, she thought she saw his eyelids flicker. She half-expected him to open his eyes, yawn, stretch and ask what was for supper, but then she watched a little longer and didn't see it again. It was just her imagination.

"Goodbye, Hero."

HERO

No, no, no. Do not go to Sidra. Do not sacrifice yourself for me. I am no more worthy than you. I do not want to be king. One day, when the time is right, I will awaken and tell you that myself.

But I cannot tell you. I am still lost in my own self: too far away.

CHAPTER FIVE

SIDRA'S HOUSE

Celene didn't sleep at all that night. She went to bed at the usual time so as not to arouse suspicion, but once in her chamber, she dressed and stood by the window, watching the rain pour down outside. Great heavy drops bounced up from the ground and formed instant puddles. The sea fought angrily back, white waves churning and thundering. She waited there, intermittently reading and just sitting, until the early hours of the morning, when most inhabitants of the palace would be asleep and no one would see her go.

It was easy to leave the palace grounds without being seen.

Guards were on watch to make sure nobody got in, but they weren't on the lookout for people getting out. She left via the back entrance of the palace, in deep darkness, with rain splashing all around. No one in their right mind would be out at such an early hour or in such weather unless they had to be, and Celene didn't pass anyone on her way to Sidra's. She simply pulled up her cloak, put her head down, and marched onwards. She would do what she had to do and be back in time for breakfast. The full moon hung overhead but Celene didn't need a torch or moonlight in these parts; she knew every path, every twist and turn.

Sidra lived right on the edge of the island. Everyone knew where. People bowed their heads when they walked past; children dared one another to knock at the door and run away. Nobody else wanted to build their own home so close to the water's edge. The house stood alone, looking as if it were about to launch itself into the sea. It was a strange building: spindly and sharp-roofed, with jutting edges like a rock. The windows were high and dark: impossible for a normal person to see through.

Celene had never expected to find herself approaching Sidra's door. A few days ago, she would have sworn it would never happen. But Sidra was the only person she had spoken to who had a solution to her family's unhappy situation.

As she drew closer, and could see more clearly, she was surprised at how normal Sidra's house seemed this close up. There were no skulls by the pathway or smoke seeping under the door. She raised the knocker, trying to quell her sense of foreboding. She was commander of the royal knights. She was brave, and Sidra was a sad, lonely woman with no friends or family who wanted to know her. At the moment, Celene had an idea of how that might feel. There was no reason to be scared of her.

Despite the antisocial hour, the door swung wide open in seconds and Sidra stood there, fully dressed, smiling with her unnaturally even white teeth. In the dim light, her purple hair looked black.

"Welcome, Princess. You have arrived, just as I predicted. Please, come in, dry yourself."

Celene walked into the room, bringing a puddle of water with her. She instinctively left the door open behind her, but Sidra swept around her and closed it with a low click.

The house was as small as it had looked from the outside. Unlike Ardis's garden-like study, it was sparse and lacking colour, with no rug on the cold, stone floor, or pictures on the wall. Candles in tall metal candlesticks flickered in the corners. A basic bed pushed against the wall was the only furniture. Celene wondered where

Sidra kept her clothes and her cooking equipment. She thought of the size of the palace with its separate rooms for dressing, eating, bathing – all that room for the three of them – and felt bad. No one else in the kingdom lived as richly as they did.

"Where are my manners? Let me take your cloak."

Sidra took Celene's sopping wet cloak and hung it from a hook that looked like it was made of the bone of some animal. She swung around, her hair and robes swishing with her. "And I should behave properly in the presence of royalty."

She dropped a deep, mocking curtsey, spreading her dress out wide. Celene narrowed her eyes, no longer feeling sorry for her. "A curtsey is not required."

Sidra smiled her mirthless smile and picked up one of the candles in its holder. "Follow me."

Celene could not imagine where Sidra would lead her – there was nowhere to go – but then she bent down, lifted a trapdoor in the floor, and stepped down into the opening. Against her better judgement, Celene followed Sidra through the trapdoor and down the steep, stone stairs, leaving the trapdoor open behind her. She was not a prisoner then, at least.

Head held high, she walked slowly, trying not to display her reticence, her boots echoing on the stone steps. They led to a cavernous cellar room. So this was where all Sidra's things were. It crossed Celene's mind that they must not be far from the sea. She listened, wondering if she could hear waves crashing, but heard nothing.

"Make yourself comfortable," said Sidra, moving around the room to light more candles as Celene took in her surroundings. It was difficult to imagine being comfortable in this cold, damp space. There were no windows and the candles cast long shadows on the walls. A single chair and spindly table were positioned right in the middle of the room. Over to one side was a long, empty counter, and behind it were rows of neatly organized bottles. Celene thought she saw something scuttling in one of the jars and her thoughts strayed to the cockroach plague reported in the east of the city. There had never been any doubt in her mind that Sidra was responsible for that. What other crimes had she plotted from this very space?

"I see you have spotted my collection." Sidra opened one of the jars and shook out a small creature on to her hand. Celene wasn't close enough to see what it was, but it was quick and had a lot of legs. Sidra cupped her hands and let it run around in there as she spoke. "I have a large variety of specimens, gathered from the darkest forests and the coldest mountains. Sometimes they help with my spells but sometimes I just like to watch them creep and crawl."

Sidra walked towards Celene, hands still cupped together as if around a small ball. Celene didn't back away. She didn't want to give Sidra the satisfaction of seeing her fear.

When she was right in front of Celene, Sidra opened her hands and flicked her palms upwards.

Celene jumped away instinctively, but saw nothing fly from Sidra's hands. She looked on the floor: still nothing. She hoped that the insect hadn't landed in her hair. Sidra dug one hand into a pocket in her robe and pulled out the jar that she'd taken from the shelf. The creature, which was a centipede by the looks of things, was back inside.

Sidra held the jar up, showing the insect running desperately up the side of the glass, towards the closed lid. "It can't escape!" said Sidra, with delight. "It's mine."

Celene shuddered. No one knew where she was, and it would be easy for Sidra to trap her in this place, like a miserable centipede destined for her cauldron. She felt her breath coming rapidly and held it for a moment, but she brought her focus back to Sidra.

"As fun as these games are, don't you think we should get to the business at hand?"

"Of course, please take a seat, Princess."

Sidra put the jar down and gestured to the single wooden chair, but Celene shook her head. She would not sit while Sidra roamed the room, producing more surprises from her collection. She would face her like an equal.

"You know why I have come." It was a statement, not a question.

Sidra smiled. "Of course. You have made the right decision."

Celene was beginning to feel really uncomfortable. She felt hemmed in, as though the empty room were full of people. Her instincts told her that someone was behind her and she turned to face them, but there was no one there.

Sidra laughed, a high-pitched laugh that went on for too long.

"Does it feel a little crowded to you?"

Celene's mouth was dry. She said nothing and Sidra laughed again. Perhaps it was a magic trick, designed to make her feel uncomfortable.

"So, I suppose you have tried everyone else? All the healers; all the magicians. Even my poor old brother could not help you."

"That is true," said Celene. "I come to you in desperation." Once again, she had a feeling of someone standing nearby. This time she could feel their warm breath on her cheek but she did not turn around. She looked Sidra directly in the eyes, showing no fear.

Sidra came towards her, so that she was standing very close. "It is strange. My brother is so respected. Yet, when he is unable to help, people come to me. They know that I am the most powerful, yet he holds the highest position. It doesn't seem quite right, does it?"

Celene didn't want to hear any more of Sidra's rantings on this particular subject. "Can we please proceed?" she asked, as politely as she could manage.

"What makes you think I will help you now? Maybe I don't want to."

Celene did not flinch. "You will help anyone who pays the price."

"Ah! You are astute! And do you happen to know what the price is?" Sidra backed away again and rearranged a few jars on the shelf.

"I think so," said Celene, quietly.

"Good." Sidra smiled broadly, although curiously, no creases appeared around her eyes or forehead. "In that case, this shouldn't take long. Take a seat and I shall prepare all that is necessary."

Sidra gestured once again to the single chair and, this time,

Celene sat. Sidra placed the spindly table in front of her, which made Celene feel even more trapped than before.

Sidra crossed the room, taking a candle with her, so that she was in the centre of a pool of light, and reached above her head to a hollow cell in one of the walls. She pulled out a scroll and unrolled it to show Celene. It was covered in tiny black writing.

"I took the liberty of preparing an agreement, in case. All you have to do is sign at the bottom, here." Sidra tapped her pointed fingernail at the bottom of the parchment, where a line was drawn.

Celene leaned forward in her chair and squinted to read the tiny writing.

Sidra laughed again, placing the candlestick on the table. She handed the scroll to her. "Here, you may find it easier to read up close."

Now that Celene could read the writing it didn't make much difference; the document was so complicated. She could see her name, and her brother's, but the sentences ran on and on without punctuation, and there was a lot of formal language like *henceforth* and *notwithstanding*.

"What does it all mean?" she asked.

"It is simple. From the moment you sign your name, Hero will sit up, yawn and stretch, as if awakening from a restful sleep. He will be well again."

Celene swallowed. That was all that she wanted.

"And what does it mean for me?" she asked, quietly.

"You get to keep your body. You will carry on as you did before."

"And what do you gain from me?"

Sidra handed Celene a fine pen, made of bone.

There was a pause.

"Your soul," she replied casually, as she might say "Your shoes" or "Your riding crop".

Once again, Celene felt the breath on her cheek, like a whisper. Someone else's soul, right there with them?

She looked around and saw then that the walls were lined with cells, like the one from which Sidra had removed her scroll. It was like the honeycomb in a beehive, but full of dark contracts, not honey. Did each one belong to a person who had signed their soul to Sidra? Were there that many desperate people in Elithia?

She thought of Madam Reddy. She'd barely known her, but even from just seeing her from afar in the marketplace, it was clear how her rosy cheeks grew pale and the humour disappeared from her character altogether. What kind of person would Celene be without her very soul?

She swallowed again.

"What do you do with the souls?"

"That is my business alone," said Sidra brusquely. "Once I own them, I can do with them what I wish."

Celene felt like she needed water, but she wasn't going to ask for a drink here. She ran her hands through her hair. "I'm not sure. . ."

Sidra drew back. "You're not sure? We are not choosing dresses in the palace now! You cannot dither and waste my time. You already rudely declined my help once in the marketplace. This is the second and final time I make the offer."

Celene couldn't think straight with Sidra directly in front of her, staring unblinkingly as she awaited her decision. After a couple of long moments, Sidra whisked the scroll from Celene's hands. "Fine. I will take this back. You said you would do anything for your brother, but it seems it is not so. I am not surprised. I often find that the higher in status my clients, the less courageous they are."

Celene stared at her empty hands. She had thought she would do anything. She loved her brother, didn't she? She tried to imagine the palace without Hero's cheerful nature. How the kind and gentle prince would be mourned by the citizens of Elithia. And their father. And Samara. Perhaps they would lose their smiles along with Hero. All in all, he would be missed more than she would ever be.

Sidra began rolling up the scroll, slowly, carefully. Celene saw the tiny black words and her one chance to be a good sister disappearing.

"Of course, I understand," continued Sidra as she rolled. "If Hero dies, it will in some ways be better for you, will it not?" She spoke in a whisper, so that it seemed her words were voices inside Celene's own mind. She spoke as a friend, or conspirator, might.

"No! What can you mean? I love my brother. I don't want him to die."

"Of course you don't, Princess. Nobody wants to see a dear sibling go to an early grave. And yet if he *did* die, you would be first in line to the throne, wouldn't you?"

Sidra's words cut like a knife. She had not been aware that anyone else knew of her ambitions. Was it common knowledge in the kingdom?

"You and I are more similar than you realize, Princess. My own brother is thirteen months older than me, like your own."

Ardis had wrinkles around his eyes, and wide brushstrokes of grey in his hair. Sidra did not show any of these signs. She must have been using her own power to stay young.

"Ah yes, I see the surprise in your eyes," continued Sidra. "I have always looked younger than my brother. Younger, cleverer and more powerful. Yet those thirteen months made the difference to everyone else. Ardis has taken what should have been mine at every step. I understand you better than you think."

Celene tried to tell herself that Sidra was manipulating her, persuading her to sign. Still, the thought of being like this sinister woman was too much for Celene to bear and she failed to keep the disgust out of her expression. "We are not alike, Sidra. And your brother was chosen over you for his attitude, not his magic. Perhaps if you had behaved better then things might have been different."

Sidra's face showed no anger although her eyelid twitched slightly. "This is what you think, Princess, but you were not there at the time, were you? You believe what they say about me – tittle-tattle from the market square – but they will be saying the same things about you in a few years. You will be known as the queen who took advantage of her brother's illness to rise to the top." She went on, relentlessly. "And your best friend, who seems so taken with him, would be yours again, would she not? All very convenient."

Celene shook her head. "No! I don't want these things. Maybe before his trip, but that was anger and frustration. Not now that I see him so ill. All I want is for Hero to get better. I don't care about the throne, or Samara. They would be a perfect match. A lovely king and queen. I would step aside."

Sidra smiled indulgently, as if she didn't believe a word. "It is understandable, that is all I am saying. All in all, your brother's death will be the most beneficial outcome for you." She tapped the scroll, lightly. "I shall destroy this and never mention it again."

Celene hated Sidra for saying these things, but a tiny part of her worried that she was right. She had wanted Hero to vanish, to step out of the way, to make life easier for her, and now that wish was coming true. There was only one way Celene could show her devotion to her brother. To prove it to Sidra. To herself. To everyone. She must show what she was willing to do.

She took a deep breath.

"I will sign."

Sidra smiled. "A wise decision, Celene. A brave, unselfish decision." She held the scroll at the top and it unfurled in one quick movement.

She smoothed the scroll over the table, pointed once again to the signature line, and Celene dipped her pen in the ink.

PEN TO PARCHMENT

Celene knew that she should not sign a document without reading it, but it hardly mattered when she was signing her soul away: there could be nothing worse. She wanted to get it over with.

Despite her attempts to hide her fear, Celene's hand trembled violently as she picked up the pen. She closed her eyes for half a second, then opened them and dipped the pen in the inkwell.

Sidra watched her intently, pale eyes unblinking, as Celene brought the pen to the parchment.

Celene wrote the first letter of her name, taking her time to draw the curve of the "C" perfectly, with her signature flourish at the top. She thought of how she, Samara and Hero had sat with their governess as children, carefully forming letters. Most children had slates, but as royalty, they occasionally had the opportunity to use fine feathered quills and parchment. Celene had enjoyed these lessons and liked the shape of the letters, each with its own story. She had always liked the way that her name looked on the page and she remembered telling Hero so.

"My initial is the best. It curves like the moon."

"Mine is like a snake," said Samara, hissing.

In the way of children, her brother had been affronted and felt the need to defend the letter "H".

"My initial is the best. It is solid and symmetrical, like a ladder."

Celene had been quick to feel anger, even then, and she had upset Hero's inkwell. She remembered how satisfying it had been to watch the black ink pool across the parchment, destroying all his careful lettering.

The governess had sat them on opposite sides of the room then to prevent the squabbling. And although the rift had soon healed, Celene had never revised her opinion: her initial was the best of them all.

Sidra's voice brought Celene back to the present. "I need your full name. Keep writing, Princess."

But Celene felt that warm breath again, brushing her cheek, and couldn't bring herself to move her hand any more. She flicked her gaze behind her and then back to the scroll. The candle flickered. A few phrases jumped out.

. . .I bequeath my soul to Sidra, in full knowledge that she can use it as she wishes. . .

. . .For all eternity. . .

. . .I accept that there is no reneging on this agreement. . .

Ardis' words from two days ago came into her mind: *"Beware my sister. Everything that Sidra does benefits her, and her alone."*

She could see the desperation in Sidra's unblinking eyes. Her hand hovered over Celene's own as if she wanted to take hold of it and form the letters herself.

"That's right – just a few more letters now—"

But Celene could not write the rest of her name. An angry pounding in her ears blocked out all rational thought and suddenly she felt as stubborn and childlike as she had all those years ago with Hero.

"No!" she shouted, "I will not sign!" She stood up from the chair, knocking the table and upsetting the bottle of ink. The dark liquid pooled from the bottle, spreading slowly and satisfyingly across the scroll like blood.

"What have you done?" screeched Sidra, and the inkblot began to hiss and fizz as though it were burning through the page.

Thick, blueish smoke emerged from the scroll and mingled with smoke from the candle, twisting like giant snakes into the sparse room. It kept coming, filling the space, and Celene put a hand over her nose and mouth to prevent herself from breathing it in. But it was no ordinary smoke and it began to reveal what had been hidden to her before. Shapes of light formed in front of it like shadows on a screen. Celene saw that they were figures: the poor lost souls of men, women and children, their faces pale, all crowded into this sorry place. All their eyes were upon Celene and they were shaking their heads, mouthing silent warnings, imploring her to get away from this place. It had been their breath that she had felt on her neck.

Celene didn't recognize their faces but no doubt all their names were imprinted and signed on the rolled up scrolls nestled in the wall. What bargains had they made that were important enough for them to end up here? She thought again of Madam Reddy and her empty eyes.

Sidra blew out the flame of her candle and all the flames in the room extinguished at once. Darkness descended.

THE CURSE

Celene saw clearly now that she must get away from Sidra and her sinister spells. "You are nothing but an evil witch. I will not sign this now. I will not sign it ever!" She kicked the table out of the way. A small square of pale light in the ceiling was all she could see in the blackness. She staggered towards it, pushing past the poor souls that thronged around her. She threw herself at the steps, banging both knees, and scrambled up using her hands as well as her feet for stability. She emerged through the hatch, breathing hard. The above ground now seemed safe and welcoming.

But Sidra followed her, slamming the trapdoor shut behind her, and stood in front of the door, blocking her way to the outside world. She held up the ink-stained scroll triumphantly and pointed to the single, unmarked letter. "It is too late, Princess! I will not let you go that easily. For you have signed part of your name and therefore part of your soul belongs to me. I can do what I like with you."

Celene had no idea if this were true but she shook her head. "Let me go now, or the king shall hear about this and you will be banished far from here."

Sidra tucked the scroll back into her robes, then threw back her head and laughed loudly.

"It didn't take you long to mention your father. You think that being a princess makes you better than me, don't you? You and your privileged family live a life of luxury while people like me are shut away out here."

Celene's hands shook. "That is not true. Your brother Ardis is a friend of the palace."

"My brother, yes, gets to share in your riches, by dampening down his true nature and conforming to your ways. But my mother raised us all in the dark arts and that will rise up in us however much we try to hide it."

She tried to push her way past but Sidra prevented her, clutching her arm as she had done in the marketplace. "You never come here, never visit. As far as you are concerned, I may as well not exist. Like the rats that make their tunnels beneath the city streets, we are always there, but hidden from view. Until you need us. Then you make the journey."

"Get off me!" Celene tried to prise Sidra's fingers from her, but they were clamped tight, bruising her.

"I saw the look in your eyes when I said we were alike. You think you are so much better but let us see how you like to hide away from people, fearful that they should gaze upon your face. I curse you! I am tempted to turn you into a rat. A cursed and lowly creature of the night, ashamed to show your face in daylight hours."

Sidra caught the panicked look in Celene's eyes and laughed. "But I do not feel that a rat is fitting to your royal status."

She let go of Celene's arm and produced a short, light wand from the folds of her robes. She pointed it at Celene like a weapon. Celene thought of Ardis's staff and the way that flowers had fallen from the plant. What damage could Sidra do with this wand?

Sidra continued to point the wand directly at her – at her heart. "I proclaim that by sunrise you will take a new form of a glorious, regal creature. The finest of beasts: a unicorn."

"A unicorn?" Celene's voice came out as a shrill squeak. A unicorn. A beautiful beast indeed, and surely better than a rat, but Celene didn't want to be a unicorn. She wanted to return home to her family and for her brother to get well.

"Yes, a unicorn!" cried Sidra, lowering the wand. "A prancing, preening princess of a unicorn that ordinary folk will want to catch a glimpse of. However, you will be a *cursed* unicorn that brings no joy, only pain and suffering. You will know real loneliness, for if you try to get close to any person, you will share your curse with them. Gazing upon you will cause misery." Her voice went lower, deeper:

"If you see the unicorn
Something will be lost or torn.
Meet twice and pain will come your way,
Be sure to run and stay away.
For if you meet three times: it's true –
The curse itself will fall on you."

Celene shook her head. What did this all mean?

"A pretty verse, isn't it? Children far and wide will recite it as they skip; mothers will use it as a warning rhyme to ensure their little ones behave. I will make sure that the legend spreads to every corner of the kingdom. No one will remember where they first heard it, but people will whisper about the Cursed Unicorn, just as they whisper my name. You will forget you ever had such a splendid life here: you will forget everything you ever knew. You will not be worthy of a person's love. You will only know running, hiding, fear and pain. People will know to stay away."

"No!" whispered Celene, shaking with fear and disbelief. There had been no sign from the wand – no flash or crackle – and she'd felt no change within her. For a moment she wondered if this was a malicious trick, but she looked into Sidra's pale eyes and knew that she meant every word. "You are an evil woman, Sidra. How can you do this to me? All I wanted was to help my brother."

"Ah yes, your brother. Don't think that he will be saved. Oh no. There will be no one to find the antidote now."

A cold shiver ran through Celene, as it had when the souls had been standing behind her. "What do you mean?"

"In return for your broken promise, I bestow a curse not just upon you, but on the whole island! When you take the form of a unicorn at sunrise, every person upon this island will slip into a dreamless sleep, like Prince Hero himself. Everyone! The cooks in the kitchen, the babies and their nurses, the nurse at your brother's side, even your kind and loving father. They will all stop what they are doing and sleep forever."

Celene shook her head again. "No, not my father. He is innocent in all this."

"I know! What did your father ever do to deserve a fate like that? But you have brought this upon those you love, my precious princess, and there is nothing whatsoever you can do about it!"

Celene tried to reason with Sidra. "How can you hurt me in this way when I have done nothing to you?"

"Ah, but you have done plenty. I know how you see me: like a pest in this city. The blame for everything falls at my door. You send your knights to spy on me, looking for any excuse to banish me from the kingdom. Now you will see how it feels, Princess, to be hated rather than respected."

"I would not want anyone to be blamed for crimes they did not commit. We can start afresh. Talk about all this. Please – take back the curse and we will find a way to live in harmony. We will give you what you want."

"Take it back? Wouldn't that be convenient for you? But the curse is cast now. There is only one way to break it."

"How?"

Sidra laughed again and recited another rhyme in an ominous voice.

> "When the moon is full on New Year's Eve,
> Elithia's rightful heir
> Must stand before the great moondial
> And cast a shadow there,
>
> "Only then, the curse will lift,
> And sleepers wake once more,
> Otherwise the curse remains
> In place forever more. . ."

"Now, go, Princess – go out into the darkness to meet your fate."

Finally, Sidra stepped aside, and Celene wrenched open the door and ran out into the night.

CHAPTER SIX

RELEASED

Celene stood out in the rainy night, listening to muffled laughter coming from within Sidra's house. She felt as though she had been released from a prison and was glad to be away from those pale souls with their grasping hands. She breathed great gulps of cold, wet air.

Was it possible that the curse was real, or had Sidra been trying to scare her? Apart from the bruising on her lower arm, where Sidra's fingers had dug into her flesh, she felt the same as she had done before she came here. Sunrise – that was when Sidra had said the curse would take effect – couldn't be far off, from the glimmer of light on the horizon.

She needed to find Ardis – he was the only one who knew enough about magic. He would tell her what to do.

She turned and ran back along the shoreline and then up the hill, in the direction of the palace. The rain began to ease and it was only then that she realized she had left her cloak behind. Her leather breastplate offered some protection, but the rain had trickled beneath it and was soaking her linen shirt.

Still, she ran on. She was almost at the city walls when she tumbled into a cloaked figure. He pulled back his hood. It was Ardis.

"Oh, Ardis, I am pleased to see you!" Celene was so relieved that she threw her arms around his neck.

Carefully, he removed her arms, stood back and looked at her. She did not know what sort of state she was in but, from the look of concern in his eyes, she guessed she must appear dishevelled. He took off his cloak and wrapped it around her, heavy and warm.

"Oh, Princess, what have you done? You went to see Sidra, didn't you?"

Celene lowered her gaze, her soaking hair dripping down her

neck. After all his warnings, she was ashamed to say what she had done.

Ardis shook his head slowly. "I awoke suddenly with a terrible feeling. I knew where you had gone, and I had to find you. Tell me I am not too late? You did not sign any dark contract?"

"No! Well, almost. Oh, Ardis, what have I done?"

Celene poured out everything, how she had nearly signed her soul away to Sidra but had backed out after writing just one letter on the scroll. He listened gravely, nodding, not saying a word.

She told him the curse that Sidra had placed upon her and the Elithian people, and the one way that she could break it. When she got to the end of the sorry tale, he sighed deeply.

Celene's heart beat rapidly in her chest as the panic built. "Ardis, will you help me now?"

"Princess, this is more serious than you can imagine. Sidra's power is strong, and she will show no mercy, as you have seen from those poor souls she keeps prisoner."

What was he telling her? That she was indeed cursed to become a unicorn? "Is there no hope for me?"

Ardis rubbed his chin thoughtfully. "Be grateful that the moon has not yet sunk below the horizon. I cannot undo my sister's magic, but there is perhaps something I can do to limit it. Come, we need to be out in the open, where the moon is most visible."

Celene followed Ardis out to the water's edge, the rain light now but the salty wind blowing her clothes around her and stinging her eyes. They walked onto the causeway that led to the mainland and Celene stood with the palace of Elithia behind her and the great full moon low in the sky ahead.

Silvery light from the early morning sky highlighted the lines in Ardis's face as he raised his hands up above his head and looked towards the heavens. He moved his hands as if he were gathering all the stars towards him. He repeated this action three times, then stood with his arms above him.

"Gaze at the moon with me, Princess – do not look away."

Celene obeyed, gazing up at the mysterious white circle. She scrutinized the dark markings upon its surface, imagining she could see a face up there. It seemed a kind face; she hoped it would smile upon her.

"I weave my own spell, a counter spell, using the power of the moon," said Ardis, and he started chanting. His indecipherable words washed over her as she continued to gaze. A couple of grey, barely-there clouds floated past the moon's face and it seemed to glow brighter, as if it were shining for her alone.

"I have done my best, Princess," announced Ardis, at last.

Celene looked away from the heavens and at Ardis, hopefully. He seemed tired, older.

She hardly dared ask. "Have you removed the curse?"

He shook his head. "There is only one way to break the curse and Sidra has already told you that."

"But it is impossible!" New Year's Eve was over two months away and she had no idea if there would even be a full moon. Besides, Hero was ill – he might die – he couldn't stand before a moondial.

"Nothing is impossible and there may be a way. Still, I have done what I can to make it better for you. You will still change at sunrise, but now there is a chance for you. Once a month, at the time of the full moon, you will regain your true form. With luck, you will remember and know what it is you have to do. You are the only person who will be able to break your own curse and that of the Elithian people."

"Is there nothing more you can do?"

"No, Princess. While Sidra keeps your half-signed scroll then she holds this power over you. And Sidra is not one to be merciful to another's plight. Wherever you go, this curse will be your burden. People will want to seek you out, to gaze upon your beauty and use your magic, but to look at you will be their misfortune. You will have to find an isolated place."

"But Sidra said that I would forget – that I would have no memory of who I am now. How will I know to stay away from people?"

"I am afraid that is true," said Ardis. "You will be more unicorn than human and will have no memory of this life in Elithia. But you will hold certain knowledge deep within; you will know to hide away."

ON THE CAUSEWAY

Ardis and Celene stood on the causeway that led from the cursed island, waves crashing around them. She waited for something more from him, some suggestion or advice, but there was nothing.

"It is the best I can do for you, my child. Now, I suggest that you get as far from here as possible."

"Where shall I go?"

"Go far, far from Elithia. Find a place where you can be alone and not a risk to anyone. Your instinct will lead you to the right place.

"I must see Hero! My father! I must go to them one more time before I leave Elithia."

"You cannot. If you fall into a slumber then there will be no one to undo this dark magic. I will do my best to look after Elithia in your absence. I have given you what you need to find your way back, and one day, we will meet again. You must do your best to regain your memories, to come back and break the curse."

"But how? If I have no idea of who I am?"

"You are strong inside, Princess Celene, and whatever you do, you do it well. You told me that yourself. I know that all must seem bleak right now, but your strength of character sets you apart from others. You will save yourself, Hero and Elithia."

"I'm sorry I didn't listen to your warnings," she murmured.

"It is too late for that. Our fates are so often unavoidable. Yet I believe there can be a happy ending for you. Take care, Princess, and leave quickly, before the causeway is submerged."

"But it is not time for high tide."

"Everything is different now, even the tides. The next part of your life is not one you will be able to schedule or plan for. You will have to wait and see what life will deliver."

Ardis placed both hands on her shoulders in a gesture of farewell. Then he turned and walked back towards the palace.

She wanted so much to run after him but she could not: Elithia was no longer her home. She took a deep breath and turned in the other direction, looking out into the black night where her future lay. Then she began to run.

ARDIS

Even with the curse that was landed upon her, he was glad that Celene had gone, out of Elithia and out of harm's way. Her new life would be hard, he had no doubt about that. Princess Celene would forget everything that she had ever known – her family, her friends, and her dreams, but at least a glimmer of hope remained. He hadn't told her the other thing he knew, which is that the last full moon to fall on New Year's Eve was four years ago. They would wait fifteen years for the next.

He turned his attentions to Elithia. He did not have long. By sunrise, everyone on the island would fall under the power of the curse. He needed to be well away by then but also he needed to protect Elithia, from looters and troublemakers. There was only one way he knew how to do that.

Once again, Ardis turned his face to the fading white light of the moon.

"Mistress Moon, hear me now. At each full moon and each new moon, you pull the tides so that the water rises up and across the waterway. This time, do not call that water back. Let your waters rest at high tide. Let Elithia remain an island. Protect her in her time of need."

As if in response, a great gust of wind swept across the causeway, so strong that Ardis almost lost his footing. Waves followed, rising high and slapping down on to the stony track. The moon had listened and was doing his bidding.

Ardis began to walk along the causeway, head down against the wind, taking great care not to be blown off course. But something made him stop. There, galloping along the causeway towards him was a familiar figure on horseback.

He put his arms above his head and waved.

She recognized him and slowed her horse as she approached.

"Turn around! Don't go any further!" he shouted.

She guided the horse towards him, looking confused. He must have looked strange out there with the water reaching for his feet and the wind pulling at his hair. Perhaps she thought him in need of help, but he saw from her red eyes and tear-stained face that she was the one who needed rescuing.

"Why are you out on your own in the early hours?" he asked.

"I have been out all night, riding. I needed to be away from Elithia. Everything has been slipping away from me. I needed to clear my head but now I am ready to come home."

"You must not return here," he told her. "Dark magic is at work in Elithia. If you care about your own future or that of your unborn child, you will leave now."

She raised her eyebrows, surprised perhaps that he knew her secret. But she didn't make a fuss. She simply said, "I cannot leave without telling anyone."

He looked pained. "Very soon, there will be nobody to tell. At sunrise, everyone on the island will fall into an enchanted sleep. The island of Elithia will be a different place to the one you know. Here, take these coins and go before the water rises."

She took the coins from him, fresh tears falling down her cheeks, and he proceeded to break off part of his staff – a twiggy section that branched from the top. "This is made from a whole Elithian mulberry sapling. When you find a place to call home, plant it. It will remind you always where you have come from.

She took the branch, and squinted into the distance. "Another was fleeing from here before me: I heard a horse leave the causeway as I was approaching from the coastal road, but when I arrived it had gone."

He shook his head and looked at her with kindly eyes. "No, not a horse, but a unicorn – the Cursed Unicorn. You would do best to steer clear of that unfortunate creature, for it is on a separate journey to you."

She nodded, a crease appearing on her forehead, and put a protective arm across her belly. "What of Elithia? What will happen here?"

"You must not worry about Elithia, Mistress Samara. She is preparing to sleep for a long time, but one day she will rise from her slumber. Then, and only then, can you return."

HERO

Minutes ago, there were voices all around me and gentle hands soothing, stroking, turning. The voices stopped mid-sentence and warm, living bodies fell to the floor, like sacks of flour at the mill. A curse has fallen and there will be no more touch, no more words.

But you, both of you, have left Elithia. I would feel it if you were here. You have gone to put this right and you will be back, I know it.

RUNNING AWAY

Water lapped at the causeway, steadily rising, but this didn't concern Celene. She would be safely across in less than a minute.

She turned and took one last look at Elithia, imprinting the familiar shape of the palace in her mind: its domed turrets and arched lattice windows. She had lived on this island all her life and she couldn't imagine being anywhere else. She pictured Hero playing the lyre, her father studying in the library. It was unimaginable that this life wouldn't continue.

She was running away, feet pounding on the hard ground, heart thumping in her chest.

Hester had been right about the dream after all: it had foretold this moment. She wanted to apologize to her for dismissing her concerned words. And for more than that: for not giving her full thanks for her loyalty and care. Now, perhaps, she would never get a chance.

She ran, not knowing where she was going, trying to put as much distance as possible between herself and Elithia. At one point she thought she heard a horse's hooves but she didn't look to see the rider. She pulled her hood over her eyes and tried not to think what people would say if they saw an Elithian princess running on her own in the early hours of the morning. If she was going to be running for some time, then she could not maintain a sprint. She slowed, breathing purposefully through her mouth, finding a steady rhythm. She was fit and healthy from all the training and could run like this for hours if necessary.

The sun began to rise. Normally, Celene would have enjoyed the beauty of the dawn sky but this sunrise meant something different for her: she knew that the curse would take effect, for her and for the whole of Elithia.

She kept running, hoping to outrun the curse, but she could not. It was difficult to tell when the change took place. At first, her legs strengthened, and running became easier. With long, swift strides she powered forwards. The muscles in her arms twitched and she felt that if she used those too, she could go faster still. She dropped her hands to the ground and saw that they were now hooves: grey-black hooves attached to her unicorn's legs, as white as the Hunter's moon at the bottom, turning golden as they stretched towards her body. She felt her face lengthen and her hair became a mane and tail, streaming out behind her as she ran. Inside, she was still Celene, but she was no longer the person she had been. Now, she was a unicorn.

HERO

Everything has changed. Elithia sleeps. I have no visitors and I can no longer hear the sounds of the city all around. I hear the sea birds calling and the rush of the waves, but no voices or man-made noises.

They are quiet now: the vegetable sellers, the town criers, the fishermen and the knights. They are all sleeping, breathing in and out, in and out. I can feel you here with me, in this space just outside of living. I know that you understand.

Sometimes I see some others, here with me beneath the waves, but I never spot the ones that I am desperate to see. They are gone. They are living new lives. Far, far away from Elithia. I know that you will return. And, I hope, you will bring the others back to me.

MY NAME IS PRINCESS CELENE

She was a unicorn now, as Ardis had foretold. But her memories had not gone. She still knew that she was Princess Celene, of Elithia, with a brother, Prince Hero, and a father, King Ellis. She told herself these facts over and over. Maybe through enough repetition, they might lodge in her mind.

She ran as she had always wanted to, galloping through the countryside, hoofbeats sounding on the ground, heartbeat in her chest. She could enjoy being a unicorn for a short time if this was how it felt.

Elithia had always been in friendly contact with the mainland for trading purposes, but still they were an island and they kept themselves to themselves. Celene didn't know anyone here; there was nowhere she could go. These rural parts were not very highly populated anyway, but she did pass a large farmhouse, all its windows still shuttered apart from one upstairs. Someone was at the window. As Celene ran closer she saw it was a small child, her palm pressed against the glass. The child smiled, eyes wide with wonder at the sight of a unicorn. Celene slowed. Her first instinct was to look up at the child, to make a connection, but then she remembered Sidra's words:

Gazing upon you will cause misery...

She lowered her head and ran.

She ran without looking back. She ran hoping that no more innocent eyes would inadvertently look upon her. Ardis had told her she must find somewhere far from people, and that is what she would do.

And as she ran, the reality of her situation hit her hard: this was not a game. The tears came, flowing freely down her face. She cried for what she had done and the mistakes she had made that she could not undo. And then guilt washed over her again. She had been unable to cry for her brother, yet here she was, crying for herself. That made her cry harder.

My name is Princess Celene of Elithia. I have one brother called Hero and my best friend is Samara. She repeated it in her head like a childhood classroom lesson, picturing the words forming on a black slate. Whatever else had changed throughout her life, these facts had always remained the same. They would never change; surely she would remember them.

She galloped through the fields in the early morning light, and saw a farmer out ploughing the field ready for his winter crop. He stopped and looked at her with wonder in his eyes – as one might gaze at a sunset or a beautiful view.

"No!" she cried. "Look away. I am cursed!" she tried to say, but the voice that emerged from her throat was not her own: it was a deep neigh. Fearful, she stopped speaking – kept running.

My name is Princess Celene. . .

There was more, she knew – names – but she couldn't recall them. She could no longer remember why she ran, from whom she ran or where she was going; all she knew was that she was alone, guilty and afraid.

Rain arrived with the early morning light: cold, relentless rain, lashing down upon her. Her mane matted to her neck and her tail hung heavy behind her.

My name is. . .

But she couldn't remember any more. She was tired now from all the running, and felt sure that she would be able to think straight once she'd had a good night's sleep. Down the hill stood a farm. She saw the farmer go to feed her cattle. When the farmer had gone, she crept into the warmth of the barn herself. The cows looked at her suspiciously and edged away, in a huddle that excluded her, but other than that they didn't pay her much attention. She could rest here, finally.

When the rain stopped, the cows went out to pasture, but she stayed in the shelter of the barn, sleeping off and on, always aware that the farmer might return. Later, when the farmer *did* return, she crept out through the barn door and off through the fields, hoping all the time that she wouldn't be seen.

BLEKE FOREST

Three weeks passed like this, running through the night, stopping only to nibble at grass in deserted fields, and drink from puddles or streams. She sheltered where she could in the daytime, avoiding crowded places. The names of the villages that she passed meant nothing to her, and she couldn't remember where she had come from. She knew that there had been some life before this one and that it had been important, but all details had vanished from her mind.

Although she didn't count the days, every night she looked to the sky and the changing shape of the moon, which waned away to a shining sliver before it disappeared and then grew again.

One morning, she was looking for a place to sleep under some blackthorn bushes. It was not the ideal spot, as the branches were spiky, but it provided some cover from the rain and the leaves were dense enough to keep her hidden. Her limbs were stiff from the cold and her muscles ached from all the running. But she stayed still and silent – there were people talking nearby and she didn't want to risk being seen.

"Over here," said one of the voices. It was the voice of a young girl. The unicorn shifted position as quietly as she could so that she could peek through a gap in the bush.

She was at the edge of a forest and there were two girls, one taller than the other – sisters or friends. They were prodding at the earth around the roots of a fir tree. They both held baskets and seemed to be searching for something.

"Yes," said the taller girl excitedly, scrabbling in the earth. "You can tell there are truffles from the darkening of the soil."

So they were searching for truffles. That made sense after all the rainfall recently. They would be able to sell them to cooks at fine houses. The unicorn couldn't remember how she knew this but it all made sense to her somehow.

The shorter girl stood up, put her hands to the small of her back and stretched. "We've cleared this area now."

The taller girl looked up at her from her digging position with a smile. "We would find more in the forest, you know. It's dark and damp in there, they probably grow in abundance."

"I'm sure you're right, but I'm not setting one toe in that place. Bleke Forest is where the cursed creatures live."

The taller girl giggled and gave her a playful shove. "You're a proper scaredy-puss."

They didn't go to the forest; they walked away with linked arms. Towards home, no doubt. Something stirred in the unicorn's chest. A memory of friendship and how it felt to share laughter with another. She was sure that she had experienced that, a long time ago.

She stood, peeking out first to check it was safe, and gazed at the forest that the girls had been talking about. Bleke Forest. *Where the cursed creatures live.* Just right for her. The girls had gone now, disappearing over the hill, and she stepped out from the bushes to take a look. Trees stretched out in both ways as far as she could see. She walked towards them, taking tiny, careful steps, and found a pathway leading in. It appeared to be an ancient forest. A cold, dark, hidden place.

She moved into the shadows of the forest. There were as many rocks as trees. Slimy, moss-covered rocks stood in piles like towers, creating narrow walkways. Trees grew in every direction, their black twisted trunks reaching like hands to meet one another, as if they themselves needed comfort in this gloomy place.

Others might have been scared by the foreboding trees and the sheer size of the place, the way that creatures hid away, eyes staring out from every hedgerow and tree. But Celene knew that these creatures meant no harm. These were the creatures with no place in the daylight. Bats and rats, trolls and weasels, ogres and beetles. These were the creatures that dared not show themselves at the edges of the towns for fear of being chased away. She could smell the fear and loneliness; the same as hers.

She trotted along the dark paths, feeling that her bright coat must stand out against all the sombre colours. Something rustled in the tangled brambles near her hooves. She turned, but whatever it was had gone.

This forest – Bleke Forest – was perfect for her, but she must find a place to hide away. She wasn't looking for comfort, just protection from the elements. She examined any likely looking gap in the rocks in her search for a suitable crevice or cave. Some were small, big enough for a rat or a fox, but not a unicorn. One was larger and she poked her head inside but a loud voice boomed, "Get out!" and so she did.

She walked a little further, starting to worry that there was no place for her. She stepped over a sad, brown trickle of water that was the closest she'd seen to a stream in this forest, and squeezed her way between two large mossy rocks. Then she found the perfect place. She nearly missed it, because the wide black mouth of the cave was covered with liana vines, twisting their way from the forest floor and over the rocks.

She used her horn to jab and thrust her way through the vines.

A memory of battling like this came into her mind. Perhaps she had once fought with another unicorn, clashing horns, although that didn't seem quite right. In her memory, she held a sharp weapon in her hand. This confused her and she shook her mane until the thought went away. She carried on jabbing and slicing until the woody vines no longer prevented her from getting through. Even though it was hard work, she was glad that she had to do it, for now she knew that there was no other creature living inside the cave. Not a creature her size, unless it had been in there long enough for vines to grow over the cave mouth.

The entranceway was wide but low. She was forced to duck her head right down and shuffle under the rock. But once she was inside, the cave opened up and was big enough for her to stand. She could not see much, as there was minimal light coming through from the entrance. The ground beneath her feet was stony and dry. She stamped her hoof hard and the sound echoed back to her. It must be a big space.

She walked in a small circle and then crumpled to the ground. For the first time in her memory, she had come to a place where she could stay, free from harm or prying eyes. Relief and tiredness hit her and she felt she couldn't move.

Nightfall was hours away. She would go out then, to explore

the forest more and find something to eat, but for now she could sleep for as long as she liked without fear of being disturbed. She curled up at the side of the cave, her legs beneath her and her face resting against the cold stone of the wall. To her surprise, tears came flooding down her face. She sobbed and sobbed, releasing all her tension and sadness, whinnying and snuffling, letting sleep come to her.

CAVELING

She awoke suddenly, unsure where she was in the darkness. Fear clutched at her heart. She had been looking for something, seeking something, but now she had found it, she worried. *Was she here forever? How would she survive?* Fresh tears began to trickle down towards her nose.

"Shush, shush, shush," said a voice, abruptly but not unkindly.

But I wasn't speaking, she thought.

"Maybe not, but you were thinking very loudly," said the voice. "And I'm trying to sleep."

She stood, looked around. Her eyes were growing more accustomed to the dim light.

A creature scuttled in the shadows and she shrank back. But it moved towards her and she was able to see that it was not something she should fear. The creature had mottled and slimy looking skin, like a frog, but it was grey and the size of a cat. It ran on four legs, but its face was humanlike and full of expression. It was a strange creature indeed and she couldn't help staring.

It stared back, sniffing the air.

Get away from me! She thought. *Look away! I am a cursed creature and bring misery to all those who meet me. If you look upon me three times, then the curse will be yours, too!*

"I do not think misery will fall upon me. Without eyes, I cannot gaze upon you once, let alone thrice."

The unicorn stared. It was true: there were little wrinkles where its eyes should have been. She relaxed a little, knowing that this was a creature with which she could freely converse and not worry about hurting.

"I don't need eyes in this place – there is nothing to see. My ears, nose and my tongue are all much more important." He paused for a moment. "Without eyes, I can't cry like you do. Why *are* you crying?"

It was a good question. She wasn't sure she knew the answer. *I am crying because I am far from home. I am crying because I can't even remember my own name.*

There was a pause.

"What is a name?"

A name? How could this creature not know what a name was? *Don't you have a name?*

"I don't think so. Am I missing out?"

Yes. It's a word by which you identify yourself. By which other people know you.

"Ah, I think I can help identify you." He sniffed again. "You are a horse-like creature but with a hint of magic about you."

That's right. I am a unicorn. I know I am a unicorn, but that is not my name. My name would help you tell me apart from any other unicorn.

"I don't know any other unicorns."

Imagine you do know some other unicorns. Do you see how a name would help?

"I suppose. I do know many spiders. There is Unusually Heavy and Clumpy Spider. And Spider Who Leans to the Side Due to Missing One Leg. And Hidey Spider."

How do you tell them apart without being able to see? she asked and then, not wanting to appear rude, added, *If you don't mind me asking.*

"They are all unique, like me. I tell them apart by their smell and behaviour. The Hidey Spider likes to hide. There is a Soporific Spider that sleeps all the time. If I smell that spider once, I fall asleep for a week. Are these names?"

I suppose so, in a way.

"Then I will call you Sad Unicorn."

Sad Unicorn? I don't want that to be my name!

"Why not?"

Because sometimes I am happy.

"Are you? That is something I would like to see. In that case I will call you Sad But Sometimes Happy Unicorn. What else do you know about yourself?"

I am a unicorn now but I don't think I have been a unicorn for very long. I was something else before, but I don't remember what.

"That doesn't seem a particularly detailed summary. Perhaps a different question would be better. What do you care about?"

She tried to remember. All she had cared about recently was finding shelter for the night, but she thought there was more to her than that.

I think that I like fairness, and order. I believe in kindness. And I like to know. All this not knowing confuses me.

"Interesting. These things are interesting, and perhaps more important than a name."

She thought that the creature had a point and that maybe he was cleverer than he looked. She wondered what he was – some kind of troll?

"I am not a troll. I might be a rock."

She hadn't realized she was thinking aloud, which was a strange thought in itself.

A rock? You cannot be a rock!

"I am grey and slimy much like the rocks in here."

But you talk! You move! You are a living thing. A unique kind of living thing. Some kind of caveling.

The creature seemed pleased and his smile widened so that she couldn't see where it ended. "A cave-ling. Yes, you may be right. You seem to have stopped crying, Sad But Sometimes Happy Unicorn. Does that mean I will be able to sleep in peace now?"

Yes, replied the unicorn, realizing he was right: she was no longer crying. And that was because even here, in the darkest of places, in the rain and the cold, with a curse upon her, she had managed to find a friend.

CHAPTER SEVEN

MOSS AND LICHEN

She slept again, for longer this time, and woke up feeling hungry. On her travels, she had been so focused on running that she had barely touched a thing. Now night had fallen and she was ready to venture out of the cave, but she wasn't sure where to go. She was sure there could be nothing to eat in the depths of this forest, where barely any light filtered through the thatch of trees. She hadn't even seen a green patch of grass where she could graze.

What do creatures eat around here? she wondered.

"Moss and lichen mainly," said the caveling. She started at

the sound of his voice; she'd almost forgotten he could hear her thoughts. It was a little disconcerting.

The slimy green stuff covering the rocks? She shuddered at the idea.

"It is not all slimy and green. You will be surprised. I am going out foraging now. You may follow." The caveling scuttled towards the cave entrance and under the hanging vines. She followed behind. The forest was not quite as dark as the cave had been and the unicorn was able to see the trees and undergrowth nearby.

The caveling kept his nostrils close to the ground as he shuffled speedily along, all four limbs working together. After a minute or two, he disappeared into a clump of ferns. She heard more vigorous sniffing, followed by little murmurs of glee and, finally, chewing sounds.

Are the ferns good to eat? she wondered.

"You can eat the ferns if you like, but the real delicacy is right here." The caveling trampled out a rough circle to reveal some purplish lichen beneath his feet. His tongue shot out, wrapped around the plant-like tufts, and pulled them into his mouth. He chewed, gulped and pattered back.

"Here, Sad But Sometimes Happy Unicorn, you try some."

She lowered her muzzle to the ground and tentatively bit off a small morsel of lichen. She ground it between her teeth, releasing the flavour. It tasted bitter, but faintly floral, like violets. And terribly moreish. She was hooked.

The caveling was delighted that she enjoyed it as much as he did, and led her on a tour of forest fungi. They uncovered ferny, feathery lichen and rubbery, mushroom-like growths. At a tree trunk, the caveling scrabbled at the bark to remove stubborn flakes of fungus. His flat, nail-less hands made it slow work, with only tiny particles falling to the floor.

Here, let me, offered the unicorn, and she lowered her horn. She was able to prise the fungus easily away. He caught the flakes gleefully and stuffed them into his mouth. "Very good, Sad Unicorn, very good. You may come foraging again one day."

She discovered dense clumps of moss and many varieties of lichen: some that were spongy and soft, others that were crusty or scaly. "Smell this," he ordered, holding out a clump of moss. She buried her nostrils deep in the springy mass and sniffed. It smelled green, fresh and damp, of life itself. Somehow, it lifted her spirits. She would have liked to nibble it and see if its taste was as good as its aroma, but the caveling snatched it away and stuffed it into his mouth. "Schtay away from the yellow lichen. Itsch poishonoush," he warned, his mouth full.

There are so many different types, observed the unicorn.

He swallowed. "Yes, in Bleke Forest we are truly blessed with fungus and moss. Both enjoy our damp, dark conditions. Now dig here, for something truly delicious."

She dug where he indicated in the soft earth. The point of her horn plunged deep until she found what they were looking for: gnarly brown balls of fungus attached to the tree roots.

"Truffles!" exclaimed the caveling, delightedly. She split the pile of buried treasure so that they had half each. She chewed slowly, enjoying the rich, earthy taste, and thought back to the two girls she'd overheard hunting for truffles. No wonder they were keen to find as many as possible.

Why don't humans come into the woods for the moss and fungus?

The caveling thought for a short while. "They do not enjoy eating these foods like we do. They enjoy mushrooms and truffles but they are scared of coming too deep into the forest – they think they will never get out again – so our sources are safe."

They think they will never get out again.

The unicorn turned that statement over and over in her mind. She wondered, if she stayed here forever, if she would change. *A creature of the night.* Perhaps if she stayed long enough, hidden away from the light, then she would become part of the forest. Moss would grow on her. Her golden and white coat would grow green and damp. Her horn would be a twisted branch and her body as sturdy as the rocks.

Part of her felt that she wouldn't mind – that it was better than running scared – but another part of her knew that her destiny lay elsewhere. She looked up at the waxing gibbous moon.

Bleke Forest was a temporary home – but for how long?

THE SYCAMORE

The longer she stayed, the more she found it difficult to remember what lay beyond. Perhaps she would never get out again. If only she could remember anything from her life before.

I wish I could remember my name, at least.

One night, she awoke with a strange kind of hunger, but it was not moss or lichen she needed. It was not food at all; she craved light. Not the warmth of the sun; she needed the cooler touch of moonlight, and then all would be well.

She peeped out of the cave and it all looked different. The forest floor and surrounding rocks were tinged with a blue-white light. The cold night air bit at her ears.

On most nights she was happy to have company for her excursions, but not tonight. She crept out as quietly as she could without waking up the caveling, and pushed between the narrow rocks nearby. She crept along the well-trodden tracks that were becoming so familiar. Up ahead, beyond the trees, white moonlight shone, casting long shadows on the ground.

It must be a full moon. Which meant a whole month had passed since the last Hunter's Moon, when she started running. But she couldn't remember anything before that.

She instinctively followed the pull of the light as a moth might, blundering her way to a large clearing: the one place in Bleke Forest where it was possible to see an expanse of sky. At this time of year, when some branches were bare, great patches of star-dusted sky were exposed. Normally she stayed away from this area, preferring to have cover if she needed it.

She stood in the clearing, enjoying the moonlight on her body. She looked down at her hooves, which glowed like silver, then up towards the sky and the perfect bright circle shining there. *A Frost Moon.* That was what it was called but she didn't know how she knew.

A tall sycamore tree stood close by, its branches reaching up like hands to stroke the surface of the moon. How she would like to do that herself, to run her fingers over its face, feeling its ripples and ridges.

What did the moon think as it gazed down upon Bleke Forest? Could it see a poor, cursed unicorn gazing back? She wanted it to notice her and respond: to touch her with its magic.

She needed to be closer to it.

Unicorns could not climb trees – she knew that – but she also knew that climbing was something she had to do. She just needed a different body.

So there, in the pale frosty moonlight, she shook her mane until it lengthened into dark, chin-length locks, and she shook her tail until it vanished. She shook away her horn, her muzzle and all the parts she didn't need. Then she stood straight and gazed at her slender front legs, which were no longer legs, but arms with hands at the end. She twisted her fingers together then spread them apart. She stretched her arms above her head and laughed. She was a human – a young woman. This body was familiar. It was hers, and she knew what to do with it. She had been this person for a long time.

She knew how to use her hands and feet to grip the branches and scale this tree. Although she wore a leather breastplate, she knew that her skin was more delicate than a unicorn's and that the branches could scratch her limbs through her soft leggings or linen shirt.

This was a good tree for climbing. She gripped the thicker branches, testing each one to see if it could hold her weight. She climbed as far as she could go, arriving right near the top where the branches grew too spindly to support her. She sat, with one arm wrapped around the trunk, her legs dangling through the pale yellow leaves, until she could see the moon above and the forest below.

"Tell me your secrets, moon," she whispered, using her voice for the first time in weeks. "Who am I, and why am I here?"

But the moon did not reply. It continued to shine as it had before.

Warm tears trickled down her cold cheeks.

And she tried to remember.

MEMORIES FLOATING BY

She stayed there all night, gazing at the moon, as if it might give her some answers. And it did help, a little. She remembered other moons, seen from a window, and from a courtyard: moons that had meant something to her.

The Barley Moon. Someone had spoken to her about such a moon, telling her that it brought about dreams. A glass had smashed.

The Mulberry Moon. It appeared when the mulberries were ripe: large, juicy tart purple fruits with a hint of sweetness. She remembered laughing, with the juice around her mouth. She had climbed a mulberry tree many times, sometimes with another girl. Or had there been three of them? They had been friends. One had fallen. Had she been hurt? She wished she could remember.

So many memories drifted into her consciousness, the way that the occasional wispy shadow passed before the moon. At first she tried to catch them, to hold on to them, by whispering words and phrases to herself, but they made no sense to her and it was frustrating. After a while, she stopped trying to catch the memories at all: just watched them float by.

Her human clothes provided less protection against the cold than her thick unicorn coat, but she still sat there all night, until the sky began to lighten and a suggestion of the sun appeared far away. The sun was not her friend as the moon was and she knew it was time for her to return to her unicorn form.

"Goodbye, moon. I will see you here in twenty-nine days."

For she felt sure that this was not a unique situation: this transformation would happen with every full moon. And she liked that idea. It would bring some order in her life – something to aim for. She climbed down from the tree and waited for the transformation that she knew was coming. She felt a tingling in her fingers and toes, as if her body knew what was coming. Within minutes, she was a unicorn again, complete with horn, mane, tail and four strong legs. But her experience had brought her strength and new hope. She galloped back to the refuge of her cave.

The caveling was there, munching his way through a small pile of fungi.

She pushed through the vines and he moved his nostrils in her direction, sniffed, and returned to his food.

She was glad to see him, although she was not sure the feeling was reciprocated. Perhaps he was annoyed that she'd been on an excursion without him.

Something happened to me. I found out who I am.

"And who are you?"

I am a woman – a girl – I am trapped in this body. Someone did this to me – cursed me – but I do not remember who, or why.

"Does it matter? Unicorn, woman. . . What do you care?"

It was a good question.

I wish I knew and could tell you why, but I do care; I think it matters more than anything.

And she curled up on the ground, determined to solve the mystery of who she really was.

She slept all day, as she had become accustomed to doing. When she awoke at dusk, the feeling of the previous night flooded back to her. It was a good feeling, of moonlight and happiness. She felt that she had travelled somewhere, and as though she'd changed in some way, but she couldn't quite remember where or how. It must have been a dream.

She stood slowly, and looked around for the caveling. He was soon there, beside her.

"How are you feeling today, Sad But Sometimes Happy Unicorn Woman?"

She looked at him curiously.

Why do you call me that?

"I know that it is a little long to say, but I do not plan on saying it very often."

No – I meant, why did you call me Unicorn Woman?

The caveling sighed. "Because you ran in last night telling me that you had transformed into a human. I am surprised you don't remember; it seemed so important to you at the time."

Her heart thudded. Of course. The full moon. The

transformation. Her limbs had been long, smooth and flexible. She had climbed a tree and sat there, remembering another life. It had not been a dream. But now she was back in the cave the memories were blurry. She knew that someone had fallen from a tree, but that might have been last night, or long ago. Back here, she could only think and feel like a unicorn, not like a person. She needed to transform again and find some way of holding on to her memories.

COLD MOON

Here in Bleke Forest, time was difficult to measure. She couldn't tell whether an hour had passed, or a minute, and a day could slip away unnoticed. Sleeping in the daylight hours, foraging at night, talking to the caveling or sitting in silence. Sometimes, the pressure of her new life bore down upon her like a heavy weight; she felt it in the muscles of her neck and back, and in her legs, which twitched to run free. But at other times, she could take comfort in the smaller things: the curved spiral of a snail's shell, or the surprising burst of nocturnal song from a robin. It might have been different if she had remembered her old life, but still those memories eluded her, as though hidden behind a locked door. And she needed to find the key.

She was desperate to transform into a person, to find out more about her real self. But a normal moon, the sharply curved crescent or shadowy gibbous, seemed to have no influence over her now: it was just a distant shape in the sky. Only the full moon – a marvellous complete disc of a moon – had seemed to have any power over her.

It was easy to forget the seasons in Bleke Forest. Her cave remained cool and steady no matter the weather. Still, the days piled up into weeks like the autumn leaves falling from the trees. When the forest floor grew soft and deep with leaves, a month had slipped away and the cold December full moon hung in the sky.

Once again, she felt its pull in every part of her body. She found the clearing and climbed the sycamore, as she had before, but she came no closer to discovering the truth about herself. It was the same during the Wolf Moon, the Storm Moon and the Worm Moon. She counted down to the night where she knew she would transform, she climbed the tree, and each time she begged the moon to give her some clue. She did remember some things: a long table, a ship on the horizon, flickering candles. By the light of the full moon, these things began to make some kind of sense, but the next day any meaning had gone. It was frustrating.

As a person, she noticed every month how she was changing.

She grew older and her hair grew longer and more tangled. Her skin grew paler through lack of light. She was completely nocturnal.

Years passed in this way and she saw no way to remember. The frustration was, perhaps, the worst part of the curse she had to bear. On one occasion, the clouds were so thick that the moonlight couldn't penetrate and she didn't transform to her human self. On that night she curled up on the floor of the cave and sobbed as she had on her first night. She needed the moon's power; she was lost without it.

Every time the orange orb of the Hunter's Moon came around, she knew that another year had passed and she still had not discovered her identity. Yet there was something special about the Hunter's Moon; it seemed the most powerful of them all.

It was during a Hunter's Moon that she sat in the branches of her sycamore tree and felt a great calm come over her. Looking up into the clear sky, with its tiny, twinkling stars, she thought that, maybe, she could be happy as she was. Little signs, like the wrinkles on the backs of her hands and the way she found it increasingly difficult to climb the tree, told her that she was older now. She was not sure how old, but too old to chase impossible dreams. She would forget about breaking the curse and would accept this life she had been given. She would live in the darkness with just the occasional burst of moonlight.

"It is enough," she told herself, aloud. "I am calm, peaceful, serene."

Serene, serene... She enjoyed the last word and repeated it a couple more times. Something stirred in her chest. A long-held memory that was important to her.

Serene ... no, not serene. But a similar word, with similar sounds.

The memory hit her hard and suddenly. She gasped and began to laugh. She climbed down the tree trunk into the clearing and turned in the direction of her cave.

She ran through the forest; the first time that she had done so as a human. Her legs felt clumsy and not as well suited to the action as a unicorn's. She ran as fast as she could, her breathing steady, white clouds of breath puffing out into the cold, moonlit air.

She ducked and crawled into the cave entrance, finding it easier to do with her new flexible limbs.

"Hello," she said. Her voice sounded familiar to her, if a little croaky.

"Hello," said the caveling, sounding unsurprised that she was using her voice and not her thoughts. Knowing the caveling, he would not be surprised if she sprouted wings and flapped around the cave. Still, she had another piece of news to share.

"I have remembered something – something important. My name. It's *Celene.*"

AN INSIGNIFICANT COUPLE OF SOUNDS

The caveling didn't respond to her great name announcement, so she prompted him. "Well, what do you think? *Celene.*" She liked saying the word, particularly the "S" sound at the beginning. To form the words aloud, feeling the vibration of air over her tongue, was a pleasure.

"I don't like it," said the caveling, wrinkling his nose as if something smelled bad.

"What do you mean? I have remembered my *name.* This is highly significant. You can't tell me you don't like it."

"I can. It is a meaningless word. Sad But Sometimes Happy Unicorn Woman creates much more of a picture for me. It is strange that a name without meaning, which is impossible to remember, should be particularly important to you. How did you acquire it?"

The caveling had a habit of picking up on the least important part of what Celene was telling him. She sat down on the cave floor with her knees drawn up. "I don't remember how I acquired it but, I should imagine that it was in the normal way and that my parents issued it shortly after my birth." She felt very sure about this and wondered why. She must have had parents once. "How else would it work?"

"It seems odd to me that the word by which one identifies is chosen by another who barely knows you. It would be more sensible if an acquaintance issued a name when they knew one better, based on learned characteristics, as I have done for you." He turned and muttered more quietly, "Not that you've done the same for me."

Celene sighed. "That is not the way that it works. But please listen – there is more. I think I was someone special."

The caveling snorted. "Special, how?"

"I may have lived in a fine house, or palace."

He looked more interested at that, and edged towards her. "What is a palace?"

"A palace is a fine building, a home, where many people live, surrounded by beautiful objects. . ." Celene trailed off, unable to remember exactly what a palace looked like.

"But you do not live in a fine palace. You live in a cave. In *my* cave."

"I didn't always live in a cave." As she said it, the image of a building with domed turrets flitted into her mind and then just as quickly disappeared. "I can't remember where. That is the next part of the puzzle."

"How strange," mused the caveling, after a moment.

"What is strange?"

"That you are excited by a name and a place to live. Are you not the same person, no matter what you are called and no matter where you live?"

Celene ran her hand through her hair. "I was not the person who decided how names work. Nonetheless, this is of the utmost importance to me. It is the first proper step I have made in years towards finding out my true identity. Will you help me remember it when I change back to a unicorn? Remind me, please, I always forget."

"I don't think I will be able to remember such an insignificant couple of sounds. I have forgotten it already. I find 'Sad But Sometimes Happy Unicorn Woman' much easier to remember. It suits you better."

The caveling slunk away into the darkest part of the cave, where she couldn't see him.

Celene wrung her hands together. "Oh, why do you have to be so unhelpful at a time like this? I must find a way to remember my name before sunrise, otherwise I will lose it again."

But the caveling didn't reply. He just muttered to himself in the shadows. She had to help herself.

Celene knew that she was able to write, but she had no pencil or paper, quill or ink. She looked down at her hands, which looked grey in the dim light of the cave. At least she was not restricted by her unicorn hooves. Various stones lay at the cave's mouth. Celene selected the sharpest one she could find and made her mark on the wall, scratching a long line into the grey rock: white and indented. She hadn't written anything for a long time, let alone with such a crude implement. It took longer than she would like, but she concentrated hard, using her time wisely.

As she slowly carved the first letter of her name, a new memory floated into her mind.

"My initial is the best. It curves like the moon."

She had spoken those words herself, during her old life. She had been speaking to someone she held dear, but who?

Another memory followed, a painful memory, of a written letter on a scroll, almost blotted out by spilled black ink. She knew that both these events were important moments in her life and she wished she could remember more. She was sure she would – in time – but for now, she concentrated only on carving the perfect letter "C", like the crescent of a moon.

LIVING THE NAME

The next morning, she awoke as a unicorn once again and the first thing she saw was her true name, etched in stone on the cave wall. *Celene.* She said it to herself over and over. Rediscovering her name unlocked something deep within her, allowing more memories to flood back.

She carried the knowledge of her name with her each day in the forest, saying it to herself. Bleke Forest was still the same, but she had changed; she had a new purpose. At every opportunity, she asked herself, *What would Celene do? What* did *Celene do?*

When she went trotting along the forest tracks, she knew that she had done the same when she was Celene. Celene had ridden a horse, possibly every day. Celene had looked after her horse, brushed him, loved him. There had been another rider, another horse, but she couldn't bring a face or name into focus.

Each shining curve of a new moon in the darkness brought further hope. As it grew from night to night, her energy increased, and when she sensed a full moon coming, she grew heated and restless. She would always know the exact time that the full moon, and her transformation, would come. On those nights, she headed for her usual space in the forest and enjoyed her transformation.

She climbed the tree to be nearer to the moon, cleared her mind and tried to allow the memories to find her.

But she no longer stayed up in the tree all night. Instead, as soon as she had a picture or word in her mind, she would run back to the cave and scratch it into the rock. She didn't even know what some of them meant but she felt sure that they were important.

During the next full moon, the image that came to her was of a bushy-leaved tree bearing ripe, fat, blackberry-like fruits. It had been the same tree that she'd remembered that first night. It took her a long time to get the shape right. A short trunk and spreading branches. Heart-shaped leaves, with jagged edges. She worked away, trying desperately to capture the image in her mind with the basic tools at hand. She described it to the caveling as she did so. Even if he showed limited interest, it helped to further ground the memory in her mind.

"I don't know why you are getting concerned about drawing a tree in a dark cave," he said.

"It's more than a tree," said Celene. "It is a memory. And I need to get it exactly right so that I remember it again tomorrow. Not any tree. It must be as I see it in my mind."

"It must be perfect?"

"Exactly."

"I'm sure you are the most perfect Unicorn Woman cave painter in the whole of Bleke Forest," said the caveling.

Celene looked at him sharply, unsure if he was being sarcastic. She ignored him and continued. Her knuckles were bleeding where they had been rubbing against the rock. She took some of the blood on her fingertips and dabbed it onto the fruits. The dark red looked just right.

"Mulberry!" she said, bringing her knuckles to her mouth and licking the sore patches. "It's a mulberry tree."

That was how she began to regain her memories. It might have been a long and painful process but she had nowhere else to go and nothing else to do. Slowly, slowly, month by month, the puzzle pieces slotted together.

An island surrounded by water, with a long straight road running to the palace gates.

Ten people sitting around a long table.

A curious circular symbol with lines marked at intervals around it, like a clock-face or sundial.

A picture began to emerge, spreading out across the wall. Sometimes, during the day, a shaft of light would enter the cave at the right angle, lighting up the scratches and scrawls. As a unicorn, these images meant very little to her, but as a woman, a full picture was beginning to emerge. One day she would understand what it all meant.

MANY MOONS LATER. . .

CHAPTER EIGHT

HERO

I don't know how long I have been asleep. Time doesn't matter to me any more. The tide rolls in and out, the moon waxes and wanes and the others continue to breathe and flounder beneath the murky depths. You, my child, are out there somewhere, living a life of which I know nothing. I wish you peace and happiness. I hope we will meet – in time.

POSSIBILITY

Tem

There were no restrictions on hunting in Bleke Forest and yet folk stayed away. It was not an inviting forest. The trees grew close together as if guarding secrets within, and the sun failed to penetrate, so it was permanently cold. The villagers had all heard the rumours of the creatures that hid in the forest: ogres, bad fairies and loathsome beasts. Even the forest's resident unicorn, the most splendid of creatures, was said to be cursed.

But these stories didn't bother Tem. It wasn't that she was particularly brave; she was just used to the forest. It was the closest to her house and she had hunted there for years, since she could first hold a bow. She sometimes saw these creatures, or signs of them, but they seemed more fearful of her than the other way around. They hid away, and as long as she didn't disturb them, she could hunt all the birds or animals she wanted. In most other forests, it was almost impossible to move without tripping over another hunter, so the rich pickings of Bleke Forest were a luxury. To Tem, the forest was a place of possibility. She knew she would never return home empty-handed after a trip there, but also, there was more to it than that: she knew that it was the sort of place where magic could happen.

In the autumn months, she tried to make the most of every dawn and dusk. She brought back as much game as she could: some to eat and some to store. On this particular trip, she had risen early and already bagged a forest grat, its warm, limp body slung over her shoulder on a stick. Her mother would be pleased with that. But, unless she was mistaken, there was another, bigger animal nearby. She turned her head in the direction of the rustling and tried to identify the sound. She was fairly sure that it was a deer, trying to stalk away. If she brought home a deer, it would feed them for a week or more. There would also be the deerskin, which they could work into a soft white leather, and take to the cobbler's for shoes.

Yes, a deer would round off this morning's hunt nicely. She balanced her earlier catch in the branches of a nearby tree and stood very still, biding her time.

SOMEONE IN THE FOREST
Celene

She and the caveling had been out feeding on moss and lichen as they did every night. Normally, Celene returned to the dark comfort of her cave by daybreak, her belly full and ready for sleep, but this morning something told her not to hurry back. She let the caveling go ahead and took her time to follow, enjoying the glittering shafts of sunlight peeping through the trees. The next night would be a full moon and she would be Celene once again: maybe knowing that was what made her bold.

But now, she regretted her decision. Someone was there in the forest. A human. She had never encountered a person in these parts but she recognized the near silent footsteps, the sound of someone trying to make themselves disappear: the sound of a hunter. She knew it deep within her soul. Perhaps in her previous life, she herself had been a hunter. But now she was the hunted and she was in fear of her life. She stopped, listening, and retreated into the undergrowth, where she concealed herself as best she could. She was patient; she could hide here for as long as it took.

WAITING
Tem

Tem would find the deer: she always hit her target. She held her bow at shoulder height and waited. She knew better than to hold her breath. Instead, she breathed quietly, steadily, through her nose and listened, listened. The creature was doing the same, but Tem was a patient person and she knew from experience that it would eventually scare and run. She waited for a couple of beats, and then she pulled back her arrow silently. She was strong enough to stay like this for a few seconds – she had to be – and at the first sign of movement, she would let her arrow fly.

THE HUNTER
Celene

Had the hunter gone? Celene had a desperate urge to be back in her cold, damp cave: she should not be here at all. She glanced in the direction of her cave, knowing that she could be back there in less than a minute. She took one step, making barely a rustle in the trees. Then she made the decision to bolt and run. But, as she stepped, she heard a quick swish of leaves and a sharp pain in her left foreleg made her cry out. The hunter's arrow had found her.

She crumpled to the ground, falling painfully on her right side, heart thumping in her chest. She shouldn't lie here. The hunter was surely on his way to finish his job. She tried to stand, but her leg wouldn't oblige. She fell back down, smelling the rich, peaty soil and looking up at the patches of blue sky showing through the close-knit trees. Such a beautiful day, but not beautiful enough to risk her life. She heard heavy footsteps. The hunter was no longer trying to stay quiet; he was coming for her.

NOT A DEER
Tem

Tem ran to retrieve her prey, but she knew she had not quite hit her target. The rustling of leaves indicated that the creature was struggling and Tem's heart beat fast as she reached for her hunting knife. She preferred to kill in one swift hit and didn't want to cause undue suffering. She steeled herself to look into the large, frightened eyes of a deer. She would kill it straight away. Her mother would be pleased.

But when she pushed through the trees, she found that the creature struggling was not a deer at all. It was a pony. Its coat was beige, but bright and glossy like gold, fading to white below the knee. Its tail and mane were also white, the finest that Tem had ever seen. The arrow stuck out from its left front leg and blood dripped below it, a startling scarlet against the white. Tem felt awful: she would never have shot at a pony had she known. It raised its head and looked directly at her and she saw the horn on its head: white, with light brown speckles, like a seashell. It was not a pony at all. It was a unicorn.

She thought of her mother's warnings, of the whispers in the village about a cursed creature. But this splendid unicorn could not be cursed. Tem felt it all over: in her fingers, in the roots of her hair. This creature was special, and she had struck it down. She was thankful she hadn't killed it.

The creature lay on its good side, its hurt leg sticking out at an unnatural angle. It was obviously in pain, and scared, but its large brown eyes didn't break away from hers as if it was warning her to stay away. No other animal had ever looked at her like that.

Tem bit her lip and looked at the arrow. Most of the arrowhead was still visible and it looked as though she hadn't badly hurt the unicorn – just grazed the outer part of its leg.

The creature closed its eyes and breathed hard through its nostrils. Tem realized she was still holding her knife in what must have looked like a threatening manner. She put it back in its sheath and held her empty hands up in front of her to show that she meant no harm.

"I hurt your leg. I'm sorry."

SEARING PAIN
Celene

The hunter burst into her hiding place, knife in hand. It was a girl: a child of around fourteen or fifteen. Celene had been expecting a big burly man, but this girl was slight, with long, tangled hair and freckles sprinkled across her face. At first Celene thought she was someone that she'd met before but she told herself that couldn't be true. She had large, dark brown, almost black eyes, which were opened wide and staring right at her. It seemed that whatever the girl had expected to find, it was certainly not a unicorn.

Celene turned her head away and closed her eyes, not wanting to meet the girl's gaze. She expected two possible outcomes. If the girl had heard tales of the Cursed Unicorn then she might turn and run. Or, if she was brave, she could kill her now – take her home as a trophy. She half-hoped it was the latter. It would take away the searing pain in her leg and the searching pain in her heart.

But the girl did neither of these things. Instead, she spoke quietly and gently.

"I hurt your leg. I'm sorry."

Celene opened her eyes and looked at the girl, who had put her knife away and crouched next to her on the forest floor.

"Luckily it's not lodged," she said, and with one swift movement, she pulled the arrow from her leg. It smarted. Celene made an involuntary sound in her throat, and then breathed through her nostrils, snorting gently as the throbbing pain dulled to an ache. The girl opened her shoulder bag and looked through its contents. She found a flask, unscrewed the cap and poured cool liquid over the painful area. Then a square of smooth bright material, coloured purple and green, which she bound around the wound. She still seemed so familiar.

"It's not as bad as it looks," said the girl. "It is good that I hit your leg and not your body – the arrow would have gone deeper there. It's strange though, I never normally miss."

Celene got to her feet, trying to bear most of her weight on her good legs. She would be able to walk, now. But she didn't walk away, not yet. She wanted to stay with this girl a minute more.

"You understand me, don't you?" said the girl.

Celene lowered her head in response. Yes, she understood.

SORRY
Tem

"I am so sorry," said Tem, not knowing what else to say. She put her hand against the lower part of the unicorn's neck. The unicorn seemed happy for her to do so. Her coat was smooth and silky. Tem had the strangest feeling, like she knew this animal: that they were connected in some way.

"I want to help you," she said, and the unicorn breathed softly.

Tem silently thanked her mother for persuading her to pack an emergency kit. For years she had questioned the use of the objects that her mother made her pack: a flask of clear water, a clean handkerchief, string. She could envisage no particular situation where any of these items would be of any use. But her mother had said, "Take them. You never know."

And now here she was, treating a unicorn's arrow wound and wishing actually that she'd brought more with her. She could do with a healing tincture. She knew the one that her mother used on her own cuts and grazes: it worked like magic.

She stroked the unicorn for a short while. Apart from its leg, it seemed fine: no sign of fever or distress. As long as they could avoid infection in that area then there was no reason it shouldn't heal perfectly.

"I'll come back and see how you are healing tonight. I'll bring a tincture."

She turned to stride away but her cloak was caught on something. She tugged and it came free, tearing the cloth as it did so.

The sound was loud in the quiet of the forest and the unicorn looked so alarmed that Tem laughed.

"It's just my cloak – no harm done. Wait for me here. I will find you later."

She gazed around at the spot, making a mental note of the layout of the trees.

And then she walked away.

SOMETHING TORN
Celene

The sound of the fabric ripping made Celene jump.

If you see the unicorn,
Something will be lost or torn.

This girl had just met her and then torn her cloak. Was it a coincidence? The only way to find out was to wait and see, but Celene knew the second part of the rhyme and she didn't want to risk it.

Meet twice and pain will come your way,
Be sure to run and stay away.

She said she was coming back with a tincture tonight.

Celene wanted to shout, *No, don't come back. I will hurt you unintentionally.* She liked this girl too much to risk that. Her eyes were kind – Celene couldn't get over that feeling of familiarity – and she felt a strong connection.

But Celene couldn't speak, either to warn her or to thank her.

The girl picked up the remains of her hunt from the nearby tree, skipped away and called over her shoulder, "I will see you again soon!"

GOLDEN MILK

Tem

Tem was still shaking with excitement when she arrived home. The temptation to pour out the whole unicorn story was strong, but she wasn't sure how her mother would react. Right now, she was tired and not sure that she could find the words. She would tell her what she had found later, over supper.

Mother was mopping the floor. Her sleeves were rolled up, and her black hair, so like Tem's, which she usually wore up in a bun, had come undone and was falling around her face. She looked up as Tem came in.

"What have you brought us today?"

"A grat." Tem put the furry body down on the kitchen table.

"Not here!" said her mother. "I've been cleaning. Hang it out the back and I can prepare it for supper."

Tem did as she was told.

"How was the forest this morning?"

"Peaceful as usual," replied Tem.

"Peaceful! Desolate more like. I don't know how you bear going in there all alone." Her mother shuddered at the thought.

Tem smiled. "I am happy with my own company and I never

have to compete with other hunters." She removed her torn cloak and handed it to her mother. "I'm afraid I tore my hunting cloak. Will you be able to mend it?"

Her mother inspected the damage. "Yes – I'll have this as good as new by supper time."

Tem tore off a chunk of bread from the fresh loaf on the side, and then retired to her bedroom to relax for a while before helping with some chores.

Her mother prepared the grat. Mother was a good cook and soon the smell of cooking onion and spices filled the small house. A few hours later, she served them both a rich, dark stew. Tem ate greedily, hungry from the excitement and effort of that morning. Grat meat could be tough, but when it was cooked for hours like this, it melted in the mouth.

Her mother laughed. "You are as hungry as my silkworms!"

Tem glanced over at the trays of silkworms, which munched their way through sackfuls of mulberry leaves and grew fatter and fatter every day.

Her mother spun their cocoons into raw silk and sold it to local merchants for a good price. Her beautiful embroidery, which she worked on for hours, never brought in much money. Tem's hunting and the silkworms helped them to live comfortably. Others in the village found it strange that they shared their living space with hundreds of wriggling caterpillars, but for Tem it was a normal part of her life.

"Are you going out hunting again this evening?" asked her mother, as she cleared the plates away.

Tem nodded. Her mother would expect her to, as it was the best time of the year for hunting, but she had an additional reason to go that night: she had made a promise.

"I will make you some golden milk to keep the cold from reaching your joints."

Tem smiled. She was not sure if her mother's remedies worked as she claimed, but she wasn't going to object to a cup of sweet frothy milk. Golden milk, gingery spices. Her mother's own recipe from childhood. She prepared it expertly, frothing the milk with a fork, and poured a cup for each of them. She slid one across the table to Tem.

Tem stared into the cup at the tiny bubbles and spices floating on its surface, then took a sip. She drank until the warmth filled her belly.

Finally she was ready to share the story of her discovery.

"I encountered a strange creature in the forest," she said.

Her mother looked interested. "Not the grat, I take it?"

"No," said Tem, with a laugh. Over the warm, milky drink, she told her mother all about it: how she had thought she'd bagged a deer and was shocked to discover it was a different, more magical animal. "A unicorn," she said, hesitantly. As soon as the word had left Tem's mouth, her mother gasped and put her hands to her face.

Tem wasn't sure which part of the story had shocked her mother most, but she continued, explaining how she was worried that she had killed it but then relieved her arrow had just grazed it below the knee.

Finally, her mother took her hands away from her face and stood up. "Something torn," she muttered, and glanced at Tem's hunting cloak, hanging by the door. She shook it out and located the rip, now mended with a line of perfect, tiny stitches. "Something torn!" she said again, waving the cloak in front of Tem.

Tem didn't know what her mother was talking about until she began to recite a vaguely familiar rhyme.

"If you see the unicorn,
Something will be lost or torn.
Meet twice and pain will come your way,
Be sure to run and stay away.
And if you meet three times: it's true –
The curse itself will fall on you."

Her mother waited a few seconds for Tem to realize what she was talking about. "The Cursed Unicorn," she said, gravely.

Tem took back her cloak with a gentle smile. "This was not the work of a unicorn's curse, mother. It was a particularly aggressive hawthorn that attacks me every other time I enter Bleke Forest. You have mended it enough times to know that."

"You shouldn't laugh about such matters."

"I don't know why you pay any attention to those old rhymes."

Her mother sighed and stood by the window, looking out at the mulberry tree.

"It was this very unicorn that brought the curse upon Elithia."

Elithia. Her mother's home kingdom. A sad place, cut off from all civilization by water and magic. It was said that within the palace walls, an entire royal court slumbered, not needing food or treatment. They were said to be under a curse. Tem knew that her mother had spent her childhood in Elithia but she didn't talk much about it. Tem hadn't asked any questions for years, mainly because she hadn't really thought about it. She was happy here with her mother and had no reason to question their life together. Also, when she spoke of Elithia, her mother got a sad, wistful look in her eye, which in turn made Tem feel sad. Overall, it had been better not to ask. Now that her mother was voluntarily talking about Elithia, Tem could hardly believe it.

Her mother didn't turn to face her, but continued looking out of the window. She spoke in a quiet, flat voice, as though reading from a book.

"The legend of the Cursed Unicorn is well-known in these parts, but nobody seems to know where the unicorn came from. However, I do know. I remember the first time I heard of the creature. There was a prince – a handsome prince – who was struck with a mysterious sleeping sickness. Shortly afterwards, a dark sleeping curse fell upon the whole island."

She stopped, swallowed. "I was lucky enough to be away from the island at the time, riding my horse. I met the royal sorcerer who warned me to turn away and not to return. And I remember his words. *If you see a unicorn, keep on riding and do not approach her for she is cursed.* I heeded those words and that is how I – we – came to be here."

"But where did the cursed unicorn come from?"

Her mother turned to face her at last, wiped her hands on her apron and pushed a chair under the table. "I believe it was some dark magic from a sorceress. Probably the poor beast made a deal with her of some kind."

"Oh," said Tem, struggling to imagine how the fate of a lost kingdom had anything to do with the beautiful creature she met in the forest earlier. "I'm sorry to hear about all that, Mother, but I promised to return to Bleke Forest tonight to check that the creature's leg is healing."

Her mother shook her head and pressed her lips together. "No."

Tem raised her eyebrows. Her mother rarely issued such a brusque command. She was normally patient and understanding. But now, she stretched her hand across the table to meet Tem's. "I wish I could make you understand the gravity of this. Elithia was such a happy place. It was known for its silk and for its circuses: happy, colourful shows. And almost overnight it was reduced to nothing. Everyone I loved was there. My family . . . everyone. Until you came along. And now, you are all I have. I will not risk your safety or happiness because of some creature's leg."

"But I plan to hunt tonight, Mother. It's a Hunter's Moon – it would be too much of an opportunity to miss."

Her mother stood to take Tem's cup before she had quite finished the dregs. "I wouldn't dream of stopping you from hunting but you cannot go back to Bleke Forest; you must find a new hunting spot. At least for a few weeks until you're sure the unicorn has gone. You may feel sorry for that creature, but it is cursed. It would have been better for the wretched thing if your arrow had struck its heart."

Tem was surprised to see her mother quite so resolved.

"But I've been hunting there for years and I've never seen the unicorn before."

"Good. Keep it that way. To see the unicorn once is unlucky, but to seek it out would be dangerous indeed. Find another forest, Tem. That's my last word on the matter."

Tem shrugged and nodded her head as if it weren't particularly important to her either way. She didn't want to disagree with Mother or to cause her any undue anxiety, but she could not ignore the steady thump in her chest when she thought about the unicorn. If it were any other creature, then she could stay away and hope that the wound would heal, but this unicorn was different. There was a special connection between them that Tem couldn't ignore: it meant something.

She knew without any doubt that she would be going back to Bleke Forest that night. Nothing could keep her away.

ANTICIPATION
Celene

Celene had managed to return to the cave, and now she could feel the pull of the moon from outside. She stood up on wobbly legs and prepared to leave.

"Perhaps you should stay here until you are better," said the caveling. "I will bring you moss and tasty lichen."

Thank you, Caveling, but I am well enough to venture to my usual spot. Her leg hurt, but tonight would be the best moon of all: The Hunter's Moon.

She stared at the wall of the cave, at the mysterious symbols and letters that she had drawn over the years. Her stomach fluttered with anticipation. Tonight could be the night that it all fell into place.

She couldn't stop thinking about the girl – the hunter – who had said she would return tonight. There had been something familiar about her, something connected to the pictures on the cave wall. But it was probably just the shock of meeting someone other than the caveling after all these years.

Celene wouldn't risk the curse falling upon the girl. She would return to the spot where they had met, near the cave, but by then

Celene would be in her moonlit clearing and they would miss each other. Bleke Forest was a big place.

PREPARATION
Tem

Tem didn't like lying, but she justified it by telling herself that her mother was being a little melodramatic about the situation. She doubted if any of the tales about a cursed unicorn were based on reality. People sometimes made up these stories to explain things they didn't understand. But, even if the words of the rhyme were true, what was the worst that could happen?

Meet twice and pain will come your way.

She had only met the unicorn once before, so a second meeting would bring her some pain, which she wasn't too bothered about. Pain was part of being a hunter. Splinters, cuts and grazes, thorns through her clothes; rarely a night went by without some minor injury.

"May I have my warmer hunting cloak, Mother?" she asked. "The Silver Woods are more exposed and I'm worried I might be cold."

Her mother found the cloak and handed it to her, eyeing her carefully. Tem suspected that she didn't entirely believe her story. She seemed to be playing the same game herself.

"Can you please bring me back a switch of silver birch while you are there? I am running low on its bark and it is so good for fever."

Tem smiled. "Of course, Mother." Perhaps her mother was running low on silver birch supplies, or perhaps it was a test. The Silver Woods were named after their tall silver trees and if Tem brought back a branch or two, it would be proof that she had visited those woods. But Tem knew that, despite its dark appearance, Bleke Forest was full of different varieties of tree, including at least two light and elegant silver birches.

Tem tried to prepare everything as she normally would, ignoring the adrenaline speeding through her veins. She bid goodnight to her mother, who would no doubt be in bed by the time she returned, and she headed west, in the direction of the Silver Woods.

Her mother waved from the doorway as she did every evening. As soon as she had closed the door, Tem pulled up her cloak, turned around and headed in the opposite direction: east, towards Bleke Forest.

CHAPTER NINE

HUNTER'S MOON

Tem

The sun was down and the moon was rising. Tem walked briskly and breathed deeply, her breath swirling in the cold night air. When she reached the forest, she gazed up at the sky.

The Hunter's Moon was bright and speckled with orange, as her golden milk had been. Above the trees of Bleke Forest, its inviting glow spread into the sky. It looked warm, like fire, although it was cold outside and Tem shivered, even through the layers she was wearing.

This moon always looked much larger than any other, but Tem

knew that it was an illusion. She straightened out her arm and blotted out the whole of the moon with her thumb. The same size as usual. Yet the light it was giving out was no illusion, as if the daylight hours had been extended.

Tem tried hard to remember the spot where she'd told the unicorn to wait. She knew there was a tree shaped like a deer's antlers, where she had hung her catch from the morning. There were two large moss-covered rocks and she had stepped over a stream to find the unicorn. She could picture it all perfectly, and didn't pay too much attention to the paths, but followed her instinct instead. Good hunters relied on instinct.

She soon realized that she had taken a wrong turning and that she was far from the right spot, but, somehow, it didn't matter. She knew that the unicorn was somewhere out in the forest and that they would meet again. The moon itself seemed to be on her side. It shone so brightly that its orangey light showed her which pathway to follow.

Tem walked carefully and quietly with her usual hunter's discretion, making an effort not to step on any branches that might snap. She didn't want to disturb any other creatures that might be out on a moonlit night like this one.

The light drew her to a place that she knew: the central clearing in Bleke Forest. Of course – if she were a magical forest creature that is exactly where she would head on a cloudless night. As she grew nearer, Tem heard a noise. She crouched down behind a holly bush and peeped through the leaves.

The clearing was flooded with moonlight, as bright as day. In the middle stood the unicorn. It was facing away from Tem, gazing up at the moon, and didn't notice her arrive.

It looked quite a different creature to the frightened animal that Tem had met that morning. Its golden coat glittered and its silken tail nearly swept the floor, rippling and ruffling in the gentle breeze.

Most noticeable of all was the unicorn's horn, which was pointing to the moon and shining with the same glow. Tem couldn't draw her gaze away. In a moment, she would approach the unicorn, check on its leg, but she wanted to enjoy this magical sight for a few moments more.

Suddenly, there was a flash of white light from the horn that was so bright, Tem had to look away. She buried her face in the crook of her arm, coloured shapes dancing behind her eyelids. After a couple of seconds, she was able to look back, but she was too late: there was nothing there.

The unicorn had vanished.

Tem forgot all about hiding and ran around the trees into the clearing, but there was still no unicorn. Had this been a trick of her imagination, or some moonlit magic at play? She felt sure that the unicorn must be near, but there was nowhere for such a large animal to hide.

Tem stood still and listened, but there was nothing. She looked all around, in the bushes and behind tree trunks. She was surprised to find that her gaze was drawn up, into the treetops. She shook her head. A unicorn couldn't climb a tree! But she followed her instinct and moved towards a nearby sycamore. She stood on the carpet of winged seeds and put her hand against the brown peeling trunk, gazing up into the branches. There was something in there, hiding. Something shy.

She threw her bow and quiver down on the forest floor.

"Hello? I won't hurt you. I am a friend."

The leaves rustled gently. Then a pair of eyes peeped out. Not unicorn's eyes, or the eyes of a squirrel, bird, or anything else you might expect to find in a tree. It was a woman.

THE GIRL FROM EARLIER
Celene

Celene recognized the voice. It was the kind voice of the girl from earlier. She hadn't wanted to be found, but now she was glad. In all the years she had been in Bleke Forest, she had not interacted with another human being. She would be able to have an actual conversation with words!

She pulled two branches apart, looked down at the top of the girl's dark head, and spoke back.

"Hello?"

THE WOMAN IN THE TREE
Tem

Tem had never seen another person here in the forest and she was almost more surprised to encounter a woman than she had been to find the unicorn. Especially a woman in a tree. The woman was swinging her legs in a girlish way but seemed to be around her mother's age. She had long black hair that fell around her shoulders and looked as though it hadn't been brushed in some time. Tem wondered if she lived here, in the forest. In the tree, maybe. She could see no signs of habitation. But, either way, the woman looked as though she knew the forest well.

"Have you seen a unicorn?" asked Tem. "It was standing right here, where I am now."

The woman shook her head and gazed down at Tem with a look that was part defiant, part scared. Tem had seen that expression before – that very morning. A strange thought came to her, that although this woman *looked* completely different to the magnificent beast she had met earlier, she *felt* the same: proud, independent, magical. Tem caught sight of the woman's left ankle, which was swinging somewhere above her head. The ankle was bound with a patterned silk handkerchief. It was dusty and folded up, so she could only see part of it, but enough of the distinctive purple and green pattern was visible. She was certain that if she unfolded it, she would see the letters E, R and K, and her mother's initials embroidered in the corner. Yes. It was her mother's handkerchief, tied with the same square knot that she had used that morning.

Which could only mean one thing.

ANKLE
Celene

The girl stared at the bandage on Celene's ankle for a long time. She obviously recognized the handkerchief that she had tied in place herself but couldn't understand what it was doing there. Then Celene saw realization dawn and the girl looked into her eyes once again, with such an open expression that Celene didn't feel the need to explain. This girl understood.

"You came back," said Celene.

DOWN FROM THE TREE
Tem

Tem was correct, then. The woman up in the tree was the same unicorn that she had encountered earlier that morning. She had heard of such things, of changeling creatures, of enchanted people, but she had never known if such tales were true. Yet, it all made sense in a strange sort of way. Tem had always known that if such things did happen, they would happen here in this magical forest.

"Yes, I came back as I promised." Tem stared at her, looking for signs of the unicorn she had met earlier. But there was no horn, and no tail. She was a normal woman in every other way, and Tem felt bad for staring. She looked down at her bag. "I brought something to help you." Tem took out the little glass bottle. She would do as she had promised, and help with the wound, before asking difficult questions.

"What is in the bottle?"

"It's benzoin oil," Tem said, holding up the bottle for her to see. "Shall I come up there and show you?"

The woman shook her head. "I'll come down."

She left her perch in the tree and swung herself down, sending a flurry of winged seeds spiralling to the floor. She wore fighting gear, like a soldier, which seemed unnecessary in the middle of the forest. Had she been hunting, like Tem? Despite the clothes, there appeared to be no weapon. Anyway, Tem could tell from this woman's dreamy manner that she was no threat. They gazed at each other.

"Do you live here, in Bleke Forest?" asked Tem.

The woman nodded.

"Have you lived here long?"

The woman's voice, when it came, was a whisper. "I am not sure. That is to say, I don't remember. I have seen many moons. . ."

She drifted off and Tem sensed that she didn't want to tell her any more. Tem lifted the bottle again. "Would you like me to put some of this on your ankle?"

The woman looked unsure – scared, even – and stepped away.

"Please don't be concerned. It will soothe the cut and help it from getting infected."

Tem pointed to a tree stump nearby and the woman nodded and sat down. Tem kneeled on the cold ground in front of her and undid the knot of the handkerchief, trying not to put undue pressure on the woman's leg as she did so. The woman's leg was almost as sinewy and strong as it had been when she was a unicorn. When she unwound the handkerchief, Tem could see, even in the moonlight, that the gash was quite deep, but it didn't appear to be inflamed. With the correct treatment it should heal quickly.

Tem shook the little bottle vigorously, unscrewed the cap and tipped a liberal amount on to a clean handkerchief.

BENZOIN OIL
Celene

The oil smelled strong, sweet and musky, like vanilla. It made her feel warm inside. A memory washed over her of a room, lined with bottles. The girl pressed the soaked handkerchief against her leg. Celene winced at the sudden sting and the memory vanished.

"I am going to tie this to your leg, with a fresh handkerchief over the top."

Celene hadn't experienced such kindness for a long time. She tried not to show any sign of pain and stared at the square of silk that the girl was unfolding. She saw now that it matched the old crumpled dressing on the ground, which she hadn't been able to examine when it was tied around her leg.

The handkerchiefs were a distinctive shade of purple and green, and some letters were embroidered in the corner of this one. They were sewn in a basic running stitch but with a child's curly flourish.

Samara.

She whispered it: "Samara" and the girl looked up, confused.

"Is this your name?" asked Celene, pointing to the handkerchief.

"No, my name is Tem."

"Tem. A short name."

"Short for Artemis, but my mother has never called me that. Samara is my mother's name. Like a sycamore seed. These are some old handkerchiefs from when she was a girl in Elithia."

Celene's heart fluttered in her chest. *Elithia. Samara.*

She felt she had seen embroidered letters like these before, with the same green silk, but in her memory it was her own name. She could remember stitching the letters as she giggled with a friend. It was a happy memory and she laughed.

"My name is Celene," she said. "It has the same number of letters."

Tem looked confused again.

"As Samara," she explained. "And they both begin with an 's' sound."

Tem raised her eyebrows and then smiled at her as if Celene were the child. "I suppose they do." She finished the bandaging and stood up. "Now, this is all finished. How does it feel?"

Celene nodded. The stinging had subsided and it felt good – secure. She took a few more steps, testing how it felt.

"I'll leave the bottle with you and you can reapply it when you change the dressing."

"Thank you but I will not be able to dress my wound. I only

take my human form on a night like this." Celene pointed to the sky.

"You mean a full moon?"

Celene nodded.

Tem's eyes gleamed. Celene could tell she wanted to know more.

"Maybe I could come back tomorrow?"

"No!" shouted Celene. "Only when the moon is full. Please. I would be a danger to you in my unicorn form." She could not risk any harm coming to this girl if they met again. She had already encountered her twice and a third time could be dangerous. *The curse will fall on you.* She didn't know what that meant but didn't want to find out. Tem was possibly too courageous for her own good.

"You should stay away from me," she continued. "I do not know where I am from or how I came to be like this, but I know that I am cursed. I cannot bring any good to another human being. Only pain and suffering."

"I don't believe that to be true. I've heard a rhyme about this curse – what is the second part? *Meet twice and pain will come your way?* Well, I have now met you in unicorn form twice, but I am not in pain." Tem wriggled in a little dance as if to show how healthy she was. "Besides, people speak only of a Cursed Unicorn, not of a cursed woman. How can it do me any harm to look at you in human form? I could help you discover where you come from."

"Perhaps." Celene liked Tem and she loved being able to talk with another person. "Come back to this spot at the next full moon. If you like."

Tem nodded and smiled. Then she picked up her bow and quiver from where they were lying nearby.

"What are you doing?"

"My mother thinks I am out hunting in a different forest. I can't go back empty-handed."

"You lied to your mother?"

"She thinks that I am putting myself in danger by coming here. She wouldn't understand."

Tem swung around, looking up in the tops of the trees for a target, her form silhouetted against the great orange moon.

"A Hunter's Moon," whispered Celene.

"That's right," said Tem.

"What will you shoot?"

"A pigeon."

Celene watched her load an arrow, pull the string back and take aim. She felt a strange envy and wanted to hold the bow. She knew what the string would feel like in her fingers and how far to pull back the string.

Tem released the arrow a second too soon and it missed

its target.

"May I try?"

"Yes," said Tem, sounding surprised.

Celene took the bow, enjoying the weight of it in her hands. She held it, shifted position a little, before firing the arrow. Her body seemed to know exactly what to do. A bird spread out its wings as it was flying in to land and she let her arrow fly.

It hit its target, and the bird fell like a stone from the air.

They grinned at each other and rushed into the bushes to find it. Celene picked the bird up by its feet and passed it to Tem who strung it to her back.

"You've done this before," said Tem.

"Yes." She was sure of that.

"Do you think you were a hunter?"

Celene shook her head. "I don't think so."

Tem frowned, confused. "Yet you are proficient with a bow? Perhaps you were some kind of athlete?"

"Not that either," said Celene, "Although I believe I trained. I can picture a straw target."

"So you were a soldier then. Or a knight!"

"Yes. Something like that."

"I would love to stay longer and try to help you get to the

bottom of this mystery, but I have to go now."

Celene sighed. "There are still hours of moonlight left. We could talk longer." She didn't want to say goodbye.

But Tem shook her head. "I will be back at the next full moon but I must return home. My mother will be worried if I am late back."

The girl was kind as well as brave. She walked away.

"Take care, Tem," said Celene.

SILVER BIRCH
Tem

Tem walked away from the clearing and looked back at Celene once, to see where she would go. But she went nowhere; she stood in the clearing with her arms straight out at her sides and her fingers spread wide. Tem half expected her to transform back to a unicorn but she didn't; she stayed like that, gazing up at the moon, and Tem went on her way.

The conversation between them had been so natural and unexceptional that Tem had barely thought it strange, but now that she was alone, her senses were heightened, and she felt giddy from the excitement of it all. She had a new friend, who was half-unicorn! And there was a mystery surrounding her that Tem was sure she could help solve.

Before she headed home. Tem had one more stop to make. Her earlier catch was only part of her cover story and she mustn't forget the branch that her mother had requested. She took a slight detour on her route home to visit the Bleke silver birches. These three trees were huddled together between other larger trees, as if in secret conversation with one another. Tem had often wondered why they were called silver, when the papery bark was white. But in this moonlight, they were as bright and shiny as the blade of her hunting knife, which she unsheathed to cut a branch.

Her mother would want as many fresh young twigs as possible, to boil up into tea: one of her homemade cures. Tem selected a bendy branch and pulled it down towards her, running her hand along it so that the leaves fell to the ground. In the springtime her mother would use the leaves as well, but not at this time of year, when they were dead or dying. She held the branch in place with her left hand and attempted to cut it at the base with the knife in her right hand. Her knife was sharp and she expected to slice straight through the relatively thin branch, but it seemed to be glued fast to the trunk.

Tem tried again, moving her left hand nearer to steady the branch. This time, she sliced right through the branch, but her knife slipped into her left thumb.

She shouted in pain, and dropped the branch. She had cut right through the soft leather of her glove, and blood now soaked the end of the glove's thumb. She removed it gingerly and saw that the cut went quite deep and a flap of skin hung off. In the silence of the forest she could even hear the sound of her blood dripping on to the dry leaves. For a moment she thought she might faint, but she breathed deeply and the feeling passed. With her unharmed hand, she rummaged in her emergency pouch.

She soaked a new silk handkerchief with benzoin-oil as she had for Celene, and wound it around her thumb, wincing at the sting. This would act as a temporary solution but her mother might need to put a stitch or two in it when she got home.

She left Bleke Forest with the pigeon on her back and the silver birch branch in her left hand, the thumb still throbbing. It wasn't the first time she had hurt herself whilst out hunting and she was sure it wouldn't be the last. Nonetheless, her mother's words played in her mind:

Meet twice and pain will come your way,
Be sure to run and stay away.

But she couldn't stay away. It was much too late for that.

BLOODY THUMBPRINTS
Tem

Her mother was still up when Tem arrived home, and she handed the silver birch branch over straight away. Its white bark was dotted with bloody thumbprints.

"What have you done?" cried her mother, and instantly sat Tem down. She unwound her temporary bandage, and reapplied salve and a new dressing. The thumb would be fine; it didn't even need a stitch.

"See, Mother – I go hunting in Bleke Forest for weeks on end without an incident but the minute I step into the Silver Woods, I hurt myself."

If she'd been hoping for a turnaround in the decision, it didn't come; her mother set her jaw and said nothing. Tem knew this look: it meant that they had discussed it and there was nothing more to be said on the matter.

Tem wasn't going to start an argument. Her cover story had worked this time, and from now on she could go hunting in the Silver Woods as her mother wanted. She wouldn't need to tell lies until the next full moon – the Frost Moon – in twenty-nine days' time.

Tem could be patient for a month. She began counting the days until she could return. In the meantime, she couldn't stop thinking about the enigmatic unicorn woman of the woods. Celene. She was desperate to help unravel her mystery. In a strange sort of way, she felt that she – Tem – was an important part of the puzzle and would somehow be able to help her put the clues together.

She already had the beginnings of an idea forming in her mind. Her mother had been convinced that the unicorn had travelled here from Elithia, and Celene had seemed extremely interested in her mother's silk handkerchiefs. Perhaps it was just that, hiding away in the forest, she had never seen anything like them before, but Tem had a feeling that there was more to it. When Tem had mentioned Elithia, there had been a fleeting spark of recognition in her eyes.

Even if there were nothing in it, Tem thought that over the next few weeks, she would uncover everything she could about Elithia. She would risk her mother's sad, faraway look; she had to know. So, a few days after she had returned from meeting Celene, she began asking her mother questions. They sat together preparing windfall apples to make apple butter. Tem's thumb was still healing, so she cut the bad parts out of the apples while her mother peeled them.

"Mother, what was Elithia like?"

Her mother stopped peeling for a minute and looked sideways at Tem. "Why do you want to know?"

"I was just thinking about it. As I get older, I wonder what it would have been like for us if things had been different and I'd grown up there."

She looked worried. "You're happy here, aren't you, Tem?"

"Yes. I was just wondering."

Her mother sighed and continued removing the peel in a continuous piece with her knife. The green spiral twisted beneath her hands.

"Elithia had everything. A beach, but also green countryside and hills. Brave knights, but rarely a war. Fine, sunny weather, but always a cold breeze sweeping in from across the sea. We were all so happy there on our little island. It was too perfect to last." That wistful look came into her eyes again. Tem nearly stopped her line of questioning, but there was more she wanted to know.

"Tell me about my father."

Her mother smiled at that and passed Tem the apple, discarding its green peel. "He was a good man. I'd known him since childhood: him and his sister. She was my best friend. He was kind and funny and easy-going. He never met you, but he would have loved you."

"And what happened? Everyone fell into a cursed sleep?" Tem had always thought the story was a little far-fetched, and had possibly been exaggerated over the years, but after meeting the unicorn woman she was starting to understand that such magic was possible.

Her mother rose and rummaged on the rack where they kept the cooking pans.

"I was lucky to escape. I believe I was the only one, apart from Ardis, the sorcerer. I left Elithia with nothing but the bare-rooted branch of a mulberry tree, a few gold coins and you, growing inside me."

"But my father died before all this?"

Her mother turned, holding a black iron pan by the handle, looking most concerned. "I never told you he was *dead*, sweetheart. He was ill, very ill, even before the curse, but I don't know what happened to him. In all these years, no one has seen any sign of life from the island. By now, he must have passed away. There is nothing in Elithia for us now. It is a lost island."

Not dead. This was a major point and Tem wasn't sure how the message had been confused. All she knew was that whenever her mother spoke of her father, which wasn't very often, she referred to him in the past tense and with a sense of regret. She spoke of him as if he had gone. But now, Tem discovered that her father wasn't confirmed dead. He may only be sleeping. And if he were only sleeping, then surely there was still a chance that he would wake up?

HERO

Years go by and my name doesn't pass anyone's lips. I do not know if they remember me at all. I feel as though I might float away. I am a legend, a story from olden times. A sleeping prince on a sleeping island that may never awaken.

But now you are talking about me. That is good. I am real and I am waiting. Never give up on me.

CHAPTER TEN

FROST MOON
Celene

Celene always felt her excitement mount in the days before a full moon. By now, she could predict when they would fall. Tonight's would be a Frost Moon: the first full moon of winter. Most years, the winter was a difficult time for Celene. Her usual mossy food was still available, but when the temperatures dropped, she shortened her night-time expeditions, preferring to huddle away in the cave, almost in a state of hibernation. But tonight, Celene knew that her new friend, Tem, would be coming to visit.

She stepped out of the cave earlier than usual and made her way quickly to the clearing. The Frost Moon was high in the sky: bright white with a blue tinge. It was cold, and it would soon be growing colder, but that didn't bother Celene. To her, even this frosty blue moonlight had a kind of warmth.

There was no one around, but this was a good thing, as she didn't want Tem to arrive too early and see her in unicorn form. That would make three times, and three times was the most unlucky of all.

She threw her head back and felt the moonlight reach her. She felt it first in her horn, as if it had been lit from some spark. She felt it in her mane, as it grew and changed into human locks, and in her coat, her limbs and her hooves as she transformed into her other self. She was a woman again. She turned in a circle, looking hopefully all around for another human. She stretched out her arms above her head, enjoying how it felt. Then she bent over at the waist, smelling the mulch below her as she trailed her fingers through the sodden leaves.

The handkerchief around her ankle had loosened and was in danger of falling off. That would be a pity, as it was beautiful. She undid the knot easily and unfolded it. The handkerchief was marked with the benzoin oil and her own blood, but she could see the pattern beneath the stains. Once again, it seemed familiar, and a memory flitted in and out of her mind, but she couldn't quite catch it.

She was in the wrong place for memories; she needed to be in her usual spot, closer to the moon, so she climbed her tree and waited: waited for Tem. Before Tem, her monthly visits to the tree had been enough for Celene. She had been content to sit within its branches, absorbing moonlight and memories as if she were part of the tree itself and needed these things to grow. But now, it was not enough. Now she felt restless and looked down at the forest floor rather than up towards the moon. She was anxious that Tem might not show up. She was a young girl. Perhaps she would grow scared and decide to stay in the safety of her own home, rather than spending her time with a cursed creature. Or perhaps something had happened to her after their last meeting. Perhaps she was lying hurt somewhere and unable to come to Bleke Forest—

A twig snapped down below. Leaves rustled. Someone was nearby. Celene tensed. She looked down but could not see anyone. She hoped it was because that person was a hunter and good at hiding.

It was.

Tem's features were immediately clear in the glow from the moon. She was looking up in the trees, trying to recollect which one was Celene's tree. Celene smiled down at her, waiting for the moment when she would look up and find her.

The joy on Tem's face made it worth the wait. She grinned, waved, and then immediately began climbing the tree, talking as she did.

"I sometimes hide in a tree when I am hunting," she said, as she pulled herself through the branches, past Celene's perch. "Is that why you come up here – to hide?"

Celene smiled; amused that Tem had not bothered with greetings or long preambles. She liked that they picked up where they left off, and she liked that she climbed the tree easily and without question.

"No. I'm not hiding. I just like to sit here, up where I am close to the moon," said Celene. "It's where I remember."

Tem soon found space for herself, higher than Celene, with her knees drawn up and the crisscrossed shadows of branches falling across her face.

"What do you remember?"

"My name was the first thing. Then other things. Buildings. Trees. Things that I don't understand but that I hope will make sense to me one day."

Celene gazed up at the round bright face of the moon, half-expecting a new memory, but nothing came. Perhaps it was different with the two of them there; perhaps Celene wasn't concentrating in the usual way.

"I remember parts of my life before. I was a young woman. I lived in a place of luxury. Sometimes I am not sure if the memories are true. Tonight, before you came, I remembered patterns painted on silk that were like your handkerchief." Celene took the handkerchief from her pocket. "It is lovely. Perhaps it was just this beautiful pattern that conjured up false memories." She stared at the handkerchief again but remembered nothing new.

"The handkerchief is yours if you want it," said Tem. "My mother has plenty. They come from her home kingdom, of Elithia. Do you think that you might have a connection to that place?"

Celene crinkled her forehead, concentrating hard. "Elithia. Elithia. I think so, yes, but I am not sure. . ."

TWO HEADS
Tem

Tem wished she could help her remember. "Elithia is an island. My mother says it had green hills and circuses. They made silk there. Mother keeps her own silkworms even now. . ."

But she stopped. Celene was shaking her head and looked frustrated; she obviously couldn't remember any more. Tem would try again later, but for now she changed the subject.

"How is your ankle?"

Celene clasped Tem's lower leg (the nearest accessible part of her), causing her to wobble in the tree, and stretched her own leg up towards Tem's branch.

"It is mending well, look!"

Tem inspected the wound, which had healed over completely and was now a bright pink scar. "I'm glad that it has healed well. The benzoin oil must have done its work."

"That oil was another thing that triggered my memories last time we met. When you applied it to the arrow wound, the smell was so distinctive that it distracted me from the stinging!"

Tem thought about her mother's well-stocked cupboard at home, filled with herbs, spices and home cures. She had learned to prepare these things growing up in Elithia. "Can you tell me about your memories? Perhaps I can help you understand what they all mean."

Celene nodded. "Of course. Two heads are better than one, after all. But we can do better than talking. Come with me and I will *show* you my memories."

Celene shuffled along her branch and swung her legs down.

Tem didn't know what Celene was doing but she laughed at her sudden eagerness.

She followed her down the tree and thumped on to the ground, which was soft with piled-up leaves. Celene darted through a gap in the trees at the edge of the clearing, checking back to see if Tem was following.

Tem felt a little nervous. "Where are we going?"

"To my home."

SHARING THE DRAWINGS
Celene

"It's a cave!" exclaimed Tem. She seemed surprised.

With one movement Celene swished back the hanging vines like a long curtain. Some things were much easier to do with her flexible human arms. Tem ventured in, her arm stretched out in front of her with a flat palm, as though she expected to bump into something.

"It's dark in here. I cannot see a thing."

Celene remembered how dark the cave had seemed in those early days.

"And it's damp." Tem wrinkled her nose.

"Yes, but you get used to it." Celene couldn't remember anything before the shelter of her cave. She found the dark comforting. Kind. But then she had the advantage of knowing the cave, whereas it must be quite disorientating for Tem. She secured the vines behind a rock to let in as much moonlight as possible.

"There is someone I would like you to meet. Caveling? Caveling?"

He did not reply. Maybe he didn't like the light and was lurking in the darkness.

Tem loitered near the entrance. Celene took her by the arm.

"I know this is not the most . . . luxurious . . . accommodation."

She pointed to the drawings, dotted over the wall like the snippets of memories in her mind. She had been busy, since that first time she scratched in her name.

"Were these drawings always here?" asked Tem.

Celene shook her head, feeling shy at the revelation of her innermost thoughts. They were strange images, cruder than she would like.

"No, they are mine. I am no artist, as you can see—"

Tem examined each image closely and pointed to one. "Is this a person sleeping?"

Celene nodded.

"Is it you?"

"No." She knew the picture was important, but she couldn't remember why. Tem kept staring for a long time. It made Celene think that she could be the one who could make the links between the pictures.

But what was the chance of the only human she had ever encountered being some kind of connection to her past? Was this just the wishful thinking of a cursed unicorn?

FAREWELL FOR NOW
Tem

She thought that the drawings might depict Elithia. Her mother thought the unicorn came from Elithia. She had mentioned a palace, a circus tent, mulberry trees, sleeping people, and here they all were on the wall of the cave. If they were of Elithia, then it was possible that there *was* a connection between Samara, Celene and Tem herself.

But then trees and sleeping people and circuses could belong to any place, at any time. Perhaps she was looking for connections that weren't there at all.

Tem's mother would know straight away if it were Elithia depicted on the wall. She wished that she could take the drawings away with her. That wasn't possible, and even if it were, her mother would be horrified to discover she had been to Bleke Forest.

Thinking of her mother made her feel guilty. She had been here longer than planned.

"It's late. Mother will have gone to bed hours ago. She will be cross in the morning."

Celene sighed deeply. Tem shared her sense of frustration. Now they would have to wait a whole month before discussing it again. Still, she couldn't stay. As well as the need to get home, she couldn't chance being near to Celene when she changed back into her unicorn form.

"Next time we'll look at the pictures for longer. We'll figure out what it all means," promised Tem.

Celene nodded.

They walked back to the main pathway together to share a few more minutes of talking time, even though Tem knew the way home. They didn't talk any more about the drawings, but instead discussed some of the other hidden sights and sounds of Bleke Forest.

Where the pathway split into a Y, they embraced. Celene

turned and headed back towards her cave and Tem went on alone, taking the right fork towards the village. She had no need to stop at the silver birches. Her mother had stopped requesting proof of her hunting trips since acquaintances had spotted her in Silver Woods. Tem had prepared a cover story to explain the late hour: Silver Woods had been so busy tonight that she hadn't been able to land a single thing. She had stayed later and later but had caught nothing. Perhaps it was time to go back to hunting in Bleke Forest.

Tem wanted to spend more time with her new friend; once a month didn't seem enough. Tears pricked at Tem's eyes when she thought about where Celene lived, in a cold, dark cave. How had she ever been able to bear it? She shivered to imagine a similar fate for herself. She wished she could do more to help, but was beginning to believe that there might be something in that old rhyme after all, and she didn't want to risk the curse. It was all getting very complicated.

THE WINGED SEED
Celene

After she had said goodbye to Tem, Celene considered going back to the clearing, but tonight, for the first time, she didn't feel like it. Instead she lay on the floor of the cave, head resting on her arms. Something was caught in her hair: a sycamore seed. She pulled it out, turned on to her back and played with it, twisting it between her thumbs and forefingers.

The caveling, whom she hadn't seen all evening, scuttled over. "You're back early. You usually spend all night in your tree when there's a full moon."

Celene raised her head a little. "I didn't feel like going back there after talking to Tem. Where were you? Didn't you want to meet her?"

She wondered if he were jealous now that her attention was diverted away from him. Did cavelings get jealous?

"I saw the other girl-woman. I didn't need to meet her. I know already that she is like you."

"Like me? She looks nothing like me."

"I didn't say she looks like you. I can't comment on what she looks like. I only said she *is* like you. There is part of you in her.

219

She belongs to you."

"She belongs to me? But Tem is a person. People don't belong to one another."

"I thought they did."

Celene let the words sink in. Of course people belonged to one another. In tight groups – families. Could Tem be a younger relation of hers? Was that the connection?

She felt sure that she was not a mother. She would know if she had a child of her own. Anyway, Tem had her own mother. But Tem was so much younger than her. She must have been born since Celene had lived in Bleke Forest.

A younger sister perhaps.

Or the child of a sister.

No, the child of her brother. Her brother. Of course.

Celene had a brother.

She looked up at the middle drawing of the sleeping prince. Her brother. How could she have forgotten? *Hero.* She felt a sudden joy at the thought, followed shortly by terrible guilt. He fell into a sleep and it was all her fault.

She stared at the winged sycamore seed case in her hands. A samara. Tem's mother was Samara. And now she remembered that was also the name of her best friend back in Elithia.

As soon as she thought it, she knew it was true. The silk handkerchief. The feeling of recognition when they first met.

Tem is my niece.

THE MYSTERY
Tem

Tem dragged her feet the rest of the way home, desperately tired and cold from her night in the forest. She managed not to wake her mother while opening the door or climbing the stairs. She slipped straight into bed, but despite her tiredness, she could not sleep. Her brain did not want to shut down: it was too full of information and excitement. Images swirled in her mind like dreams. The symbols on the cave wall. Her mother as a small child. Snippets of things Mother had told her. Her father's family and the mystery around them. Elithia.

She got out of bed, pushed aside the drapes at her window and gazed out on to the mulberry tree. Her mother had told her that was all she had brought with her from Elithia.

The stem of a mulberry tree, a few gold coins and you, growing inside me.

Her mother had planted that tree and watched it grow as her daughter did, never returning to Elithia. She had left everyone behind, including Tem's father and his sister, her best friend. Tem wished that she had asked this best friend's name. It could have been Celene, couldn't it?

Her mother thought that the *unicorn* was cursed by Sidra, but if it was actually a *person* from Elithia who had been cursed, then it might have been someone her mother knew. What if the unicorn was her mother's best friend? She would never have known.

Tem couldn't wait any longer; she had to know if she was right. She left her own bedroom and went to her mother's room. She was fast asleep, clutching the sheets just under her chin as she always did.

Tem knelt by her bedside. "Mother," she said softly, her hand on her upper arm.

Her mother opened her eyes, looking panicked. "Tem? What is it? What time is it?"

"Nothing's the matter. Everything is just fine." Tem spoke soothingly. "I just wanted to know: what was the name of your best friend, back in Elithia?"

Her mother looked confused, as if she couldn't quite remember. Then she spoke, her voice thick with sleep. "Celene. Her name was

Celene. I loved her very much." Then she shut her eyes and began breathing steadily again.

Tem's pulse quickened and she stood up, thoughts racing.

If Celene was her mother's best friend. . .

If the unicorn was Celene and she had been running away.

If Celene was a princess and her father was the brother of the princess. . .

Then Celene would be her aunt.

It all seemed obvious now – the pieces of the puzzle slotting together.

She was suddenly sure it was true, and it couldn't wait another month: she had to tell Celene. The moon was still out and if she ran then she could reach Bleke Forest before sunrise.

She tiptoed carefully from her mother's room. If Tem knew her mother, she would fall back to sleep and wouldn't even remember being woken up. She didn't stop to go back to her own room or dress properly, but pulled a cloak over her nightshirt and boots on to her bare feet. She clattered down the stairs, opened the door, ran out past the mulberry tree, away from the village, out into the fields and towards Bleke Forest.

SUNRISE
Celene

The caveling didn't reply and she repeated her words, but more to herself than to him:

Tem is my niece.

This was her most important breakthrough so far: it was the key to everything. And she must make sure she remembered it. She couldn't rely on the caveling, and so she had a choice: she could draw it on the wall, at the risk of forgetting what it meant; or she could tell Tem right now.

The decision was easy and she left the cave without telling the caveling where she was going. Above the trees, the sky was lightening, the promise of morning at the horizon. Tem would be back at the village by now. Celene wasn't sure, but she thought she had just enough time before dawn to get there and find her.

She didn't stop to question what she was doing. She ran through the forest, navigating the familiar twists, turns and tree roots, and grabbing on to tree trunks as she went. The unexpected sound of her running in the still morning sent birds fleeing from the trees and unseen creatures darting into the bushes. There were human footprints in the damp muddy tracks that Tem must have left a little while earlier.

At the edge of the forest she gazed out at the fields that separated Bleke Forest from the village. She hadn't ventured this way, or left the forest at all, since she arrived here all those years ago. She was used to hiding in the shadows. But she had to reach Tem and tell her this news before the sun rose.

So she continued running, the morning frost making the grass crispy under her feet. The open space felt so liberating that she wondered why she had not ventured out here before in her human form. But then the golden sun peeped over the horizon and she knew it was too late. She squeezed her eyes shut, desperate to block out the sunlight, to stop the inevitable. She couldn't risk losing this newfound memory.

"No," she cried. "Not now." Out in the fields there was not so much as a bush to hide behind: she would be exposed to anyone who happened to see her.

But it was now. As the sun peeped up over the horizon, her arms became legs. As the yellow morning light warmed the sky, she grew a glossy coat over her smooth skin. And as the birds began to sing, she knew that her human voice had left her until the next time.

She stood on the hill, wishing the curse away, wishing that she could return to her true self, knowing that she would never remember her discovery.

And then she saw a figure, running from the direction of the village, towards her. Who would be out here at such an early hour? Straight away, she saw. It was Tem, her friend, her *niece.* Why? What was she even doing here at this time in the morning? Celene's heart lifted at the sight of her. Maybe, just maybe, Tem had been coming to find her with news of her own. Perhaps she had worked out the truth at exactly the same moment as Celene. Their eyes met. Celene's heart plummeted as she realized that Tem had gazed upon her as a unicorn for the third time.

TOO LATE
Tem

Tem checked the horizon and realized that she'd been overambitious in thinking she would reach Bleke Forest. The black shapes of houses looked like cut-outs on a colourful screen. Layers of yellow and orange sunlight were building behind them. The sun would be rising in moments and she would never make it in time. Tem stood, catching her breath, frustrated that she hadn't worked out the puzzle earlier. She knew how happy Celene would be: this could be the secret of her identity. But it was too late and Tem had no choice: she would have to wait until the next full moon and their next meeting.

And then, before she turned around for home, she saw Celene, at the edge of the forest. Tem had no time to ask her why she was there, no time even to tell her what she had deduced, for shafts of sunlight were spreading across the sky. Celene was changing.

The first time this had happened, in the clearing of Bleke Forest, the light had been so bright she had missed the metamorphosis from unicorn to woman. This time, the metamorphosis was the other way around, and Tem didn't look away. She squinted into the light, fascinated to see Celene's tail, horn and mane growing; and her light, bright coat tinged with the warmth of the winter's morning light.

Tem knew she shouldn't look – according to the rhyme she had used up all her chances.

For if you meet three times: it's true –
The curse itself will fall on you.

But it was too late. She had seen, and she couldn't turn away.

"Celene, I have something to tell you," Tem cried. But she was at a distance and couldn't be sure that Celene had heard.

Then, it was if some great force from above had struck her

between the shoulder blades.

She gasped, tried and failed to shout to Celene again, and then crumpled to the ground.

CHAPTER ELEVEN

CURSED CREATURE

Celene

Celene galloped over to Tem, who lay slumped on the cold ground, head resting on her outstretched arm. Tem had been trying to tell her something, but what? Celene nudged at her shoulder with her muzzle and her body rocked a little but she didn't respond. She was alive: her warm breath appeared in the cold air like smoke. So she was sleeping. Was this what the rhyme meant? Had Tem now fallen under the sleeping curse like the Elithian people?

Her mind flew back then, to her brother's bedside. Hero. He had been taken sick and lay slumped like this. She had tried, but there had been nothing she could do for him. And now, there was nothing she could do for her niece.

Why, oh why had she risked everything to speak to Tem? She had known that she would change. She could have waited one more month. If she had remembered once, then she would have remembered again.

Her mistake was thinking that she could escape from who she was. This is why she was out here in Bleke Forest. This is why she was far away from people and should stay hidden in the shadows. Celene may have begun to imagine herself in a different life, in an old life, in a palace, but this couldn't ever be. She was a cursed creature and she would stay a cursed creature.

The lowest of creatures. A cursed creature that brings no joy, only pain and suffering. Not worthy of a person's love.

She turned to slink back into the shadows but she realized she could not leave Tem here, exposed to the cold. She might not be found until it was too late.

Yet what could she do?

She thought of attempting to drag Tem back to her cave, but that seemed like an impossible task, and who would help her there? The caveling was unlikely to be of much assistance.

The only other way was the village. It was at the bottom of the hill and she could be there in minutes. Tem had a mother who would be worried about her if she didn't return. And if Celene was correct, this was her old friend from Elithia – Samara. Just the name filled her with a feeling of warmth and comfort: a feeling of home.

Yes. She would find Samara.

Celene found some leafy branches nearby and tucked them around Tem like a blanket for warmth and comfort. She wanted to speak to Tem, to reassure her, but her human voice had left her for another month. Instead, she thought aloud to her as she did to the caveling.

I'll be back as soon as I can. I'll bring help.

Tem's eyelids fluttered lightly but there was, of course, no response.

BLEKE VILLAGE
Celene

Celene trotted down to the village, hoping that she could go unseen at this hour. Places had a personality to them, as much as people, and straight away Celene got a sense of this village. It may have been a little way away from the forest, but it shared many characteristics. The shuttered windows and tall fences told Celene that this was a place where people came to shut themselves away. People wouldn't ask questions here.

There were so many houses that her first thought was despair – how could she ever know which one belonged to Tem? They were small, simple cottages, with identical white walls and each with a patch of land. Some were better kept than others. Some had sills crumbling away and upturned pails outside. Others had neatly painted shutters and roses climbing around the door.

Then Celene saw the tree. With its proportions of short trunk and long branches she recognized it straight away as the one she had drawn on her cave wall. A mulberry tree. This must be a sign that she had found the right house.

The mulberry tree was taller than Celene but with a young, slender trunk: not like the old tree in her memory, which she could barely circle with her arms. She had climbed the branches of that one, and tasted the juiciness of the sharp fruit exploding in her mouth. There was no fruit left on this tree, and it had lost most of its summer leaves. Still, she stood beneath its branches, breathing in its familiar musty smell, grateful of some cover.

Downstairs, inside the house, the shutters were open early and she could see a figure – a woman – moving around inside. It was too dark and shadowy in the house for Celene to tell if it was Samara. Then Celene heard her call urgently: "Tem? Tem!"

So it *was* the right house. And Tem's mother had realized that her daughter was missing. Celene's heart went out to her. She wondered what to do, unsure if she should knock at the door with her horn, or make some other kind of noise. She didn't want to alarm the woman, although that seemed unavoidable.

She stayed where she was and after a few moments the door swung open, and the woman stepped outside, her slim brown feet bare on the stone pathway.

It was Samara.

Celene's heart thumped in her chest as she stared at the familiar, yet unfamiliar woman. How could she have forgotten her best friend? She was older now, with one or two streaks of grey in her long hair, which she wore swept up in a bun. Her face had lost some of the plumpness of youth, although her beauty remained evident.

A sob rose up in her chest and throat. How had she not known in one instant that Tem belonged to her? Those big eyes and the strong, dark brows, were the same.

Poor Samara, who had been such an able knight and so loved by all. How did she come to be here all alone? Had she been happy here, with her daughter and her silkworms? Had she missed Elithia? Hero? Celene?

Celene wanted to run to her, to hold her tight and to weep on her shoulder for all that they had lost, but she knew that Samara wouldn't recognize her. Perhaps she made some involuntary movement because Samara looked towards her. She gasped and brought her hands to her mouth.

Of course she did. All she saw was the Cursed Unicorn, so close to her doorstep. An unloved creature, an unlucky sign, not a dear friend from the past.

Celene stepped out tentatively from behind the tree. She wanted to show Samara that she was friendly, but she didn't know how. She lowered her head and lay on the ground in a submissive gesture.

Samara didn't move from the doorway but she lowered her hands. Her voice when it came was quiet and husky. "You! I should have known that you had something to do with it. I tried to keep her away from you and I *knew* she was lying. I should have trusted my instincts." Then she closed her eyes, as if she wanted the world to disappear.

Yes – trust your instincts, Celene wanted to say. *Listen to your heart and you will know, like Tem did, that our meeting was meant to be. There was nothing that could have kept her away. We were drawn to each other as the ocean's tide is drawn to the moon.*

But Samara was not like the caveling; she couldn't hear Celene's thoughts. She opened her eyes. "Where is she? What have you done to my daughter?"

My niece. I will lead you to her. Perhaps, if she felt it enough, then Samara would understand. She gazed steadily at Samara and then turned away.

Follow me.

Samara seemed to understand. "Wait," she said. "I will follow, but let me put something on my feet."

She disappeared into the house and then reappeared with boots, warm clothes and other useful items: a lantern, food and a blanket. She always was well prepared. But she was missing something. "I have a thick rope, which I keep by the door. I can't find it."

She was looking at Celene with narrow eyes and Celene couldn't understand why, until she realized. Samara was familiar with the rhyme.

Something will be lost.

Celene wanted to say sorry. For the missing rope, for her missing daughter, for everything. But she could not. She would just have to put it all right. She turned in the direction of Bleke Forest, and Samara followed.

LEAFY BRANCHES
Celene

Celene led Samara away from the village, out into the fields, and up the gentle slopes that headed towards Bleke Forest. The morning sun was too low and Samara's lantern provided a circle of orange light. She walked inside its glow without speaking, her eyes focused on the ground and her mouth set in a determined line. Once upon a time, Samara had owned a smile that brightened a room, but Celene hadn't seen this older Samara smile once. She spoke only once.

"What happened in Elithia? You have done so much damage. And why did you come here? I wanted to lead a quiet life after everything that went before."

Celene could not reply of course, although she wished desperately that she could. It seemed that Samara thought she was responsible for the sleeping curse in Elithia. No wonder she hadn't wanted her daughter to spend time with her. To Samara, Celene was simply the cursed creature that was to blame for her daughter's disappearance.

They reached the other side of the hedgerow where Celene had left Tem. Celene half-expected Tem to be on her feet by now, to see her strolling through the gap in the hedge, explaining to her mother what had happened. But it was not to be. As they grew nearer, there was no sign of Tem or anyone else.

They reached the gap in the hedgerow and walked through.

Celene stopped – looked.

Tem was not there.

The leafy branches that Celene had used to cover her were still on the ground in a neat pile, but Tem herself had vanished. Perhaps she'd recovered, as Celene had hoped. She looked around, but there was no one about.

Samara seemed to understand instantly. "You left my daughter here?"

Celene bowed her head in a nod, although it seemed so heartless. She wished she could explain what had happened. They both turned to look around, but it was just the two of them in the cold morning.

Samara began to call out. "Tem, Tem? Where are you? You can come out now, it's safe."

Celene tensed at the sound. She was so used to hiding away. Shouting seemed a foolish thing to do: something that might draw unwanted attention to them.

After a few moments, Celene noticed that Samara had stopped again, bringing her hands to her mouth as she had done at her own front door earlier.

Celene followed Samara's gaze across the open fields and towards the darkness of Bleke Forest. An animal was there, peeping out from between the gnarled, but familiar, tree trunks. And without having to peer too closely, she knew exactly which animal it was.

The animal emerged fully from the woods and stood in the misty morning light. It stood taller than Celene, with a silver grey coat and a bright white mane, tail and horn. This animal was like her: a unicorn. *That* was the curse that had fallen upon Tem.

TWO UNICORNS
Celene

Samara seemed to know straight away who the other unicorn was, and ran towards her. The brown leather boots, which she had put on in a rush, were not fastened, and flapped around her ankles as she ran. She reached out her arms in front of her and the unicorn stepped awkwardly into them. They lowered themselves to the ground and Tem nestled her head in the crook of Samara's arm.

Samara patted Tem's neck, ran her fingers through her mane, and whispered soothingly into her ear, although Celene was too far away to hear the words. As she grew nearer, they both looked up at her and she could see, that even now Tem was a unicorn, she had the same dark eyes as before. Samara's eyes.

Samara's were fixed on Celene. "*You* did this and now you have to help us."

Celene wished that there was some answer that she could give, but she didn't know how to break the curse. All she could do was show her the pieces of the puzzle as she had herself discovered them. Perhaps Samara would understand them better than she or Tem did.

She stood close to her, voiced the thoughts clearly in her mind and willed Samara to understand.

You must come with me, to my cave. I have drawings, letters, words. I hope that they hold the secret of how to break the curse.

To Celene's surprise, there was a reply. A small voice, sounding not through her ears, but straight to her heart.

Do you really think that will work? asked the voice. Even though Samara might not be able to understand her, Tem most certainly did.

Celene's heart leaped at the thought that she and Tem could talk to each other, just as they had done as humans. Tem stood, left Samara's lap and walked towards Celene. Celene put her nose close to Tem's. *My niece. I am sorry. I never meant to do this to you. I should have stayed away.*

Tem shook her head. *It was not your fault. It was foolish of me to come looking for you.*

But you fathomed out our connection as I did, didn't you? That's why you turned around towards the forest?

Yes. My dearest aunt. I am so glad to have found you. Tem stepped away and breathed long and hard through her nose. *Some things are unavoidable. They happen as they are meant to. And I think I am meant to be like this to help you break the curse. Could that be possible?*

I do not know, but I hope with my whole heart that you are right. I also think that your mother might be able to help us understand some more.

Tem nodded and Celene realized that Samara was watching them closely. "You are talking... You can communicate, can't you?"

They both turned to her, nodded again.

Tears were in Samara's eyes. "Help me to understand too," she said.

Celene looked back at Tem. *We can do that,* she said. *We need to show her the markings in the cave. You lead the way and your mother will follow.*

So Tem turned in the direction of Celene's cave, her long white tail swaying behind her, and Celene, then Samara, followed.

BACK IN THE CAVE
Celene

Celene put her head through the curtain of vines and then stopped for a moment.

Caveling, it's only me. I have brought another friend – two friends – with me this time.

She stepped into the cave and looked around in the shadows, but the caveling did not appear.

Tem followed her.

He is shy, this cave friend of yours, said Tem. *Can we speak freely or will he be listening?*

He may listen, but it doesn't matter – the caveling keeps to himself.

Samara stepped into the cave behind them, holding up the lantern. A warm yellow light instantly illuminated their faces and the wall. Celene remembered Tem's reaction when she first saw the cave. She'd thought it dark and damp and Celene had expected the same from Samara, but she looked quite excited.

"It's cavernous in here," Samara exclaimed. Then she stopped, and turned in a slow circle, gazing at the walls.

Even Celene was surprised at how much of the cave wall her drawings covered.

Samara blinked, stared at the markings, then walked slowly towards them.

"It's Elithia," she whispered, as she put her hand against the stone. She touched all the pictures gently, as if she could magic them into life.

The island surrounded by water.

The mulberry tree.

The full moon.

The girl with the chin length hair.

The sorcerer with his hands held aloft.

The unicorn running away.

How Celene wanted to understand what it all meant. The look on Samara's face suggested she *did* understand. As Samara studied the drawings, her eyes widened in disbelief. She traced a finger over the letters of the large, unmissable word that Celene had first scratched into the wall. Her name.

Samara turned, with tears in her eyes.

"Celene. She was the princess."

A princess? She was a *princess*. Of course. Her father was the king. Hero was a prince. Their home was the palace. How could she have forgotten these things?

"My friend. So brave and strong. We were friends for years and years and we never quarrelled, not until just before I left home. Do you know what has happened to her?"

Celene wished she could speak, could explain everything. All she could do was look Samara in the eye and hope that she would recognize some spark of the old her.

Samara parted her lips as if she were about to say something, but then stood in silence for a moment.

Tem stood by Celene and nudged her forward. *She knows, I am sure of it.*

Samara looked from one to the other, recognition dawning. "Celene," she said, again. " It is you . . . isn't it?"

Celene nodded. *Yes, it's me. Oh Samara, how I've missed you.*

Samara laid her hand gently against Celene's flank as if the answers could somehow transfer from skin to skin. She looked at Tem, who nodded, giving her support.

A tear trickled down Samara's cheek. "You were the Cursed Unicorn, all along. When I left Elithia, I wondered what became of the unicorn. I think, without knowing it, I followed you here – always a few miles behind. When I heard tales of the unicorn living in Bleke Forest, I thought it just a coincidence. But I didn't know then who you really were. All these years, we were so close and I didn't know."

But Tem found me. Your amazing daughter.

"How did you get like this? I wish you could tell me. I wish I could help."

Samara put down the lantern and moved into the shadows to stand close to Celene. She reached out her arms and Celene rested her chin in the crook of her arm as Tem had done earlier. They sat on the floor of the cave and stayed like that for a while, the three of them, until Samara spoke again. "How I've missed you, Celene. All these years, I thought you were asleep in the palace with the others. I thought I was the only one to escape."

She paused.

"I have heard people speak of Elithia. It is different now, you know. The causeway is lost under water and it is a true island."

Celene thought of Ardis, calling in the waters as she left. And so it had remained that way ever since. She couldn't imagine her home cut off from civilization in such a way.

Samara stared again at the cave wall. "And all of this ... you didn't know who you were?"

Celene shook her head.

"But you do now?"

Celene swayed her head from side to side, in an attempt to communicate the idea that she was unsure.

"You remember only some of it? Then let me tell you everything, even if I risk repeating what you know. It has been so very long. Look at this drawing here. This is the kingdom of Elithia and this palace, right here, was your home, Celene. You were the commander of the royal knights. . ."

They sat, the three of them, in the cold gloom of the cave, in the circle of light from Samara's lantern, and Samara talked. She talked for a long time, as a mother might tell a bedtime story, but instead she read the markings on the wall. Tem and Celene both lay with their limbs curled under them, listening, enjoying her words and her voice. And as Samara read the story that Celene had written, the pictures came to life in Celene's mind and she remembered the sights and sounds of Elithia. Samara's memories triggered her own, like the sun encouraging spring bulbs to poke through the cold earth.

The palace, her father, the brave knights of Elithia. How had she ever forgotten? The moondial, the mulberry trees, the Elithian silk. She remembered all of these things as if they were yesterday.

Tem didn't say a thing to Celene; she listened, enjoying the tale of her history and her origins.

Samara even made amendments and added some of her own drawings. She drew the faces and names of all of the Elithian Royal Knights. "This is all wrong. Nyaal had a much bigger nose, don't you remember?" She amended the picture with a smile. Then she drew Celene at target practice. "No one out there was half as accurate as you, Celene." She patted her on the flank.

Apart from you, thought Celene, remembering.

When she came to the sleeping prince, Samara stopped and rested her hand on the picture. "You know about Hero – Tem's father?"

Celene and Tem both nodded and Samara let out a great, juddering sigh.

"I miss him every day."

Celene remembered how he had looked, lying helplessly in bed, the swollen bite on his arm.

I miss him too. That is the painful part of regaining my memories: remembering all I have lost. Celene tried to send this message to Samara.

Samara looked back at the wall, at the sharp-roofed house with its stairs leading down, the scroll and the lost souls. "I recognize this house. And I see from the drawings that this was all Sidra's doing. She cursed you, didn't she?"

Sidra. Yes, that was the name of the dark sorcerer. Her strange house, the flickering candles, crawling things in jars, and the wide eyes of her stolen souls. Celene shuddered and nodded. Sidra.

"Is there anything we can do to break this curse?" asked Samara, a look of urgency now crossing her face. "I need my daughter back the way she was. And you, my friend, after all these years."

But although everything else was falling into place, that was still the big question: how to break the curse.

BREAKING THE CURSE
Celene

When she had talked for a long time, Samara traced her finger over the crude picture of the unicorn. "What a shame I didn't know that we fled Elithia together. We could have been together for all of these years; maybe I could have helped you."

And I could have helped you, thought Celene. Samara must have been desperately frightened, leaving the city where she had grown up, a new life starting within her.

But neither of them had known. Life had led them down quite different paths.

"Life has gone quite differently to the way we planned it, all those years ago," said Samara, as if she had read Celene's mind. "I wouldn't change it, for there is much that I love about my life." She put her arm around Tem. "But I feel for you, Celene. You have had nothing, when you wanted so much, and worked so hard. I know that one day you hoped that the throne would be yours."

The throne.

Those words were like a spark to her memory. A clear picture of the Elithian throne with its mulberry leaf carvings appeared in her mind. And Sidra pointing her wand.

The night that Celene left Elithia, Sidra had cursed Celene, but she had also told her exactly what she must do to undo it.

She turned to Tem. *I remember now. I know how to break this curse. And if I do it, then you will not have to endure years trapped in the wrong body as I have done.*

How?

I can't remember the exact words, but a shadow must be cast upon the moondial in the palace, by the light of the full moon. Something to do with the last day of the year. The next true ruler of Elithia.

Yes that was it; Celene remembered now.

Then Sidra's curse will be broken and we will both be free of it. The citizens of Elithia will awaken and we can return to our rightful home.

The last day of the year? said Tem. *And on a full moon...*

She didn't have to finish her sentence. The last day of the year must surely be in about a month's time. And it was a full moon now, which must mean that the next full moon was also about a month away.

This could not be a coincidence. Meeting Tem here in the forest, the timing being right. Surely this was meant to be and it was their time to return to Elithia.

And it was possible that she, Celene, was the next true ruler. She always had been, but she had been shut away out here, not remembering. How could she have forgotten? This was the most important thing in the world to her.

Tem tapped urgently on the hard ground with her front hooves. *Let me come with you.*

No.

Please. There is no place for me here. I cannot go home with my mother and I do not want to stay in this dark cave all alone.

Celene understood. She knew she would feel the same and she

nodded to Tem. She would love to embark upon this journey with her niece. But she couldn't whisk her away with no explanation. How she wished she could tell Samara where they were going. She brought her muzzle close to the drawing of the island and touched it with her nose.

"You are going back there – to Elithia – to break the curse?"

Samara understood. Tem came and stood by Celene and they both looked at Samara, a question in their eyes.

She sighed. "You want Tem to accompany you, don't you?"

They both nodded together.

"Then she must go." Samara turned to Celene alone and looked at her directly. "I cannot come with you for fear of invoking the curse."

The expression on her face was pained: she looked older than her years. But she nodded slowly and held Tem's face in her hands. "Go. Keep safe."

She turned to Celene. "My daughter is special. I know that every mother thinks that about her child, but Tem has an extra something about her. Promise me that you will look after her – your niece – as if she were your own."

Celene bowed her head towards Samara in gratitude. *I promise.*

FAREWELL TO THE CAVELING
Celene

Tem and Samara made their way outside the cave to say their goodbyes, while Celene stood and stared at the carvings. Nearly fifteen years' worth. Samara had taken the lantern outside with her so Celene could only half-see them, but by now she knew and remembered each one like marks on her own body.

As she traced her fingertips over the familiar lines, the caveling came scuttling over. She had known he would, now that the others had gone.

I am going. Back to Elithia with Tem, she said.

"This is no surprise. I overheard much of your conversation and had surmised as much."

Did you hear Samara say that I was a princess in Elithia? I was Princess Celene. She felt proud and a little shy telling him.

"So now you have two forgettable names?"

No, the princess part is not exactly a name, it's a title. A princess is somebody born to royalty, who lives in a fine palace or castle and rules over ordinary people.

"Ah yes, I remember. You talked of palaces before."

That's right. You were unimpressed then and you remain

unimpressed. But it matters to me. It is my life – my real life – and I must return.

The caveling said nothing.

I wanted to say farewell, and to thank you for everything you have done for me. I will miss you.

"How strange."

What is strange this time?

"You didn't miss me before we met, so why is it that you will miss me now? No doubt your life will go back to being just the way it was."

I hope not. I think that perhaps I have changed from this experience. Perhaps you have taught me new things about myself. That is why I will miss you.

"Interesting. Perhaps I will miss you too."

That's the nicest thing you've ever said to me, Caveling.

"It is of course possible that I will be a lot happier with you gone. I still have the spiders for company and I will certainly gain a few more hours sleep at night without your loud thinking. And there will be a lot more room in the cave—"

Maybe stop at the "miss you too".

"Very well. Farewell, Sad But Sometimes Happy Unicorn Woman."

Farewell, Caveling.

Celene ducked her head to leave the cave.

"Stop!"

She thought perhaps she'd left something behind but it was as empty as ever. The caveling pattered right up to her feet.

What is it? she asked.

"I would like a name. I've changed my mind about names. What is your favourite one?"

Various names flitted through Celene's mind, most of them belonging to people she knew. Samara, Tem... But her very favourite name was the one that she had forgotten for a long, long time.

How about . . . Hero?

"Hero. Hear-o. Yes, I like it very well. Does it have a meaning?"

Celene thought for a moment.

Yes, it does. A hero is someone who is brave and strong inside. One can rely upon someone called Hero.

"Interesting. Those characteristics apply to me. I choose Hero as my name."

Well, in that case, farewell, Hero.

"Farewell, Celene. Oh, and Celene?"

Yes?

"I am glad to have a name, even though it is unlikely that anyone will ever call me by it. However, I know that what really matters is who you are inside. Do not forget that."

Celene nodded. She glanced once more at the markings on the walls, wondering if she would ever see them again, if she would ever return to this cave, or even to Bleke Forest.

But some things were impossible to know. Sometimes you had to wait and see what life would deliver.

CHAPTER TWELVE

BACK TO ELITHIA
Celene

They began the journey back to Elithia. Samara told them which way they should go.

"You are travelling east in a straight line to the coast, so travel towards the sunrise and away from the sunset."

They followed her advice, taking the back way, through fields, rather than the main road. Celene recognized some of the landmarks. The house where she had seen a child's face at the window, the farm where the farmer had gazed at her in awe. The last time she had travelled that way was nearly fifteen years ago and she had been lonely, disorientated and afraid. Back then, her memories had slipped rapidly away from her, but this time, they were returning, and her feelings were different. She was excited, tense and not at all lonely. This time she was glad to have Tem at her side. She felt bad that her curse had fallen on Tem, but she couldn't help rejoicing that, after all these years of being alone, there was another like her.

Now that they were two, they could talk to each other and ensure that they wouldn't forget what they had learned.

It was a long journey. In the last fifteen years, Celene had barely ventured out of the woods. Cocooned in her grey, damp world, she had forgotten how beautiful the world was. She had forgotten how autumn leaves changed to the colour of a warm fire, how white blooms flowered on the wild ivy, and how birds flew in formation against the vivid backdrop of the sky.

They might be on an impossible quest. Perhaps she had misremembered Sidra's words (for everything back then felt like a dream). But right now, as they galloped along dust tracks and through long grass, Celene felt that they could do anything. She knew that they would break the curse together.

HERO

I hear the clatter of hooves; I have not heard anything for such a long time. You are drawing nearer. I know I will meet you soon.

BEAUTIFUL WORLD
Celene

The journey together was special. Although they had both always felt a deep connection, now that they knew they were related, they could understand it more. The way they spoke, without any sound, was easy, and Celene was happy to answer any of Tem's questions.

How to you feel about going back to Elithia, Aunt Celene?

Aunt Celene. Her heart warmed at those words. She had been a sister, a daughter, a friend, but never an aunt before. She liked it.

I am a little scared that it will have changed from the place I used to know. But I am determined to break the curse, and once I set my mind to something, I don't fail.

Tem trotted beside her. *I know what you mean. It's the first time in my life that I've spent a night away from home, so I'm a little nervous, but I'm also excited about all manner of things. I can't wait to see Elithia. This place is part of my history, part of who I am, and I know so little about it. Why do you think my mother did not tell me that my father was a great prince? I didn't even know his name. For years, I thought he was dead.*

She was probably trying to protect you. There was nothing you could have done about it, after all. Sometimes, when you are powerless, it is best not to know what you are missing. Like before, when I was in the forest. I was almost happy before I started to remember.

They trotted on for a while in silence.

I am still sorry, Tem.

What for?

That you are like this – like me – and that we need to make this journey. It may be dangerous.

There is no need to be sorry. I thought that my mother was my only living relative but now I find that I have you – and I am glad.

Celene was glad, too.

ALONE AT THE WINDOW
Samara

Samara stood alone at the window of the cottage, looking at the winter skeleton of her beloved mulberry tree. When she had found this place, the very first thing she did was to plant the tree. She remembered thrusting the branch into the earth, patting the soil all around so that it stood firm, watering it and willing it to grow. Her piece of Elithia. For fourteen years she had watched it grow alongside her daughter, both of them living memories of what she had left behind. Part of her heart had remained with Hero in Elithia. And now, her daughter and her best friend were heading back there, with the hope of saving the kingdom from its curse.

In the distance, she heard the sweet sound of a fiddle and people singing a wintertide song. Friends and family would be gathering together to celebrate over the next week or so, eating and merrymaking with the ones they loved.

And so, she asked herself, what was she doing standing here alone at the window?

Upstairs, in an old dusty trunk, lay the outfit that she'd worn when she fled Elithia. Her leather training armour, cracked with age but still serviceable. She shed her outer garments and put the musty-smelling armour on over the top of her cotton tunic. With some loosening of the ties, it fitted, although it felt strange, like putting on a past life. She took a few paces around the room, remembering how it felt to be a knight, to train and fight. Her weapons were long gone, but Tem's hunting gear lay downstairs. She would arm herself and borrow a horse. Then she would be ready for anything.

QUESTIONS
Celene

The journey to Elithia took longer than expected. After a couple of weeks of travelling, the winds began to howl and the rain blew in their faces. The weather got so bad that the unicorns were forced to take shelter. They stayed in a deserted barn for days, huddled together for warmth. When they ventured out again, Celene guessed that they had only about a week left before the end of the year.

They didn't pass many houses, but those they did had green wreaths hanging on the doors and candles burning in the windows.

What was wintertide like in Elithia, Aunt Celene?

Celene closed her eyes and pictured the great hall strung with cedar and eucalyptus and the fires blazing. *It was warm. And beautiful*, she said. *We all had so much, but we didn't know it.*

Maybe the thought of wintertide was making Tem homesick. Or maybe it was because they were drawing closer to their destination, but Tem seemed to be overflowing with questions.

You were a princess. You must have lived in luxury.

Celene nodded. *Yes, but I don't suppose I appreciated it. It was normality for me.*

You must have had cooks and maids and cleaning staff ... everything you ever wanted.

Celene nodded. A picture came into her mind of a kindly maid with a sweet nature who helped her get dressed every morning. Hester. How could she have ever forgotten Hester? It was like that: every so often, a trigger would bring a new memory back to her, which returned crisp and whole as if it had never disappeared.

And what was it like to have a brother?

Tem had grown up without siblings. A very different childhood to her own. Celene wanted to answer honestly. *It was fun ... and frustrating. He meant the world to me, but sometimes he irritated me tremendously. He always knew just what would anger me. I miss him.*

Tem listened and Celene wondered how much of that she could possibly understand.

So you always had someone around. It must have been hard for you out there in the forest for so many years without company, said Tem.

Yes. Thank goodness I had the caveling. Without him, I would have been decidedly lonely.

Tem said nothing for a few hoofbeats and then said delicately, *Ah yes, the caveling. You mentioned him, but although I visited your cave twice, I never saw him.*

Celene knew what her niece was hinting at. Tem thought that, in her solitude, she had invented an imaginary companion. She wanted to say no, that the caveling was as real as you or I, but somehow she wasn't quite sure. Now that they were out on the open road and she was leaving her nocturnal ways behind her, Bleke Forest felt like a distant dream. She simply said, *The caveling was shy.*

Tem didn't question it and they both kept galloping in the direction of Elithia.

CHANGE APPROACHING
Ardis

Ardis had been alone for many years, but not lonely. He knew that this period of time, like any other, would come to an end, and it was his job to wait and watch for change. In the meantime, he had the sea, the drifting clouds and the birds for company.

This morning, Ardis felt different, deep within his bones. The full moon was on its way. He looked to the sky. Change was coming.

He hadn't been counting the months, but he realized the end of the year was approaching with the moon. This was a rare event, which happened only once every nineteen years, so it was Celene's first opportunity to break the curse. He knew she wouldn't disappoint.

Princess Celene was strong and clever. She was coming home. And he would be there to meet her.

SOMETHING IN THE AIR
Sidra

There was something in the air: she could feel it, even from the darkness of her cellar.

Sidra summoned the souls. They surrounded her, like a cloud of smoke, each desperate to be chosen: to escape from their prison for a time. Sidra made her selection. She whispered to them, "Help me see what this full moon is bringing to Elithia."

They flew out of the window, from her house, across the sea, along the coastal road.

It didn't take long until they were back, with information. And Sidra was very interested indeed.

"So, the princess is returning. I wonder how that can be. Celene should not remember a thing, yet somehow, she has discovered her true identity and is coming home. I suspect my brother, with his strange link to nature, is behind this. But, wait. Two unicorns running side by side? Fascinating. The curse has spread."

In the silence of her cellar, she laughed aloud.

"Oh, my cursed unicorn, you must see that you are no threat to me. This is simply a challenge, a little fun to make my life more interesting. I'm excited that you've come back and I look forward to seeing you again."

A STRONG SALT BREEZE
Celene

Days passed, and Celene knew that they were nearing the final day of the year, and the full moon. They had to be at Elithia by that evening. They travelled at trotting pace, off and on, for most of the morning, until they reached the coast. They were high up, on a deserted cliff top, scrubby with brown gorse.

We are drawing close. I feel it, said Celene. She felt a sudden familiar chill at her neck and shuddered, watching a wisp of blue smoke fly past her. She looked to see if Tem had noticed, but her head was turned towards the sea. She had grown up so far inland that she had never once seen the sea and she couldn't take her eyes off it. After fifteen years away, Celene knew how she felt. The pale noon winter sky, almost white with rolling cloud, contrasted with the agate blue of the water. A strong salt breeze ruffled their manes. Celene tasted home.

Celene also kept her gaze on the water below, expecting to see an island emerging from the water. So far, all they had seen was foam swirling around the rough, uneven rocks. Just as she was beginning to imagine that the sea had swallowed the island, the ground dipped, they took a sharp right turn, and there was Elithia. Her towers stood proud and tall, just as Celene had carved them on the wall of her cave.

Elithia! Tem saw the island at the same moment. Her thoughts were full of excitement and disbelief, but Celene found she couldn't reply. She could only gaze upon the island of her childhood home, slowly letting herself believe it as tears welled in her eyes. She felt an urgency to be there, to see her family – even if they all lay asleep and uncommunicative.

Despite their tired legs, the unicorns sped up to a canter, sending pebbles flying with their hooves as they followed the coastline around and down. They arrived at the point on the shore opposite Elithia where the main road led straight into the water. A wooden jetty jutted into the water, next to a smallish hut. Celene didn't remember these being there before, and she tried to imagine who might live in the house – a ferryman, perhaps. Right now, its door was locked and its windows shuttered, giving the impression that nobody was home.

They stood and stared across at the island, their breath still coming hard and fast after the long run. They had finally made it.

Celene was home.

But how things had changed.

Elithia was surrounded by water. The connection to the mainland had been severed and you wouldn't even know a causeway was there. Samara had already told her this but it was still shocking to see her homeland changed in such a way. Unless Celene's memory was misleading her, the water level was much higher and the island looked smaller. It was if it was being slowly swallowed up by sea. If this curse was not broken, then maybe the sea would get higher and higher until Elithia was lost altogether.

What's wrong? asked Tem, who always had a good sense of how Celene was feeling.

The water is so deep.

She realized then that she'd thought they would be able to gallop through the water; she hadn't prepared for it to be like this. *Perhaps it will be better at low tide.*

Tem peered out to sea. *Perhaps.*

Celene knew that Tem was trying to understand, but she couldn't really help in this situation, knowing little of the sea and tides. Time would tell. They would wait and see; at least it would give them time to rest and to plan their next move.

Tem stood right at the water's edge, letting the waves crash and break into foam around her hooves. She pricked up her ears. *It sounds so . . . big.*

The sea?

Tem nodded.

Yes, I thought that as a child.

Celene joined her, the icy water on her dusty legs rejuvenating as she stepped and splashed. For a moment she considered how conspicuous they must look – two unicorns paddling – but no one was likely to see them here at the edge of the earth. They hadn't encountered a soul all morning; it seemed that Elithia had been abandoned to her fate.

Tem was still gazing out across the waves. *How far is the island?*

A couple of miles. It might as well have been up on the moon, as they had no way of getting there. For the first time, Celene spotted a boat floating on the water beside the jetty. It was well kept and there were no pools within to indicate a leak.

It looks seaworthy, but it would never carry two unicorns.

Tem joined her. *We could wait until we transform tonight.*

So Tem had assumed that, like Celene, she would also turn back to her human form in the full moon. Celene had thought the same, but was still surprised that Tem was so sure.

If we did that, would we leave enough time to reach the moondial?

It was a conundrum, but surely not an impossible one. They had not come this far to be defeated by a stretch of seawater.

THE FIGURE ON THE ISLAND
Celene

As they continued to stare across at the island, Celene noticed something that she hadn't before. Off to the west there appeared to be a tiny, separate island, with a single strange and spindly building built upon it. Sidra's house. It had always been right at the water's edge, but the higher water level meant it was now cut off from the main island.

Tem was looking in the same direction. *I can see someone.*

Celene too thought she saw a flash of someone dressed in black, darting towards the house. If someone was on this island, then it meant that not everyone had succumbed to the curse. The only person who would surely be immune was Sidra, who had cast it. Celene's heart raced. She tried to focus in on the figure, but it disappeared and did not return.

Sidra, she said.

Do you think she saw us too? asked Tem.

I don't know. They gazed at one another, not sure of their next move.

Shall we go back up to the cliff tops and wait under the cover of those trees? Celene still felt exposed when she was out in the open for too long, and the possible sighting of Sidra after all these years had made her nervous.

We could knock on the door of the hut. Just to see, suggested Tem.

They both looked at the shoreside hut, assessing the possibility of anyone responding to a knock. As if in response, the door shook. Someone was turning the handle inside.

Celene tensed and stepped back a couple of paces as the door creaked open, the image of Sidra still in her mind. But it was a familiar face that emerged, more creased and more weathered than ever, but at once reassuring and wise. He looked delighted, and not at all surprised, to see two unicorns standing by his front door.

"Welcome home, Princess Celene," said Ardis.

SAGE TEA AND SLICED CARROT
Celene

Celene could not stop looking at Ardis. His hair was sparser than before and was now all white. He was also thinner and tireder-looking, but his voice was the same. Calming, reassuring. How had she ever forgotten him? They could not speak to him, of course, but Ardis had always been the type to understand.

This is Ardis, explained Celene. *A friend.*

I know, said Tem. *The evil sorcerer's brother.* Maybe her niece was also the type to understand without lengthy explanations.

Ardis stood for a few moments, smiling. Then he spoke again. "I would invite you inside but I'm afraid there is nowhere for us to sit."

Celene saw where he pointed through the door that there was very little room inside: a crumpled bed and not much else. She wondered if this was his permanent residence or if he just slept here now and again.

"Luckily there is no rain this evening. Let us have some refreshments out in the open air."

He brought cushions and blankets out from the hut and bade them sit down, near the water's edge. The waves lapped and the pale afternoon sunlight reflected off the water, and Celene felt the urgency of their mission ease a little. If Ardis was talking about refreshments, then time couldn't be as tight as she had imagined. It was a relief to have him here, taking charge. She had been making all her own decisions for so many years, and for once, she could sit and rest as instructed. He poured them each a bowl of fresh water from a flagon. Then he sliced a carrot into chunks on a tin plate. Celene nibbled a piece. After years of moss and lichen, it tasted sweet and decadent. He boiled up a pot of sage tea for himself, which filled the cool air with a herbal aroma.

When they were comfortable and relaxed, he smiled. "I am glad you have finally made it home. I hoped that you would. At every full moon I thought of you. I spoke to the moon and asked her that she might give you back your memories."

"And now here you are, with a friend." He turned to Tem. "Samara's child?" Tem nodded and looked inquisitively at Celene. *How did he know?* she asked.

He always knows, she replied.

"When you left, I sought help from the moon and she raised the water up. The sea has remained this way, to protect Elithia and the people within. I made my home here, acted as guard, prevented people crossing and offered an explanation to any who sought it. *Elithia is sleeping.* That is what I said, countless times. And people stayed away, for there was nothing for them here: no trade, no entertainment, and no circuses. Elithia became nothing more than a tale to them. A forgotten island."

Celene stared at the rowing boat, tethered to a mooring behind the hut. She wondered if Ardis had been back to the city; if he had seen her father, Hero, any of them. Ardis followed her gaze.

"You have seen my boat. I return to the island daily. The crossing takes a couple of hours as long as the current is with me. Most people do not need me. They are caught in a moment of time, suspended as though they are statues. They do not require food or drink and they do not age."

Ardis took a sip of his hot tea, slurping to cool it.

"The main reason for my visits is to attend to the prince."

Celene and Tem both pricked their ears forwards at this.

"Ah yes, Prince Hero lives."

My father.

Celene could sense Tem's joy at this confirmation that her father was still alive. Celene had never doubted it.

"His affliction, of course, is different to the others. He is the same as ever, although he ages like we do. His needs are small, but I like to check on him, to talk to him. I feel that he hears me, wherever he is."

Celene's heart was heavy in her chest at the thought of her poor, sleeping brother, and she tried to concentrate on the rest of what Ardis was telling them. It sounded as though Ardis hadn't ventured far from this spot for fifteen years. All alone in a shed. She saw a fishing rod leaning up outside. He must have found his own food. Celene had thought her own life, in Bleke Forest, had been lonely, yet he had experienced the same isolation. He had chosen this lifestyle, when he could have gone anywhere, done anything, offered his services to another royal family, lived a life of luxury.

He had displayed such loyalty to this lost kingdom.

She wanted to thank him, but could not, and tears sprang up in her eyes.

Are you all right, Aunt Celene?

She nodded and blinked the tears away. Now wasn't the time for sentiment.

I will be. All we can do for now is to concentrate on the task at hand, which is to get to Elithia.

Tem nodded and stamped her hoof. *As quickly as possible!*

Now that she had heard he lived, Tem was more desperate than ever to set eyes on her father.

Celene understood her frustration. *I'm sure that Ardis will have a plan to help us reach the island.*

Again, as though he had heard their words, Ardis spoke.

"You are here to break the curse." He offered the words as a statement, not a question. "This is good. The time is right."

He stood and began to recite the words that Sidra had spoken all those years before, that Celene had relayed to him.

"When the moon is full on New Year's Eve,
Elithia's rightful heir
Must stand before the great moondial,
And cast a shadow there.

"Only then, the curse will lift
And sleepers wake once more.
Otherwise the curse remains
In place forever more. . ."

Celene shuddered at his words: the first time that she had heard them since that terrible night.

"Your timing is right," he said. "Today is the last day of the year and tonight will be a full moon. Sundown is early during these winter months, but we still have a couple of hours to reach the palace before night truly falls. The only problem is that I am not sure if the weather is on our side. A clear night would have been perfect, but this evening you will have the clouds to contend with."

He stared at the clouds for some time, as if he could read them.

"We need a clear and bright moon to cast a crisp shadow. If I predict correctly, then those drifting clouds will not let through much moonlight tonight."

He thought for a little longer and then looked long and hard at them both. "I may be able to help with the moonlight, of course, but the other factor that you should address is who should stand before the moondial. I wonder if you have discussed this. You should carefully consider the phrase *next true ruler.* Ask yourselves honestly who that is."

My father, surely? Tem asked Celene. *He was next in line to the throne was he not?*

Celene nodded. There was much more to it than that, of course, but there was no need to have this conversation now. There would be plenty of time to talk later if – or when – they made it to the moondial.

Ardis walked to the water's edge and they both rose and followed him there, waiting to see what he would do. He gazed at the city he had been protecting for so long and he seemed to address her directly.

"Elithia, you have been asleep for many years, but it is time. You must awaken to a new dawn."

As if in response, the sea seemed to come to life: the waves building and tumbling towards Ardis upon the shore. Both aunt and niece looked across the choppy waters but Tem was distracted by something to the west of the island, as she had been before. *Look – I see her again. The sorcerer we saw earlier. What is she doing?*

Tem was right. Sidra was back, and this time she was rowing in a small boat towards the island. She had seen them. She was waiting for them.

Ardis followed their gaze.

"Ah yes, I see that Sidra has noticed you. Well, let her notice. We are coming her way, and nothing she can do will stop us. Remember that: we are strong and we are working together."

They both nodded to indicate that they were ready, although for what, Celene wasn't quite sure.

CHAPTER THIRTEEN

PARTING OF THE WATERS
Celene

The sun was dropping from its high point in the sky and dark waves continued to lap at the shoreline as if they wanted to be close to the sorcerer. Ardis raised his staff as he had done when he had brought the waters across the causeway all those years ago. Was he casting another spell now?

Although he spoke to the sky, the spell seemed to be affecting the water. The waves rose in great peaks, crashing and foaming as though in the midst of a storm. But the waves weren't coming in to meet them in the usual way of the tides. The waves were travelling the *wrong way*, swishing from right to left in front of them, perpendicular to the shore.

For a moment, Celene thought Ardis was bringing the water level up even higher. Tem obviously thought the same thing.

What is he doing? Trying to drown his sister?

I hope not, replied Celene. If he were to do that, then Sidra would only retreat further into the island and Ardis would have to flood the whole of Elithia. But as Celene watched, she realized that Ardis was not raising the water level at all: he was dividing it. Half the waters rushed east, half the waters rushed west, and a path opened up. This was not the natural parting of the waters that came at low tide when the causeway was revealed. This time, it was as if some giant was slicing their way through the water and pulling the two sides apart with his hands. The causeway, which had not touched the air in fifteen years, gradually reappeared from under the water, a wall of water at either side.

Ardis lowered his hands, looking tired now, and nodded to them. It was done. The path was clear enough for them to cross. The two unicorns looked at each other. They didn't have to wait for the full moon or a big enough boat. The way to Elithia was clear and they could be on the island in minutes.

Celene walked slowly to the start of the causeway, front hooves edging towards its flat stones, which were still dark and wet. The waves were at head height and rushing, rumbling on either side. Tem stood beside her, looking for reassurance. There was no reason to delay, so Celene nodded. *Let's go.*

"You know what you have to do – there is no need to wait for me," said Ardis.

They set off side-by-side, tentatively at first, and then broke into a full gallop. Ardis made his way behind on foot.

The unicorns did not talk as they galloped along the causeway, as the sea was so noisy. Because the path was arrow-straight, it was difficult to tell how far they were progressing. It was no longer possible to see Elithia: the tunnel was too narrow and the opening at the end too far away. Celene concentrated only on her senses: the pebbles beneath their hooves; the smell of the sea, murky and green; Tem's breathing beside her.

Then, as they were about halfway across, Celene clearly saw a figure at the end of the causeway.

Is that her? asked Tem. *Is it Sidra?*

From this distance, her features were unclear, but Celene knew from the way that she stood with her wand held aloft, that it was.

Yes. Celene turned her head to check with Ardis whether they should continue, but they had left him too far behind. And Celene knew the answer without asking: of course they had to keep on going.

KEEP GOING
Celene

Celene began to feel uneasy. Why was Sidra standing there, waiting for them? She didn't appear to have a weapon, a horse or anything of use – just her wand – yet it was difficult to believe she wasn't plotting something.

And as they galloped nearer to the island, Celene thought she could see the expression on her face: Sidra was smiling.

She looked at her niece, who returned her gaze, worry creased around her eyes.

What is she up to? she wondered.

Sidra lifted her wand, hands above her head. She was saying something, chanting perhaps, although they were too far away to be able to hear the words. But whatever she was doing, she was having an effect on the water, just as Ardis had. She brought the waves up higher and higher until they arched inwards, rather than away, and crashed on to the causeway from both sides.

Celene tensed, looking into the tumbling waves. She half expected some sharp-toothed sea monster to emerge from the depths, but there was nothing, just a rough sea.

Their one route to Elithia was filling with water.

Celene slowed, and then stopped. Tem followed her lead.

Do you think we can gallop through before it gets any higher? she asked.

I don't know. Maybe she means to drown us, said Celene. She spoke lightly but she was worried: what was stopping Sidra from bringing the waves crashing down on top of them?

Can we swim? asked Tem.

I don't know, said Celene. She knew that her human self could swim – they all could on Elithia, where they were surrounded by water – but in all her time as a unicorn, she had never tried. *Perhaps we are about to find out.*

As if in response, the water began rushing in, getting higher and higher, and then pouring towards them.

They both reared up at the same time and turned and galloped back to Ardis.

He was still some distance away, supporting himself with his staff as he hobbled towards them. He clutched his side as he grew out of breath; he was not of an age for running any more.

He shouted and gestured towards them: great circling hand signals.

They couldn't hear what he was saying but they understood.

"Turn around. Keep going!"

They looked back in the direction of Elithia. At first Sidra was just about visible, her arms raised, but she soon disappeared from view and it was just water ahead of them.

How can we keep going? asked Tem. *There is nowhere to go!*

But Ardis pointed his staff in the direction of the water – in the direction of his sister. He said something else that looked and sounded like, "Trust me!"

He would never let harm come to us, said Celene. So they didn't retreat. They stayed, facing the high wall of seawater. Celene momentarily closed her eyes, and when she opened them, the water had changed. It was no longer rushing towards them, but had stopped. And where Ardis pointed his staff, a circular whirlpool appeared, rushing around and around and then disappearing in on itself.

It was burrowing, drilling into the seawater, creating a tunnel for them.

I think Ardis means us to go through there. Celene turned to check with him but he stared at the tunnel, concentrating hard.

When she looked back again, Tem was sitting back on her hind legs, her muscles tense, preparing to jump. She made eye contact with Celene and then sprang up, thrusting her head forward and raising her forelegs up in one smooth move.

Tem, her brave and beautiful niece who had never even seen the sea before, had put all her faith in Ardis and jumped right into the tunnel through the waves.

And Celene had no choice but to follow.

TUNNEL THROUGH THE WAVES
Celene

They galloped through the tunnel. Celene couldn't feel anything beneath her hooves – they weren't running but they weren't swimming either. Something magical powered them through.

It was dark and the water rushed and whooshed in their ears. No: it roared. The water was roaring, like a wild animal, about to swallow them whole. It felt unnatural to go forwards, as though heading right into its jaws.

Celene followed Tem closely, focusing on her powerful back legs and her white tail swishing from side to side. She could see nothing else: not even the light at the end, where Sidra waited to meet them.

She looked behind to check on Ardis but the swirling mouth to the tunnel had closed and it was a wall of water. Ardis was on the other side and they were on their own. They had to trust that his magic would hold and that the great weight of seawater wouldn't collapse on top of them as Sidra intended.

Then, as the claustrophobia was threatening to become too much, Tem seemed to stumble in front of her, her head and mane falling out of view. But she wasn't falling; she was jumping out of the tunnel. They had made it to the shore.

The sudden change of light was blinding. Although the sky was darkening, the yellow ball of a sun was still bright as it dipped below the clouds, reflecting on the rippled surface of the sea. Celene blinked as her eyes adjusted, standing close by Tem, feeling her warmth. *We made it,* she said. Tem nodded as she looked around, taking in their surroundings. They stood on a walled gangway. The first thing Celene noticed was how they were completely dry, and then how quiet the island was now that they had left the roar of the water behind them. There was no flower petal welcome, no shouting from the city, and no fishing boats at the port. Just the occasional sea bird screeching overhead.

And Sidra. She stood in the centre of the gangway, facing them. Sidra's face was in the shade but her smug smirk was visible, and it was clear she hadn't aged a day since their last meeting. Celene couldn't help wondering why she was smiling when they had ruined her plan. It made Celene think that she had something else in store for them.

"Welcome to my island. It is good to see you again!"

Celene felt anger rise up in her. *Her island? Elithia is not her island.*

Sidra threw back her head and laughed, and Celene was instantly transported back to her house, on the night of the curse. She could see the place now: strange and spiky, on its little island to the west.

With the memory came all the feelings: the panic, the pain, the fear.

Are you all right? asked Tem.

Celene nodded. She had known she would see Sidra; she had to keep control and try not to let her manipulate them.

"So, you have come. Someone must have helped you regain your memory. I suspect that my brother was the one who gave you that chance." She looked Tem up and down, still smiling.

"I see you have not managed to heed my words and you have

passed on your curse to another poor innocent soul. Was it too lonely for you, Princess? Did you find it difficult without your maids and your silver dishes? Perhaps your need to find a friend outweighed your concern for their well-being."

Celene felt a stab of guilt but she tried to ignore it.

Tem was at her side. *Don't listen to her.*

Sidra was trying her best to provoke – that was what she did – but Celene would not let her. Yes, Celene had passed on the curse to Tem, but she would also undo it: that was why they were here. Sidra continued. "Self-preservation always takes priority for you, doesn't it, Princess? You could have saved your poor brother, but you were too frightened to make the sacrifice."

Celene couldn't stop the guilt. If she had signed away her soul to Sidra, perhaps Hero would have recovered. The rest of the kingdom would have avoided the curse. Tem would have grown up in luxury rather than in a simple cottage by the woods.

"It is funny to think how these events spread, like ripples on a pond when a stone is thrown in. A spider bites your brother, you fail to help him, and before you know it, an entire kingdom has fallen!"

Please ignore her, Aunt Celene. Let's get on with what we have come here to do.

Sidra stopped for a moment and stared hard at Tem. "*Aunt Celene? That is most interesting!* Your friend here is not just any friend but another precious royal baby!"

Celene turned to Tem, who looked panicked. *She understands us!*

"Of course I understand you! The lovely Princess Celene almost signed her soul away to me. She only signed one letter, but that was enough for me to have power over a little piece of her soul. Enough for me to understand. And now her curse belongs to you too, her niece, so I can read you in the same way."

Celene's heart sank. It could have worked to their advantage that Tem's identity was a secret, and that they could speak secretly to each other, but now both of those advantages had gone.

We don't care if you understand us, said Tem. *That doesn't mean that you can defeat us.*

Sidra laughed again. "She has a fighting spirit. What a relief! She might have grown up lazy, like her father, happy to let others do the work while she enjoyed the benefits."

Tem tensed, ready for the fight. *Don't talk about my father that way.* She looked to her aunt for back-up, but Celene was unable to concentrate on what either of them was saying. Her mind jumped back to something that Sidra had said, a minute before.

A spider bites your brother, you fail to help him, and before you know it, an entire kingdom has fallen...

How do you know? she asked in her mind.

Know what? replied Tem.

Sidra. How does Sidra know it was a spider that caused Hero's sleeping sickness? No one knew what had bitten him. Not Ardis, not the sea people or the countless healers who'd visited his chamber.

Sidra looked delighted at the chance to share this information. "Oh, Princess! Did you really think that the little spider found your brother by chance? The only part I left to chance was whether it found your brother or the king first."

Celene thought back to Sidra's house, to the trapped creatures in jars on her shelves. However had she not realized before? *You planted it on Hero?*

"Of course! It may be complicated to break into a royal bedchamber, but it's easy to slip unnoticed on to the royal ship. The soporific spider is fond of dark places like royal boots and jacket sleeves, but dislikes being disturbed. Its bite proves that. The spider dies once it has bitten but leaves enough poison to make a person sleep for eternity."

Is she saying that she caused my father's sleep? asked Tem.

Yes. Of course. It was Sidra all along. Celene should not

have been surprised. Sidra had always been behind any trouble in Elithia; Celene just hadn't realized quite how far she would go.

A new surge of anger rose within her. To think she had ever blamed herself. Sidra had surely known that Celene would visit her, desperate to help her brother. She had probably planned the whole thing.

Sidra seemed to be behaving strangely now, turning around and looking towards the palace.

Tem watched her intently. *Aunt Celene, forget all of this for now. She is trying to distract us from what we have come here to do. She is up to something.*

It was true. Celene turned to Tem. *Stay still for now, and then whatever she tries to do, we will wait until the last minute and run past her.*

"Run past me! Do you think I would allow that? My Royal Knights will soon arrive to protect me." Sidra raised her wand and shouted, "Come now, it is time to fight!"

CHAPTER FOURTEEN

PUPPETS

Celene

Tem looked at Celene with wide eyes. *Royal Knights? What can she mean? I thought that you and my mother were Royal Knights – that they fought for Elithia.*

But Sidra stood laughing, her wand held high. "Your Royal Knights now fight for me. Look!"

Behind her, two figures marched towards them; it seemed that not everyone in Elithia was asleep. Knights, in full battle gear. Both unicorns tensed but then Celene saw the purple and green colours of their shields and the intertwined letters, ERK. *Elithian Royal Knights.*

Do you know them? Tem asked.

It's hard to tell. If these were true Elithian Royal Knights, then Celene should know them; she had been their commander, after all. At a distance, and with their helmets pulled low, it was hard to identify them but there was something about the way they walked. They were marching together exactly in time, their steps mirroring each other. When one knight put their left foot forward, the other stepped forward with their right.

Celene's heart thumped. She only knew one pair who walked in this way. *Rohan and Jade.*

You do know them? Tem's eyes were bright.

Yes, they are two of my knights – and friends. Friends who were still alive. And awake! Could it be that Ardis had been wrong and the curse had not swept across Elithia? Or had someone broken the curse before them?

The two knights' visors were raised and she could see their faces in detail. It was definitely the twins, but the strange thing was, they didn't look a day older than she remembered. Celene reared up on her back legs and both unicorns rushed forwards to greet them.

But Jade and Rohan did not change their stride or slow down. They both drew their swords and continued to march with purpose. Something was wrong. *What are they doing?* Celene didn't understand; she had known them all her life and now they were acting as though they wanted to kill her.

Tem began backing away first. *They don't recognize you, Celene!*

Of course they didn't. To the knights, Celene and Tem would look like two strange unicorns, which had appeared uninvited on their island. Still, Elithian Royal Knights would never attack visitors, especially unarmed visitors. Maybe they had heard of the Cursed Unicorn and thought, as Samara had, that the unicorn was responsible for the sleeping curse. That could explain their aggression. She wished more than anything that she could communicate: to shout out a greeting, explain who she was – anything. If there were some way that she could show that she meant no harm.

But Tem was looking unsure. She took a few steps back, nostrils flared. *There is something not right,* she said. *They are not behaving ... normally.*

Celene immediately saw that Tem spoke the truth. Jade and Rohan were not the Jade and Rohan she knew. Their faces were blank, like the puppets she played with as a child. There was no expression and no voice; they moved forward automatically.

It's as if someone's controlling them with strings, said Celene.

Tem turned to look behind her. *I know who the puppet-master might be.*

Sidra, of course.

Sidra was gleefully muttering to the two knights as she coaxed them forwards with her hands, moving closer and closer to them.

"Yes, it's me! The poor souls that I hold in my house are so desperate that any body will do. And now they have found bodies, they will do whatever I bid them."

What does she mean? asked Tem.

Celene stared at the knights. *Jade and Rohan are still asleep, under the effect of the curse. Sidra has sent her souls to possess them and now she is controlling their movements. They will do whatever she commands.*

Celene and Tem took a few steps back.

We must fight them!

We can't! Jade and Rohan are two of my oldest friends!

Sidra is counting on exactly that. They will kill us, even if they don't know what they're doing. We must defend ourselves.

NAMELESS KNIGHTS
Celene

Tem was right. The knights were drawing closer and they had swords.

In her human form, she would know what to do. She felt sure that even after all these years, she would not have forgotten how to fight. She thought about that time with Tem in Bleke Forest, when she fired the bow. Tem, too, was a hunter.

But as unicorns, they had no weapons: they were helpless to defend themselves. They had the choice of retreating into the sea or pressing on towards the knights.

As the panic built inside her, Tem lowered her head, horn sticking out, ready to charge. Celene stood with her. Tem was right; it was the only way. Celene tried to think of them as nameless knights.

Jade and Rohan continued advancing, but Celene and Tem charged, horns lowered. The knights stepped out of the way, but immediately swung around to counter attack. This time, the unicorns leaped out of the way. It was more like a dance than a fight, with the knights moving stiffly and predictably.

Despite this, they weren't going to let Tem and Celene past. It could go on forever unless someone brought it to an end.

They have no intelligence: they are following Sidra's orders, said Tem.

Celene knew what she meant. But to trick the knights, she would have to trick Sidra too, and Sidra could hear everything they said to each other. They would have to use physical clues. Celene made eye contact with Tem and then tilted her head to the right. Tem did the same and tilted her own head to the left. She had understood: this time they would run in opposite directions to confuse the knights.

The dance continued. The knights walked towards them, still mirror marching. But this time, Celene galloped one way and Tem the other, kicking up great clouds of dust as they each turned in a circle.

This seemed to have the desired effect of confusing the knights. Sidra couldn't issue commands to both at once. They stopped for a moment, unsure which way to turn, and then set off again, Jade aiming for Tem and Rohan for Celene.

But Tem and Celene both ran wide, so that the knights were forced to follow, running behind. Then, as the unicorns were about to meet, they turned in the middle, before cantering off again.

This puzzled the knights, as Celene had hoped. They clashed

swords noisily, but they were so synchronised that each always guessed the other's move: it was a fight that neither would win.

"No, no, you fools!" cried Sidra, rushing over. "Fight the unicorns, not each other!"

But the two knights were finished. They stopped as if their strings had been cut, crumpled at the knees and collapsed on the ground, helmets askew and swords pointing inward.

Celene winced at the sight of her old friends defeated in this way, even though she knew that it was not really them. She stared for a moment before realizing that she and Tem had won. This was their chance. She began galloping again, in the direction of the palace, turning to check that Tem was with her.

But as Sidra's laugh rang out behind them, she realized it was not going be as easy as she thought.

"You thought that all you had to do was to defeat two knights? You thought that when I talked about an army, that was my effort? Oh no, princesses, I can do better than that."

They both looked around. Which army was she talking about?

There is nobody here, said Celene.

But to their surprise, Sidra turned away from them and waved her wand towards her house in the west.

"Now I summon every soul
Whose name is scrawled upon a scroll;
A sleeping form will make you whole
Find one now and take control!"

"Come, souls!" she shouted "I need you *all* now! Come and do my bidding! Sweep into the palace, the houses, and the market. Find sleeping bodies and make them yours. Come and fight upon the shore."

The unicorns stopped for a moment, confused.

Across the water, the door of Sidra's house swung open. They were too far away to see what was inside, but Celene stared, squinting to see.

Tem stood so close that Celene could feel her breath. *What is she doing?*

Celene kept her eyes on the door. Something grey and wispy, like smoke, emerged from the shadows and grew into an enormous cloud.

Can you see that? she asked Tem, not sure if it was real, or in her imagination.

Tem nodded, tensing beside her. *What is it – a spell of some sort?*

No, said Celene. She knew what it was, or she thought she did. She remembered what she had experienced in the cellar of Sidra's house, fifteen years before. *It's the stolen souls. And this time it is more than two.*

It was a cloud of souls.

Sidra guided the misty greyness, coaxed it over the water towards her, then she turned in the direction of the palace and shot out her wand arm as if throwing a ball. The souls rushed towards Celene and Tem, who began to gallop again, up from the coast and along the path. The cloud rushed up behind them, pushed between them and flew ahead, along the main road towards the palace. Both unicorns shuddered and a feeling of dread rushed through Celene from nose to tail.

This time, they knew exactly what Sidra was going to do with her army: she had sent her souls to look for bodies to inhabit.

They watched the cloud of souls as it dispersed into numerous smoky trails, each disappearing in a different direction.

Tem turned to Celene. *What is she doing? Where is she sending them?*

Sidra laughed her grating laugh. "You will soon find out, Princesses. My poor lost souls are looking for new homes!" She continued to look up the path as if she were waiting for the souls to return, muttering under her breath.

Celene and Tem took the opportunity to have a private conversation while she was distracted.

I wish I knew what she was doing. Celene looked between Sidra and the path, waiting to see what would happen.

She also looked behind her. Somehow, while they had been fighting Jade and Rohan, the water had sunk back down, revealing the causeway, the water calm and still at either side. Ardis must have used his magic to undo his original spell, but where was he now?

As Celene grew more agitated, Tem seemed to be calming herself, focusing.

Sidra's display with the souls could all be for show – she could be trying to scare us off from the palace. We have to do what we came here to do. Let's go, anyway – let her try to stop us.

Celene looked skywards. The sun had not yet dipped below the horizon, but the moon was up and the clouds were drifting ever closer, threatening their chance to break this curse. Ardis had said that they might only have minutes of opportunity between the sun going down and the clouds obscuring the moon.

She nodded. *To the palace, then.*

But people were beginning to appear on the walkway.

More knights! said Tem.

Celene steeled herself to meet more of her old friends possessed by Sidra's stolen souls. She quickly realized that these people were different.

They're not all knights.

There were one or two knights: some from the training school, and a couple in full armour, with their weapons at the ready. But as well as that there were ordinary people: maids, grooms. Some wielded weapons of sorts: pans and scythes, but others were empty-handed. Celene recognized faces from her childhood, faces from the marketplace, faces from the past. She thought she saw one of the girls from the docks, who'd come to welcome Hero. They came in pairs down the walkway from the palace and then stepped to the side so that they formed a long human wall.

It's not so bad – we can break through that line. If we aim for a weak spot and run as fast as we can...

But Tem trailed off, and Celene could see why. Another line – a new wall of people – was forming behind the first. And another behind that.

SIDRA'S ARMY
Celene

Individually, these blundering people would not be the most fearsome foes, as Rohan and Jade had demonstrated, but as a group they would be impossible to get past.

If only I had my bow, said Tem.

Celene knew how Tem felt. But even if they were in their human form and able to fight, she knew she would not be able to bring herself to harm Elithian people.

Let's go around the back way, said Celene. Sidra was surely far enough away that she wouldn't catch this thought. *Sidra will think that we're retreating along the causeway, and then at the last minute, we'll change direction along the shore road and around.*

Tem nodded, and they turned back to where Sidra stood looking up the hill, muttering directions to the people.

Sidra shouted up to Celene and Tem, "Maybe you can avoid my soldiers, but for how long? I have countless souls in my home and all the people of Elithia at my disposal, whereas you are just two unicorns: do you think you can fight off this army forever?"

Celene tried not to listen. Sidra was trying to exhaust them not only physically but also mentally, with these mind games.

But they could also play mind games.

Let's go, quickly, back along the causeway! said Tem.

But Sidra was not that easy to trick. She stared at them, eyes narrowed and then shouted up to her army, "Block them! Stop them accessing the shore road!"

Tem was concentrating hard, watching the people stream towards her.

We need to divide ourselves as we did with Jade and Rohan, she said. *They can't follow us both at once, so you go to the palace and I'll stay here. If it all gets too much, then I'll flee back along the causeway.*

This time Tem was not trying to trick Sidra; this time she meant it. Celene looked at Tem, her strong, noble niece. Celene could run to the courtyard, break the curse, and be back to fight again by her side. And yet Tem was still only a child. Celene had to ask herself if that would be fair.

She remembered Samara's request to her before they left. *Promise me that you will look after her – your niece – as if she were your own.*

She had made that promise, and it was a promise she couldn't break. If something happened to Tem while she was under Celene's charge, she would never forgive herself or be able look Samara in the eye again.

Yet time was running out. If they didn't reach the moondial tonight, it would be nearly twenty years until another opportunity came her way. Some of the most important years of Tem's life would be lost to the curse.

What can we do? Celene asked, more of herself than Tem.

But Sidra shrieked back an answer: "Leave your niece with me, Celene. She'll be safe here!"

For the first time since they had gazed upon the island, Celene considered turning back.

Tem was looking at her with large, round eyes. She had offered her solution and it wasn't one that Celene was prepared to accept. Yet she had no solution of her own. She wished for someone to come along and help. Ardis, her father, a friend.

And then, somewhere in the mist, she heard hoofbeats. She turned. Was it her imagination? But no, someone was coming on horseback along the causeway. She squinted to see who it was, but all she saw was an arrow, which flew straight and true right past her left ear.

CHAPTER FIFTEEN

HERO

I am closer to the surface than I have ever been before. I see the sunshine (or is it moonlight?) dappled above. Three faces gaze down at me. Two, I recognize. They are blurred and distorted, but I do not need details; I would know them anywhere. The third – yours – is equally familiar and yet I have never set eyes on it before. All I have to do is to reach out. To break the surface with my hand, pull myself up and breathe again. But I do nothing. It is such a wonderful sight that for now, I just lie here, enjoying the calm.

THE ARROW
Celene

Sidra's scream was more piercing even than her laugh. The arrow stuck out of her right shoulder and she was doubled over in agony. She held its shaft with both hands, so it was difficult to see what damage had been done, but Celene didn't have to imagine the pain. She knew how much it had hurt when Tem's arrow had grazed her lower leg.

Celene snapped her head around to see where the arrow had come from. Had the arrow been meant for her? For Tem? Or was this someone on their side?

It was another knight, this time dressed in training armour. This knight wore no helmet and her long black hair fell in disarray around her shoulders. Somehow, it was Samara.

"You!" cried Sidra, still writhing in pain. "Another royal knight – an imitation princess! I might have known that you would come to the aid of your daughter."

Samara looked just as Celene remembered: a brave, highly skilled knight, gazing down at them from her horse, still holding the bow in her hand. Tem's hunting bow.

Tem stood and stared. *Mother?*

Careful, said Celene. Although her heart had lifted at seeing her friend, she knew this could be another one of Sidra's tricks. Hadn't she been just as delighted to see Rohan and Jade approach?

But Samara's face was soft and warm, and tears ran down her cheeks. She was no puppet.

What are you doing? When did you get here? Celene and Tem had so many questions they wanted to ask, but Samara could not hear them. Lengthy explanations would have to wait. For now, Samara smiled at her daughter reassuringly, and said simply, "I couldn't be away from you, so I am here to help. Leave me! You must go and do what you have to do to break this evil curse."

Sidra had broken off the shaft of the arrow and was muttering an incantation over the wound. Celene nodded to Tem.

Come on, let's go now. We'll see your mother again soon.

Tem couldn't seem to take her eyes off her mother, who was looking different – magnificent – in her armour. *I don't know if I can leave her...*

Samara didn't need to understand the words to sense her daughter's hesitancy.

"I insist. You must go now. I have a full quiver of arrows here, and Ardis is following behind. He has told me everything. I can hold this army here. Go! Both of you!"

Samara backed her horse along the causeway as they came at her in droves. Every so often she sent an arrow towards them to prevent them getting too close. A gap – an opportunity – opened up for Celene and Tem. They took it, rearing back and setting off as quickly as they could towards the palace and the moondial.

TO THE PALACE
Tem

Tem was still reluctant to leave, but her mother was right, this was an ideal moment. With Sidra injured, the rows of possessed people had no one to direct them as they stumbled along. They barely seemed to notice when the unicorns changed direction.

Straight to the palace – follow me, said Celene. Tem was close behind, head level with her aunt's hips as they galloped off up the hill.

The moon hung expectantly over the palace, and the sun touched the horizon, leaving hints of orange layers in the sky. Adrenaline coursed through Tem's body. She had felt ready to drop to the ground and give up, but now her energy was returning.

The sun is nearly down, cried Celene. *It is time!*

Should we find my father first? asked Tem. She had been

desperate to see him since Ardis had confirmed he lived. And surely this was the moment.

But Celene didn't seem to agree. *There is no time for that now. We will visit him, of course. First we must break the curse, free ourselves and all those poor people possessed by Sidra's souls.*

Tem was confused. *But do we not need my father to break the curse? The curse will only be broken when the next true ruler of Elithia casts their shadow on the moondial. Surely the next true ruler is my father?*

Celene didn't turn around or break her stride.

Do you remember what Ardis said outside the hut? He advised us to ask ourselves honestly who the best and true ruler would be. I cannot believe that it is your father. I have never been able to picture him on the throne. I think that the next true ruler is me. I brought the curse upon Elithia and I must fix it.

Tem's eyes were wide. This was all new to her and she couldn't believe that her aunt hadn't shared these thoughts before. *What if you're wrong? This is our one chance.*

Celene sighed. *I promise you that this is not about me or what I want. But I am sure that Hero never wanted to be king. Even as a child, he didn't want to be a knight or a ruler of anything or anyone. Trust me.*

Celene was right. There was a great deal that Tem couldn't

understand about the father she'd never met. She would just have to trust her aunt, who had never let her down before.

Celene continued explaining. *Besides, Hero is in a deep sleep and cannot move: we have no way of bringing him to the moondial. Unless we want to wait another nineteen years, for the full moon to fall upon the last day of the year, then this is our only choice.*

Tem nodded. This was also true. *I do trust you, Aunt Celene. It's just I did want so much to meet my father.*

I know. And we will. I want to see him again. We don't have long to wait now.

Tem hoped her aunt was right. If not, Tem might find this decision difficult to forgive.

They galloped onwards, stopping briefly at the brow of the hill, the palace before them. Tem had seen it from a distance, but up close it was even more magnificent, and just as Tem had imagined. They gazed back towards the shore. It was difficult to tell from that distance, but Tem couldn't see Sidra or, more worryingly, her mother. The army had turned around to face them and were marching up the hill.

Sidra must have taken control again, said Celene.

Tem nodded. *I hope my mother and Ardis are not in trouble.*

Your mother is stronger than you think. Remember that she

*was a great knight when we were younger. We'd better go. Sidra's
army will be much slower than us on foot, but we still don't want
to waste any time.*

They set off again, galloping towards the palace with purpose,
but Tem found it difficult to put her mother out of her mind.

She couldn't help but think of the second line of the unicorn
rhyme:

Meet twice and pain will come your way,
Be sure to run and stay away.

Down by the shore was the second time that her mother had
looked upon her as a unicorn. When Tem had met her aunt in
unicorn form for the second time, she'd cut her thumb. She hoped that
whatever pain she brought her mother wouldn't be worse than that.

FACING SIDRA
Samara

Samara stayed where she was, out on the causeway, watching
Celene and Tem gallop towards the palace. She hoped they could

break the curse. They had to do it, for her, for Hero, for the whole family. Meanwhile, she would keep Sidra and her army at bay. With Ardis – when he managed to get there.

Sidra wasn't out of action for long. She returned to an upright position, her shoulder healed and purple hair glossy in the twilight. She glowered at Samara: her pale face and gritted jaw giving away her rage. Then she shouted at her army of people.

"Turn around! Follow the unicorns! Quickly! They are heading for the moondial. Prevent them!"

They turned and began marching away from Samara, on to the island and back up the hill. Samara knew they had no chance of reaching Tem and Celene unless there was some delay.

She was more concerned about Sidra, who was walking towards her with a stony expression.

Then a voice came from behind her: "Samara! Well done! Thank heavens you came to help."

It was Ardis. He had finally arrived and stood beside her horse, leaning on his staff and breathing heavily. Sidra looked at her brother and laughed.

"Such an old man now! Do you really think you'll be any match for me?"

"The question is, whether you are any match for all of us, Sidra.

Together, we are strong. Princess Celene and Princess Artemis are no doubt at the moondial by now and your curse will soon be undone."

"That is what you think," she said, and turned to Samara, her expression soft.

"You have changed little, Samara. All those years away have not dampened your skill at all: you are still such a strong knight."

Samara raised a suspicious eyebrow.

"Oh, I have changed, Sidra. I had to. I had to start my life all over again. You might have been trying to hurt Celene and her family, but you have hurt so many others. You have taken fifteen years of my life from me. You took my best friend and my true love when I needed them. Now I see you trying to harm my daughter."

"But you are a sensible person, Samara. Perhaps we can do a deal. When Celene came to see me all those years ago, she was desperate to save her brother's life. And he still lives, Samara. In that tower over there, he sleeps as he has always done. It would be easy to wake him, if only you knew the secret."

Samara turned away, blinking back tears. The thought of having Hero back was overwhelming, but she knew she could not trust Sidra.

"You have never done a thing for anyone else. Your actions

serve you, and you alone. If I were to let you cure Hero, then there would no doubt be something in it for you."

"Of course, but I am sure we would find a solution that benefits us all. I want what I have always wanted, which is to be the royal sorcerer here, with the power and respect that the role brings. I wouldn't need to rule the kingdom. That would be your role. Stop Celene from reaching the moondial and you can be queen, Samara. You and Hero would reign over Elithia, and your lovely daughter would have everything she wanted. The only person standing in the way of that is your so-called friend Celene. She never did a thing for you."

Samara told herself this was not true. Celene did care for her, always had. She also cared for Tem. Whereas all Sidra ever brought was trouble. She would twist and turn anything to make it fit her purpose.

"No," she said, simply. "No. I will never make a deal with you."

Sidra nodded slowly, looking from Samara to Ardis and back again. "Thank you for making that clear. It is most sad, because now you will have to die, followed by my brother, your best friend and your daughter. The next queen to sit on this throne will be Queen Sidra!"

Samara's hands were instantly on her bow and she sent another arrow flying towards Sidra. She would make sure that she couldn't wreck any more lives.

But Sidra cackled as she reached out and caught it in mid-air. She snapped it without taking her eyes off Samara and Ardis. "You think that arrows will defeat me? Your last one may have taken me by surprise, but they will not surprise me again."

Sidra walked towards them, pointing her wand first to one side of the causeway and then to the other. "You must realize that my powers are greater than yours," she said. Giant waves reared up and crashed back towards them.

Samara held her ground, but the horse was scared by the combination of Sidra and the waves. He reared back on his hind legs and although Samara was a natural on a horse, she couldn't calm him. Ardis made a grab for the reins, but the horse was out of control, and bucked violently. He reared up again and twisted, throwing Samara off his back from a considerable height. She had been thrown countless times but this time she had no helmet and fell awkwardly to the side, hitting her head hard on the ground. She lay as still as if she had fallen under Elithia's sleeping curse.

THE LOST STAFF
Ardis

The horse bolted, running along the causeway, past Sidra and on to the island. The sun was down and the only light was from the Cold Moon. Ardis ran to Samara's side, cupped her cheek in his hand.

"Can you hear me?"

She was still breathing, eyelids flickering, but unresponsive to his words. Ardis looked up to the moon, whose power was at its strongest tonight, and whispered, "Do not take her. It is not Samara's time. Give her strength to fight this."

Then he looked back at his sister, who was raising her wand above her head, muttering her incantations. If she brought up the water level, then Samara, in her unconscious state, would be swept away. Yet he couldn't fight back with a spell of his own without abandoning her.

He saw the intent in Sidra's pale eyes – he knew that look well – and he chose to stay with Samara, leaning over her so that his cloak protected them both.

Sidra sent a wave crashing down next to them. The water soaked Ardis from head to foot, but he managed to shield Samara from the worst of it and they kept their place on the causeway.

He stood and turned to use his magic, but Sidra laughed.

"You seem to have lost something!" She pointed out to sea and he saw that his staff was gone, swept away by the waves. He saw its familiar shape floating far away and knew that he was beaten, for without his staff there was little he could do.

"It's time you realized whose magic is greatest," gloated Sidra. "You never should have tried to fight me."

Ardis didn't reply. He felt nothing but tiredness. He had lived a full life and had done his part for Elithia. He had helped Princess Celene and Princess Artemis get this far and maybe that was where his role ended. Maybe it was his time to give up, although he still found it difficult to accept that it was Samara's.

"I'm sorry, Samara," he said, to her prone body, and he turned to face Sidra's next attack, ready to accept his fate.

Sidra waved her wand furiously, chanting and muttering. He knew that the next wave was going to be a monster.

Once again, he sent a silent message up to the moon.

Take me, but spare Samara. Give her strength to defeat this.

The wave roared and rushed, building into a great wall.

He closed his eyes and waited for the impact.

It didn't come.

He didn't feel the force of the ocean or any more water landing upon him.

He opened his eyes.

Samara had somehow woken. She was on her feet, hair flying out behind her and a determined look on her face. She held one hand up to her head, where it had hit the ground, and the other arm straight out with her palm flat, as if she were pushing against the water.

And it worked. The towering wave began to fall, cascading down with all the force that Sidra had intended. But in a different direction: towards Sidra herself.

The moon was powerful indeed.

A FAIR FIGHT

Samara

As the wave thundered down upon Sidra, the sky lit up in a bright white flash and Sidra screamed: a horrified, angry sound.

The force of the water swept her legs from underneath her and she was carried out into the dark sea.

Samara held her breath as she disappeared from sight, but then she rose up again, hair spreading around her like exotic seaweed.

"Ardis! Help me, brother!"

But Ardis couldn't help. His staff was far away at sea. No one could help Sidra. The moon and the sea had their own plan, and they could be unforgiving.

She dipped below the water and then reappeared, this time stretching up her wand arm, trying to gain control. But another wave came, and another, until they obliterated her voice, and her face, everything, from view.

Sidra was washed away.

They continued watching, waiting for her to emerge but she did not rise back up above the water.

The sea calmed until there was barely a ripple on its surface. It was like dark glass, reflecting the night sky and the giant moon.

Ardis stood for a long time, gazing out to the spot where Sidra had been. He didn't smile or blink and it was difficult to interpret his expression.

Samara walked up and stood beside him. "How are you feeling?" Sidra had been his sister, after all.

Ardis put an arm around Samara's shoulder. "I feel nothing," he said a little sadly, and they turned and walked along the causeway together.

CHAPTER SIXTEEN

THE MOONDIAL
Celene

Celene and Tem finally reached the palace and galloped single file along the tiled walkway. The ornamental pools on either side were murky and the topiary balls were untidy after years of neglect, but the scent of the bay was fresh and familiar. Even in its unloved state, the palace was undoubtedly grand. Tem's eyes grew wide. *Where is the moondial?* she asked.

In the central courtyard on the ground floor, in a straight line through the palace. Do not stop for anyone.

There were no guards at the entrance, sleeping or otherwise.

Jade and Rohan must have been guarding the doors on the night of the curse, which is why they had walked down the hill in full ceremonial battle gear. The doors were wide open and someone had hacked through the thick bindweed, presumably Ardis on his visits.

The unicorns ran up the steps, through the great doorway and down the tiled corridor, not worrying about their muddy hooves.

The palace was emptier than usual. Sidra's souls had possessed the first people they found. Celene and Tem passed just one sleeping person: a maid, who must have been dusting some paintings when the curse struck her. She lay on the floor as though she had been overcome with tiredness, one arm bent like a pillow under her cheek, the other still clutching a feather duster. For a moment, Celene thought it was Hester, and nearly stopped to check, but she had to remind herself to keep going. There would be time for reunions later, when all this was over.

Celene and Tem burst through the swinging doors to the courtyard. Celene thought back to the last time she had stood here: when she led the last Knights' meeting. The place had changed and nature had moved in. Ivy trailed out of planters and over balconies, bird mess covered the walls and spiderwebs decorated the dried-up fountain. Trees had shot up towards the sky and their roots had caused floor tiles to warp and crack.

The sky was almost dark. A mere glimmer of the sun's brightness remained. In the evening's silver light, the place looked like a jungle. The only part that was untouched was the moondial, standing proud in front of them. The perfect full moon hovered above them, although the clouds were drifting dangerously close.

They had made it. They danced in a little circle around each other, nose to tail, and then stood, gazing at the sky.

What do we do now? asked Tem.

It was their last chance. The last moon of the year. The last moment for the magic to happen. Celene felt light-headed with panic. *We must act before the moonlight disappears. The next true ruler of Elithia must cast their shadow on the moondial.*

She had been so sure, but now she was not, and she saw her doubt reflected in Tem's face.

Are you sure the next true ruler should not be my father? We don't have time to get this wrong.

Tem's words hit Celene hard. This was their one chance in twenty years to break the curse. They couldn't fail.

She thought of Ardis's words. *Search inside yourself, Princess, and you'll find the answers. Ask yourself again, who is the true ruler of Elithia?* Again, she tried to picture her brother on the throne and could not. She was as sure as she had ever been that Hero would

322

never be king. Whether he survived or not, he was not a leader.

But suddenly, she was as sure of something else. She could not picture herself on the throne, either. Her father had tried to tell her many years ago but she hadn't listened. Her brother would not make a good ruler, but then neither would she. *Rigid and controlling,* her father had said. She would not want to negotiate and would rub people up the wrong way. She did not know how to compromise. Perhaps she had changed after her years in the forest, but actually, she wasn't sure she wanted to give up that part of her personality. Perhaps it was the idea of the throne she should give up. She was no longer sure she wanted to be queen.

Aunt Celene? We have to do something!

Tem was right. Once again, she wished that Ardis were by her side to help, but he was back with Samara, fighting a whole army. He would not be able to help her now.

She looked in the direction she always did when she wanted answers: towards the sky – the moon.

Despite the clouds hovering nearby, the moon was shining brighter than Celene had ever known. The moon was on her side. The moon would give her answers, as it had always done. She gazed towards it, squinting. She wanted to get nearer as she did in the forest. If she had been in her human form then she would have climbed a tree, or stood on the balcony: anything to be near its glow.

Rays of moonlight emanated from the bright white fullness. One long and gleaming ray pointed towards Elithia, to the palace, into this very courtyard.

The ray fell upon Tem.

Her grey coat was white in the moonlight, her white mane was whiter still, but her horn glowed like the moon itself.

The moon had given her answer in no uncertain terms. She had pointed to the true ruler of Elithia.

Tem.

Her brother's daughter. The king's granddaughter.

Celene thought of how Tem risked her own safety to come back to Bleke Forest and help her; how she accompanied her to Elithia without question. There was no doubt that Tem was brave and kind. But she also thought of Samara's parting words before they left the forest: Tem was special. Tem may have grown up in a tiny cottage with just her mother for company, but perhaps she was the one who was destined for the throne.

She remembered the way that Tem had tended to her wounded leg; her hunting skill; the way that she had leaped without question into the tunnel of water. Tem had inherited her father's charm and unflappable nature; and her mother's kindness and technical skill. There was no question: Tem would make the perfect ruler.

Celene considered what this would mean for her. If she were right, then she would never realize her dream of becoming Queen of Elithia. And, standing in the courtyard with her wonderful, recently discovered niece, she realized that it didn't matter to her any more. The caveling's words came back to her: "Your name is not really what matters. It matters who you are inside. Do not forget that."

At that moment, Celene felt the sun disappear from the sky and the night begin. She knew from her time in the forest what that meant. The moon was taking over now and they would feel her power. The clouds began moving again, touching the moon's outer edges, waiting for permission to cut across. Celene hoped that the moon would stay on her side.

She turned to Tem.

It's you!

What?

The next true ruler – it's you, Tem! The moon is moving. Do something!

Me? It can't be me!

But Celene had never been more sure of anything. She looked at the direction of the moonlight. *Stand up here on the table. Cast your shadow on the moondial and break the curse.*

The doors to the courtyard banged open and Sidra's possessed people burst in, wielding their axes, pitchforks and skillets.

Tem looked from Sidra's people to the table and back again. If she didn't move quickly then they would miss their chance. Celene galloped over and butted her into position. Tem looked shocked but she took her prompt and climbed ungracefully up on to the stone bench and then on to the heavy stone table.

Celene edged as far as she could from the advancing crowd and watched Tem, hoping above hope that she had made the right decision.

Tem stood motionless, a sharp black silhouette of the perfect unicorn. The moon behind her was bright white and perfectly round, as if it were there for the sole purpose of framing Tem in this moment. There was a moment of silence. Celene knew then that she had guessed correctly and that Tem was in the right place at exactly the right time.

The moon was on their side. She seemed to glow brighter than ever before, casting a shadow down on to the moondial. The curve of Tem's back, her still legs and tail, the crisp outline of her muzzle and crest were cast on to the stone, covering the shadow cast by the gnomon. Her straight, magical horn, looked longer than ever in shadow form, and its pointed tip fell on the moondial, pointing up.

The sky flashed like sheet lightning and Celene thought she heard a scream.

Sidra's people stopped abruptly and slumped to the floor as Jade and Rohan had done earlier. Asleep.

Tem began to change, then. She reared back on her hind legs and stayed there. Her horn shrank, her mane lengthened and she became her true self again, the girl that Celene had met in Bleke woods.

Celene changed too, from her unicorn self to her human self. She managed to keep her eye on the moondial, though, on Tem's shadow, which didn't look quite the same as the girl standing on the table. The shadow that was cast upon the moondial was undoubtedly Tem, in the same position as she was standing now, but the figure in the shadow had a crown upon her head. Celene recognized the crown: the delicate beaded structure and the refracted light around it. It was the crown that she had gazed at and coveted since childhood: the glass crown of Elithia.

And it was Tem who wore the crown. Celene's hunch had been correct, and the next true ruler of Elithia would be Queen Artemis.

Sidra had said that Celene would hate anyone else who inherited the throne, but Sidra had been wrong. Celene looked at her niece, standing there, looking younger and more vulnerable than ever, and she knew she had made the right decision. The right person would become queen, and it wasn't her.

Then the moon was so bright that Celene could no longer see anything. She crouched down on her haunches, with her arms folded over her eyes.

When it was over, she straightened herself and stood. Tem was facing her, still standing on the table, blinking, and looking confused. She looked all around her, at the courtyard bathed in gentle moonlight. "What happened?" she whispered.

"You broke the curse," said Celene.

AFTERWARDS
Celene

She helped her niece down from the table and they embraced.

"One day, you will be queen," said Celene, into her hair.

Around them, people were waking, rubbing their eyes, wondering what they were doing in the palace courtyard, reflecting on their strange dreams.

But Celene and Tem only had eyes for the last two people to

run in: Ardis and Samara. They rushed to greet them and Samara held her daughter tightly.

Ardis put his hands on Celene's shoulders and smiled. "Well done," he said. "You made some good decisions. I won't ask what you saw on the moondial, but so that you know, it was a vision of a future reality. What fell upon the moondial tonight will be reality the next time that a full moon falls on the last day of the year, in nineteen years' time."

Celene nodded. So Tem would be queen, but not just yet.

"And Sidra?" asked Celene.

"Gone," said Ardis.

"Lost at sea," said Samara.

That was all that Celene needed to know. She thought back to the knights' meeting long ago, when Alard compared Sidra to a cockroach. Cockroaches were notoriously difficult to kill: you might think them drowned but they could be holding their breath. Maybe Sidra was just as indestructible, but she was gone for now and, with luck, they would not see her for a long time.

Her thoughts were interrupted by a new confused and sleepy person wandering into the courtyard. King Ellis himself.

"Tem! Come and meet your grandfather!" cried Celene.

CHAPTER SEVENTEEN

BACK AT HERO'S BEDSIDE
Celene

Celene and Tem sat by Hero's bedside.

Celene had been startled when she first saw him – his hair and beard were unruly – but when she looked more closely she saw that his face was still her brother's. He was the same, but older. Like Samara, and, she supposed, like herself.

She knew by the surprise in others' eyes that she was an older woman than she had been before. Fifteen years ahead of them, which was strange. "You're catching me up now," said Thorran.

It also seemed strange that although they had broken the curse, and restored most things to just the way they were, Hero was still asleep. Everything in his room was the same as the last time Celene had visited. The cerulean silk coverlet, the gilded chairs, even Dev the nurse, who was alarmed to wake from a nap and find his patient fifteen years older.

But there was something new: hope.

Now that they knew his sleep had been brought on by a spider bite, they just had to find *which* spider.

The knights combed Sidra's house from top to bottom and gave the creatures from the jars their freedom, but they didn't find any spiders. They went back to the east to find every variety they could. One day, they would cure him.

But it seemed sad that Tem's first meeting with her father should be like this.

Tem studied his face, looking perhaps for similarities to her own. She wouldn't have to look for long. His nose and the curl of his hair were the same as Tem's. And their smiles were identical. If only he would smile.

Tem turned to Celene. "What was he like, when he was my age?"

Celene smiled. "He was funny. Charming. Lazy! Loveable. Everyone loved him. Not just when he was your age, though. He was like that aged six and aged twenty."

"Maybe he will be like that again," whispered Tem.

"I hope so," said Celene. She paused. "I was jealous of him sometimes ... often. The last words that I spoke to him before he fell ill were not kind. I felt that I'd somehow brought all this about."

Tem laughed a little, kindly. "But that doesn't make any sense at all! All siblings argue, don't they? Why would you blame yourself?"

Tem was right. Surely after all these years of running, hiding, and searching for the truth, she could forgive herself for a few angry words.

She nodded and Tem continued, "with luck, they will find an antidote soon."

An antidote.

Something stirred within Celene, as it used to under the moon in Bleke Forest when a memory returned.

A soporific spider. That is what Sidra said had bitten Hero.

And she had heard of that somewhere else.

A soporific spider. Fragments of memories replayed in her brain searching to fit together, as they used to on the wall of her cave.

Trust yourself to know the answer.

The caveling. That's where she'd heard of it: he had talked

about soporific spiders in the cave. His voice came back to her. *Soporific spider that sleeps all day. If I smell that spider once, I can sleep for a week.*

What if Hero hadn't been bitten by a spider from the east after all?

Sidra had said that her lovely helpers were *collected from the darkest forests and the coldest mountains.* The sea people hadn't recognized Hero's bite because it hadn't been a local species! The spider was from Bleke Forest. She was sure of it. Celene could picture Sidra there, hood pulled high, at home amongst the cursed creatures.

Tem stared at her curiously.

"You've gone quiet – what is it?" she asked.

Celene was surprised that Tem had noticed. Perhaps their connection as unicorns had left them with the ability to communicate via their thoughts.

"I think, after all these years, I may have finally discovered what bit my brother."

And Celene told Tem everything.

She sat, patiently listening, nodding every so often, then she looked at Celene with bright eyes.

"If the spider *is* from Bleke Forest, we don't have to send out a royal search party – my mother will have the antidote in her medicine cabinet!"

HERO

Your voice. The touch of your hand. The smell of your hair. I thought it had been such a long time but maybe I am mistaken. Maybe I last saw you yesterday and this has all been a peculiar dream.

I am ready now. I want to wake up.

FATHER
Tem

Tem had seen her mother in every possible mood: loving and patient, tired and frustrated, even as a brave knight on horseback. But she had never seen her quite like this.

When Samara walked into Hero's chamber, her face seemed ten, twenty years younger. She was shaking slightly, through nerves, or excitement.

Celene had opted to stay away. She would be out in the corridor in case of any news. Now Tem wondered if she should have waited with her aunt. It felt like a moment from many years ago: a moment that didn't include Tem. She hung back, near the door, watching her mother greet her father after so many years apart. At first, Samara sat by his bedside, gazing at him. Hero's hands rested, one on top of the other, on the blanket. Samara placed her hands on top of his, and whispered something – Tem couldn't hear what.

Then Samara opened her bag with trembling hands and removed a small bottle. She unstoppered it, filled a dropper, and applied some drops under Hero's tongue. She stoppered the bottle, put it back in her bag and waited.

Tem waited too.

She leaned against the doorframe and closed her eyes. Could an antidote work, all these years later?

The seconds and minutes ticked by.

If her father never woke, then she would not be missing anything. All of those years, her mother had been enough for her. She had an aunt now. And a grandfather, who was king! She could have a horse, a beautiful bedchamber of her own. So many people had nothing. Was it fair of her to wish for a father on top of all this?

Still, she kept her eyes squeezed shut and hoped.

She was never sure what made her open them again. Perhaps it was the change in Hero's breathing, or a gasp from Samara, but when Tem opened her eyes her father was sitting up, running his hand through his hair as if waking from a puzzling dream.

Her mother was motionless, apart from the tears running down her cheeks.

Tem walked slowly towards them as her mother spoke.

"Hero, it's me – Samara."

He nodded. "My love." He put a hand to the side of her face.

"There is someone you should meet. Your ... our ... daughter, Tem."

He looked up towards her, confused at first, and then he smiled, and it was like looking into a mirror.

BROTHER
Celene

Celene waited. Let Hero have his moment with his new family (not that they were really new – Tem was nearly fifteen). It seemed that this was the longest wait she had ever had to endure, despite being away from her home for so long. In her mind, she was back in Bleke

Forest, peeping out of her cave and waiting, hoping, for the sun to disappear and that first glimmer of moonlight.

She knew he would not be angry, not really, yet she felt the dry mouth and palpitations of nervous anticipation.

Then it was her turn. She barely looked at Samara and Tem as they exchanged places: she took the place by her brother's bedside and they waited in the corridor.

"Hello, brother," she said, and took his hands.

He'd had a shave since she'd visited with Tem, and he looked even more like the brother she remembered.

He smiled, and his smile was unchanged. "Sister!" he said. "It's been a long time, I understand."

"Too long," she said. "I am so, so sorry for everything."

He smiled again. "There is no need for you to apologise. Samara has explained. It was Sidra's hand that caused all of this."

"I know, but if I hadn't been to see her, then maybe the curse could have been avoided—"

"—And if you hadn't all ended up in Bleke Forest then perhaps we never would have found the antidote."

Celene nodded. "Of course, and yet I wish also that I had been kinder before you left for your sea trip. I was so worried that my last words to you could have been such angry ones."

"But we are siblings. We are supposed to fight and be jealous of each other."

"Of each other?" Celene had always felt that the jealousy had been rather one-sided (on her side). Jealousy of his easy, likeable nature and his lineage to the throne.

"Of course. It wasn't easy having a perfect sister – good at all the things I was supposed to be good at: fighting, leading, strategy. And you had Samara, of course. Why do you think I kept you waiting for an answer about the throne?"

Celene smiled ruefully. "Well, now neither of us have the throne and Samara is yours."

"That's not true. We both have Samara, but in different ways. And Tem. We are all family now."

"Yes," said King Ellis, beaming as he came into the bedchamber. "And don't forget me; I'm not planning on going anywhere just yet."

TWO MONTHS LATER

CHAPTER EIGHTEEN

SNOW MOON
Celene

She was back in Bleke Forest but she wasn't scared or lonely any more. Her family were with her. Samara and Hero sat in the clearing, a blanket on the ground and a small child tottering between them. She and Tem were unicorns again. Snowdrops carpeted the forest floor and rays of sunlight streamed through the trees. They chased each other around the clearing while the small child pointed and giggled. Someone was calling from far away...

"Your Highness! Your Highness! Time to get up now!"

Celene blinked her eyes open to see Hester's concerned face looming over her. It was funny to think that she and Hester were now about the same age; Hester had always seemed so much older.

"I didn't like to wake you, Your Highness, as you were in the middle of a dream, and a Snow Moon dream is always so vivid. But I know you don't like to lie in."

Celene smiled. "I seem to remember you saying that the Barley Moon was the strongest, Hester."

"Well, I'm no moon expert, Your Highness, but I would suggest a full moon at any time of the year is a powerful force."

"I can agree with you there," said Celene, sitting up in bed. "Thank you for waking me. That breakfast smells delicious."

Later, Celene stood at the training ground, with her bow and arrow. She had started her training almost as soon as she had returned home and was nervous that she might have completely forgotten what to do. After the lack of practice, her shoulders and upper back did ache after these sessions. But her eyes were as sharp as ever, her aim was true and her body remembered exactly what to do.

She pulled back the string of her bow and sent the arrow flying towards its target. It hit the white ring, just outside the centre.

Acceptable, but she could do better. She picked up another arrow and prepared to shoot again.

"Strong shot."

Celene turned at the sound of the familiar voice. Samara. She had been so focused on her training that she hadn't heard her approach.

"Morning. Where's Hero?" she asked. Samara and Hero had been inseparable since he awoke. Ardis had married them within the week and they had been spending as much time together as possible.

Samara smiled. "He's with Tem, attempting to teach her to sail."

"How's that progressing?" Celene couldn't imagine Tem on board any kind of boat.

"I'm not sure that she's inherited his seamanship. She is a child of the forest, not the sea, but it's a good chance for them to spend some time together. I was wondering if you want to go out on the horses this morning?"

Celene looked out at the bright blue sky. It was a beautiful late winter's day, crisp and bright with patches of snow dotted in the grass. She knew that it would feel good, to be out in the fields on horseback with her dear friend and sister-in-law.

But Celene needed to work hard if she was going to get back to her previous standard. She nearly shook her head and raised her bow to take the next shot, but she stopped herself. She and Samara had many missed years to catch up on. She had already trained hard today. The rest could wait for another day.

Celene lowered her bow.

"I'd love to join you," she said.

THE OLD MULBERRY
Celene

Samara was right; it was beautiful out on the hillside and Celene knew that she had made the right decision. Their horses, Morus and Breeze, were still around for them, having slept for fifteen years with the rest of Elithia. Riding Morus was like travelling back to her girlhood. Although Celene had not ridden a horse for years, she found it as natural as ever. Her years as a unicorn had given her new muscle memories: her body knew what it was like to run with four legs rather than two.

A low sun cast long shadows across the fields. Although they were some distance from any houses, the smell of wood smoke drifted over and mingled with the salty air. The ground was hard and snow patches crunched under hoof.

They galloped to the top of the hill and dismounted by the old mulberry tree. Unlike the horses, it had aged with them and was more gnarled and twisted than ever.

The last time they had been at this spot, there had been tension between them, but that was all gone now. All that was left was the deep love of friends and sisters.

Samara removed her riding hat and let her hair fly behind her in the breeze. Celene had cut her own hair short – shorter than before – within days of returning to Elithia. She no longer needed a mane. Samara wouldn't suit short hair, though. She still had a girlish air about her, despite the fact that she was a mother, and now a wife, and approaching middle age. "Do you ever think of all the years that we missed – all the things we could have done?" Samara asked.

Celene nodded. "All the time. Not just for myself, but all of us. Hero missed Tem's early years, you missed out on having your husband with you. Even Ardis sacrificed so much to protect the island."

"I do too, but I am trying to think instead about what we've gained. I feel like we've all been given a second chance, and this time I'm going to focus on what's really important in life."

"You're not coming back to the Royal Knights, are you?"

"No."

"Why not? You were so good at every part of it." She thought of the way that Samara had appeared under the full moon, fifteen years after she had been a knight, looking as though she had never stepped out of her armour.

"Maybe. But it never made me happy."

"What will you do instead?"

"I would like to learn more about healing and the magic of nature. Ardis is getting on in years and he won't be able to carry on doing what he does forever. He needs to hand over his duties to someone soon. Would you consider letting me take on that role?"

Once, Celene would have argued with Samara. She would have said that she was her best knight – that she needed her. But now she saw the sense in what her friend was saying.

"Of course. It is the right decision for you."

"He needs a new staff and he says I can go with him to choose one of my own."

Celene laughed at that. "I'm not sure I can imagine you with a magic staff."

"It can't be that different to a lance."

"Ah, in that case you should be fine – you were always better at the lance than me," said Celene.

They stood in silence and let the horses graze a while. Morus sniffed at the moss under the mulberry tree and Celene smiled, thinking of how fresh green moss sustained her in Bleke Forest for so many years.

"What will you do, Celene?" Samara asked, gently.

Celene understood what Samara meant. They all knew now that Tem would inherit the throne. So Celene's hopes and dreams of becoming queen would never be.

Years ago, she hadn't realized how quickly everything could change. But now she knew she should appreciate what she had, because it might not be the same tomorrow.

"I see how fragile life is – how quickly it can all fall apart and upon how little it all rests. A tiny spider living its life in a cave miles from here set off a chain of events that affected the course of all our lives for so long. I also know that if I hadn't been so intent on controlling everything and everyone, then things might have worked out differently. We could have worked together and somehow cured Hero fifteen years ago."

"But then we might have all fallen under the same cursed sleep in the palace. You wouldn't have been able to come back and save everyone. And I would never have known about the antidote if I hadn't moved near Bleke Forest."

"Perhaps. Ardis once told me that we have to trust everything will work out as it should. Perhaps we were all exactly where we were meant to be. We will never know for certain."

They paused and listened to the throaty chirp of a solitary robin.

"So what *are* you going to do with your future?"

"I thought that I needed to be queen, but now I know that my identity is about so much more than that. I know that Tem will make a great ruler of Elithia, maybe the greatest we have ever seen. I believe that it is my role to train her. Thorran used to train our knights, but was getting ready for retirement before I even left Elithia. Tem will take his place within the Knights and train for the role of commander and queen. As Tem finds her feet, I will step back from the role of commander and enjoy the trainer's role."

Samara laughed at that. "Poor Tem! Does she realize how hard she's going to have to work?"

"If anyone can do it, Tem can. She is already used to early mornings, and she can shoot an arrow more accurately than any of us. Most of the time, anyway, fortunately for me!" She felt the silver scar on her ankle with her fingers. "She will be our youngest ever knight, younger even than Alard. But age doesn't matter in the Elithian Royal Knights. She will be judged on her skill alone."

"You will be an excellent trainer, Celene. And you will be happier without the punishing schedule you put yourself through."

"I hope so. I suppose what I am trying to say is that I don't know exactly what will happen, and that is the way I like it. "

"And it might not happen for many years to come."

"You're right. As my father says, 'I'm not planning on going anywhere yet.'"

THE END

EPILOGUE

As everyone knows, a curse, once cast, never quite disappears.

Sidra had gone, her house knocked down, and her souls back where they belonged. Celene's heart lifted whenever she saw Madam Reddy's smiling face in the marketplace, back to the way it was before.

Although there was no longer any sign of Sidra's presence in Elithia, Celene often thought about her. If she walked to that part of the island, or the moon was full, Sidra's words played in Celene's mind.

You will only know running, hiding, fear and pain.

But that was no longer true. Now she had family, security and love.

Still, Celene's life had once been governed by the moon, and now, when it was full, she found herself unable to resist its pull. She would lie in bed, unable to sleep, thinking only of the gentle glow of moonlight on her skin. On nights like that, she would crave the twisted trees and shadows of Bleke Forest, which had welcomed her when she had nowhere to go. She knew she would never return, but she would get as close as she could to the wilds of nature, into the Elithian hills, away from the city and away from people.

When the moon was full, Celene no longer turned from a unicorn to a woman; she turned from a woman to a unicorn. And the transformation was no longer a curse. She enjoyed the sinewy strength in her unicorn legs, and the silky feel of her mane and tail. These days, she was never scared and alone. These days, she had company. Trotting up the hill was another unicorn, silver grey with a bright white mane.

I thought you weren't coming tonight, said Celene.

Of course I was coming. I will always be here when the moon is full. It draws me in a way I cannot begin to understand.

Tem. Her beautiful niece, who understood her like nobody else.

Acknowledgements

Halfway through writing this book, the world went into lockdown, which made for a very different writing and working experience all round. Thanks to everyone at Scholastic for making things happen despite all the new challenges and restrictions. Liam Drane for the amazing cover art, Pete Matthews, Louisa Danquah, Harriet Dunlea, Laila Dickson, Lucy Page and Tina Miller for all your hard work on this book and the other Unicorns. And Fiz Osborne, of course! I'm glad we've been able to keep in touch via the power of technology and I hope for a face-to-face meeting soon.

Thank you also to:

Emma Young, who has helped me shape all three books;

The London Library for your amazing postal service. Although I'm writing fiction, I enjoy reading books related to my themes and I found some inspiration for this story in the following books: Cashford, J. (2003), The Moon: myth and Image; London: Cassell Illustrated. Moore, P (2006), Patrick Moore on the Moon; London: Cassell. Feltwell, J. (1991), The Story of Silk; NY: St Martin's Pr.

Simon, Clara and Tom for more help than ever before – there has been just no getting away from my questions – I included the double "a" and the staff just for you.

Readers of *The Midnight Unicorn* and *The Darkest Unicorn* for your emails and letters. It's lovely to know that you're out there enjoying my books and I've had you in mind while writing this one. I hope you enjoy it and I wish you all safe and well.

HAVE YOU READ
THE DARKEST UNICORN?

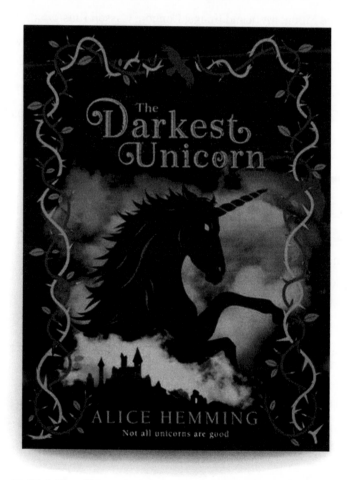

READ ON FOR AN EXTRACT...

CHAPTER ONE

LULLABIES FOR THE COWS

Linnell took the wooden pail from the hook by the door and stepped out on to her porch, into the brand new morning. It was early, and the sky was the colour of orange hawkweed. She tended to her little bird, scattering some seed in his cage, then she turned and breathed deeply, treating her lungs to the cool, crisp air and her eyes to the spectacular mountain view. The great giant, Mount Opacus, stood strong and tall, its peak shrouded in thick cloud whatever the weather, and guarded on either side by smaller mountains known as the Sentries.

Her own home was opposite these giants, on the lower slopes of the Grey Mountain, but on a day like today, its name was hard to comprehend. The bright sky contrasted with the dark green of the pine trees and the lush green of the meadow. Green mountain would have been a more appropriate name.

Maybe those who named the mountain long ago lived on the other side– the Essendor side – where it was said to be grey and rocky. Essendor was the capital city after all. But Linnell had never been to the other side of the mountain. There was no real reason to go. Besides, there was no tunnel through, the journey around would take days, and Linnell's father said that only a brave man or a fool would travel upwards, crossing the mountain peaks.

The nearest village of Arvale was just a few miles downhill but Linnell couldn't really claim to live in the village at all: where she lived was more of a hamlet. Just a few dilapidated farmhouses clustered together. But despite the low population and the early hour, she passed no fewer than three people on her way to the cow barn.

Piet, the old farmhand, stopped shovelling hay and nodded his head in polite greeting. "Good morning to you Linnell. I like the way you are wearing your hair today."

Linnell touched her hair, which she had braided and twisted

around her head. "Good morning, Piet. Thank you."

Across the way, Madam Lavande was rocking on a chair on the porch, a crocheted blanket on her lap. "I bid you good morning, Mistress Linnell. I do like your hair plaited in that way."

"Thank you, Madam Lavande."

And, just as she reached the barn, little Johan jumped out at her from behind the hay cart, making her start. "Boo!"

"Be off with you, you imp!" said Linnell, chasing him away.

She made her way into the cow barn, where she could finally hide away. Here it was dark and warm and smelled of manure, hay and the cows themselves. The strong smell might have bothered some, but not Linnell, who had grown up with it. She found Nettie, her favourite cow and led her to the milking stall. Nettie clomped along happily enough and began munching the grain in the manger. Linnell pulled the milking stool up close, wiped Nettie down and began milking.

Her hands worked automatically and the milk squirted into the pail. She sighed heavily. She would like to be able to part her hair whichever side she chose and braid it in whatever style she fancied without it being a talking point for everyone.

Linnell had lived in this out-of-the-way place all her life and nothing had ever changed. Every day, her father farmed the meadows, tended to the animals and prepared food for the markets. Every afternoon, Linnell helped with the farm and every morning she studied her schoolbooks.

Nettie must have sensed Linnell's mood and shuffled her feet. The waiting cows mooed unhappily. Disgruntled cows made her job much more difficult, so Linnell began to sing. The cows liked her singing and her voice echoed pleasantly in the barn. She sang her favourite song – the one her father had written for her mother and her mother had sung to Linnell in her cradle:

To me you are a diamond
To me you are a pearl
To me you are an emerald
To me you are the world

I'd give you a diamond to shine the whole day long
But I have no diamond, so I give to you this song

Linnell sighed again. She had never seen a diamond before, or an emerald, but she would surely like to. She would like to wear a dress of silver brocade, encrusted with tiny pearls. She would like maids to wait on her and style her hair however she chose. She continued singing and the cows stood by peacefully.

To me you are the mountain
To me you are the sea
To me you are the forest
You're everything to me

Linnell loved the pictures that the song brought into her mind, of snowy mountain peaks and the billowing sails of great ships on the ocean. She would love to be free to explore, to travel and see the world, but she knew that she would not. In just a few short years, Linnell would leave childhood behind and start working on the farm permanently. Her father was old and he couldn't bear the weight of their existence alone. With no siblings to share the responsibility, Linnell knew that her route in life had a fixed course.

As if conjured up by her thoughts, Linnell's father came into the barn. He leaned just inside the doorway, listening to her song. Then he joined in, his voice deep and powerful.

I'd give you a diamond to shine the whole day long
But I have no diamond, so I give to you this song

When they had finished, Linnell thought she saw tears in his eyes. "Your mother's song."

Linnell nodded. Her mother had died when she was a small child.

"You sing so well – better than she did, even. Your voice is a true gift."

Linnell smiled, wistfully. Her father told her this often. Which was nice, but what good was a sweet singing voice when she was stuck in a cow barn near a village that no one had heard of?

"She was my diamond and you are my pearl, Linnell. The most precious things in the world."

Linnell embraced her father. He was so sentimental. Foolish, really. But it was a good moment to ask for a favour. "After I have finished my chores for the day, may I go to the meadow or the forest?"

"What about your schoolwork?"

"I shall take my schoolbooks with me. It's going to be such a lovely day that it seems a shame to stay cooped up inside."

"Then, yes you may, Linnell. You're a good girl and you do

so much for me. I don't know what I'd do without you. Just make sure you don't stray too far, be back by lunchtime and don't talk to anyone you don't know."

At this, Linnell laughed. The chance of meeting anyone she did not know was so remote that if she did, she would probably be struck mute from the surprise.

THE SINGING FOREST

Today, Linnell chose the shade of the forest over the openness of the meadow. It was going to be a hot day and she had more chance of concentrating on her schoolwork without the sunshine reflecting off the bright white paper of her books. There was also something about the forest that stirred Linnell's curiosity. She had heard people talk of sightings of the Midnight Unicorn, which was rumoured to roam these parts and protect the citizens of Essendor. Linnell doubted that the unicorn would come to Arvale, let alone venture up into the foothills of the mountain, but if it did, she was more likely to encounter it here in the depths of the forest, rather than out in the open meadow.

She sat on a treestump, took a small stack of books from her satchel and opened the first one. History. Not her favourite subject, but then none of them were. Apart from music, of course. She could see the use in learning to read and write music, whereas the other subjects seemed like a waste of time. She failed to see how history or arithmetic would help her milk the cows. She flicked through the pages. It was all about kings and queens. She ignored the long chunks of text and gazed at the illustrations instead . The royals wore such fine clothes, in fabrics that she'd never seen: velvet, mulberry silk and linen.

She would probably never meet a queen, even though she was just a few miles away from the royal city of Essendor where Queen Audrey ruled. She was a popular ruler, unlike her uncle, King Zelos had been. It was rumoured that he had killed his sister, her husband and the twin babies in order to take the throne as his own. But the twins had survived and returned to claim their birthright. Sometimes she imagined that she was a lost princess. How fine that would be, to discover that she was born into royalty. She could have anything she wanted. A great castle and gardens in which to play, delicious food and elegant clothes. She could wear her hair braided, or curled, or swept up with sparkling hair combs.

She traced a finger over the floral pattern on one of the dresses. Just beautiful. She glanced briefly at the words, which listed the many achievements of these great royals who had lived so many years ago. Row after row of dates and battles. Linnell couldn't concentrate. She rested the book on her knees.

She gazed at the flowers dotted around: celandine, dandelions and merrybells. Weeds to some, but Linnell thought them rather beautiful, their bright blues, pinks and yellows enhancing the beauty of the shadowy forest like jewellery worn against bare skin. If she would never see real jewels, then these would have to do. She let her book fall to the ground and began to pick a bunch of sturdy leaves: the ones with long flexible stems. She wound three stems together and then gradually added more and more to the row, poking yellow and white flowers into the gaps. The melody from earlier was stuck in her head and she sung it again.

"To me you are a diamond
To me you are a pearl..."

Her voice sounded different in the forest compared to the echoing stillness of the barn. Out here, the notes drifted away from her to mingle with the other sounds of the forest: the chorus of the birds, the light breeze in the trees and the buzz of nearby insects.

She wound the strip of leaves and flowers into a circular crown.

"...To me you are an emerald
To me you are the world..."

She placed the flower crown on top of her head. Now she really did feel like royalty. The white and yellow flowers would bring out the golden highlights in her hair. She began to dance slowly, with her hands raised high above her head, imagining herself performing in a real theatre, in front of the queen.

"I'd give you a diamond to shine the whole day long..."

Linnell sang, but then stopped suddenly when she heard music. She had the most curious sensation that the forest was singing back to her.

THE COLOURFUL STRANGER

Linnell slowly turned her head to listen. The notes were quiet, but she could definitely hear them, drifting out from the trees. Was someone singing along with her? It sounded magical. Maybe it was a unicorn. Did unicorns sing? But no, it was the sound of a pipe. Someone was playing along to her music. She sang the next line:

"But I have no diamond, so I give to you this song"

The sound of the pipe matched her singing, note for note. How could that be? This was her own special song that her father had written. She followed the music, taking small footsteps and singing as she went. She recognized the instrument: the music was coming from a wooden fipple pipe. It was beautiful. Then she peeped through the bushes, watching and listening.

The pipe player was also beautiful. He was young and slight, with slim limbs and skin the colour of a walnut shell. She could tell from the brightness and cut of his clothes that he was not from around here. Dark blonde curls peeped out from under a red alpine hat and he wore a long jacket of striped patchwork.

As he played, he danced, skipping lightly from one foot to the other. This, combined with his sharp features, gave Linnell a fleeting feeling that he was not entirely human; he must have some fairy in him. But then he turned and she saw he was a boy. Just a boy.

She stepped from her hiding place and he caught her gaze, but carried on playing to the end of the song. She sang along; it seemed like the only thing to do. Then he stopped playing, lowered his pipe and smiled, showing even white teeth. "You sing well."

Linnell smiled too. "You play well. How did you know the tune?"

"I can play any song I hear." He picked up the pipe and played another, merry tune that she didn't know.

She tapped her foot along to the rhythm and then clapped when he'd finished. They gazed at each other until Linnell felt the need to break the silence.

"My name is Linnell. I live over there," she said, shyly, pointing towards the village.

The boy took off his cap and bowed low. "Sander. Pleased to make your acquaintance." He looked in the direction she pointed and shook his head slowly as if puzzled. "I can't imagine living out here."

The heat rose in Linnell's cheeks. "There is a village a few miles away. We are not as remote as it might appear."

"Still, it is a sleepy place."

Linnell wished she could defend her home but it was true. It was beyond sleepy; it was dead to the world. "Why, where are you from?"

"I am from nowhere and everywhere. Today I am from this very forest. Yesterday, I was from the mountains. I go wherever I want and do whatever I please. I live only for adventure."

Linnell let this sink in for a moment. Adventure. Just the word sent a thrill right through her. "What sort of adventure?"

"Any sort of adventure. For a time, I slept on a homemade raft, floating down the river. When it drifted ashore, I would get out and explore. When it did not, then I just stayed afloat for days."

Just drifting. For days. So different from Linnell's own life, with its unvarying sequence of chores and activities. "Don't your parents mind?"

"I wouldn't know, I've never asked them." Sander stopped and picked up a large, shiny beetle from the forest floor. It scurried up his arm and he laughed, transferring it to his other hand and then back on to the ground, where it disappeared under some leaves. "It would be easier to tame that beetle than to stop my wanderings. I cannot imagine another way to live."

Linnell could not imagine how such a carefree lifestyle would be possible. "But how *do* you live? How do you eat … clothe yourself?"

"Sometimes, I play my pipe for people in taverns or at festivals. A few coins in my hat go a long way. Sometimes, I tell stories.

People pay to hear my tales of the mountains and the things I have seen: fairies, dragons, flying wolves..."

Just imagine. Sander had experienced more excitement on his journey than Linnell had in her entire life. He spoke only of doing what *he* wanted, with no care for anyone else's wishes. How she would love to be that free.

"Are the stories true?"

"All my stories are true. You wouldn't believe the things that I've seen just moments from here. The Midnight Unicorn of Essendor roams freely if you know where to look—"

Linnell gasped. "You have seen The Midnight Unicorn?"

"Yes, I've had the pleasure to see it dancing in the moonlight on many occasions; but the Midnight Unicorn of Essendor is not the greatest sight you will see. What does that horned horse even *do*? Rescue people from rivers? Save sheep from wolf attacks? The Midnight Unicorn does nothing that you or I couldn't do; its powers pale in comparison to those of the Greatest Unicorn."

"The Greatest Unicorn?"

"Yes. A more powerful and majestic beast. Of all the sights I have witnessed on my travels, it is he who takes my breath away."

"Then why do ordinary folk not speak of him? I have not heard a single tale of his great feats."

"He is hidden away in a castle in the clouds. Only a true adventurer would ever find him."

"What does this unicorn – the Greatest Unicorn – look like?" whispered Linnell.

Sander lowered his voice to match Linnell's. "He is white. No, not white. Clear. He is translucent – like ice."

"Like a diamond?"

Sander smiled. "Yes, like a diamond. But not hard like a diamond. Strong and sinewy but still soft. And his mane shimmers with gold. He has real power."

"Power?"

"Oh, yes." Sander picked up his pipe and played another pretty tune. Linnell wished he wouldn't. She wanted to hear more about the unicorn. The *Greatest* Unicorn. She waited patiently until the end of the song and then, before he could play any more, she asked, "What power?"

Sander smiled. "If he chooses, the Greatest Unicorn can grant wishes. He can make any wish come true."

Any wish. Linnell thought of all her hopes and dreams of getting far from here. Of beautiful jewels, fine clothes. And freedom.

"What would you wish for, Linnell?" asked Sander.

Linnell shrugged. She felt foolish saying her dreams aloud. Sander played a few notes on his pipe. Her song.

To me you are a diamond
To me you are a pearl

He put down his pipe and gazed directly into her eyes. "Diamonds around your neck? A dress decorated in exquisite seed pearls? Just imagine. If you looked like that, you could do anything you wanted. You could travel to great kingdoms and sing for royalty. They would pay you handsomely and then you could buy more fine clothes."

Linnell nodded, slightly unnerved by how easily he seemed to read her dreams. "I would love to live a life like that."

"Then live it. There is nothing to stop you. If there is something that you want, just do it."

"How? How could I just do it?"

"Well if you wanted it to happen right away, you could ask the unicorn."

"I *could*? But how?"

Sander ran a hand along some long grass. "I could show you where to find him. He can grant any wish, as long as something is given in exchange."

Something in exchange. That was the problem. Linnell had nothing. No money or even belongings that she could sell.

"What does the unicorn take in return?" Linnell asked.

Sander sighed. "Oh dear. Are you one of *those* people?"

Linnell didn't know what she'd said wrong. "One of which people?"

"One of those sorts of people who like to ask questions. 'Why?' 'How?' And 'Why' again. If you ask too many questions then you end of talking yourself out of what you really want. If you want something then you must grasp it and not let go. Forget the questions."

Just imagine the freedom if Linnell just thought about herself and what *she* wanted for a change. What sort of life would she lead if only she could experience that? Her father would find help with the farm, or maybe he wouldn't need the farm anymore: she would keep him in luxury too.

Linnell could go and see the unicorn – ask him to grant her wish. The idea was so liberating that she laughed out loud before she asked, "May I come with you?"

"Well you *may*, but I will be surprised if you *do*. I meet many people on my travels but few have the inclination to venture very far past their own doorsteps. As far as I know, I am the only person who has ever set eyes on the Greatest Unicorn."

"I am different from the others," said Linnell earnestly. "I really want to come and meet him. Please may I accompany you?"

Sander looked pleased. "Of course, it's not too far." He picked up his pipe and bag, brushed himself down and turned towards the trees. "This way."

Linnell's heart beat faster. Surely he wasn't going straight away? "I must let my father know where I am going."

"That's a shame." Sander began walking further into the forest.

Was he really leaving this very minute? He couldn't expect her to just walk after him without telling anyone, could he? "It will only take me a few minutes. You could come too." It would be worth it to see Madam Lavande's face as Linnell walked past her cottage with this colourful stranger.

Sander stopped, turned and sighed. "A few minutes will easily turn into a few hours. Your father will no doubt refuse to allow you to go, you will protest and barricade yourself in your bedroom. He will start up with the Whys and the Hows, then in all likelihood you will never go anywhere at all. I understand. Some of us are not made for adventure. But as for me, I am leaving now. So I bid you farewell."

Sander walked off towards the trees and Linnell watched him leave, startled by his impatience. She could not – should not – follow a stranger into the forest on a whim. After all, what would her father think if she didn't return home that afternoon? Sander began playing his pipe once again: a sad, wistful tune. As he drew away and the notes grew quieter, panic rose in Linnell's chest. What if she was letting her one chance for real adventure slip away? She would regret it forever. If the unicorn did grant her wish of freedom then her father would not be cross – he would never have to work again. And if the unicorn did not grant her wish, or she wanted to return, then she would just return home straightaway. Sander said it wasn't far, after all.

"Wait for me!" she cried and sprinted after him, her flower crown tumbling to the ground.